### *"My name is Alyssa***

"Billie."

"But...but Billy is a *boy'*

"Only if you spell it *B-i-l-l-*

"There's a boy in my class," Alyssa said from the backseat, "and his name is Billy– Daddy! Look!" His child pointed across the street. "Isn't that little white dog the cutest thing ever?"

If he ever said yes to a dog, it sure wouldn't be a yappy ankle-biter like that one. "Uh-huh," he said. When he had been forced to leave her favorite doll at the airport, Noah had soothed her tears by promising to replace it with a kitten.

"If I had a dog," she said, "it would be big. Like the one you had when you were a little boy, 'member, Daddy?"

How could he forget the gentle giant that had been more sibling than pet? "Cash. My dad named him Cash Money, because he'd been abused before we adopted him, and cost a fortune at the vet's."

Noah glanced over at Billie, and for a moment there, the woman in the passenger seat looked mildly interested. She pointed left. "You just passed my street," she said.

Noah groaned. That meant driving up to Hamilton Street to make a U-turn in the post office parking lot. Halfway there, traffic on Main Street slowed, then came to a grinding halt. Noah gripped the steering wheel until his knuckles ached. Trapped at a dead stop between parked cars and the constant flow of traffic heading east, he and Alyssa–and Billie, too–might as well have bull's-eyes painted on their foreheads....

Dear Reader,

How many times have you wished you could escape your life and all its travails and tragedies? Or wanted to hop a plane or a bus–or just start walking–to get away from whiny kids, demanding bosses and inconsiderate neighbors, at least for a little while?

If you're like me, the answer is "A lot!" At least, that *was* my answer, until I researched the Witness Protection program (WITSEC) and interviewed inspectors with the U.S. Marshals Service. These brave and dedicated people helped me understand that whether a witness goes undercover because he's a bad guy turning state's evidence or a good guy whose testimony will help get bad guys off the streets, life in the program is anything but easy.

Imagine receiving completely new identities and documentation, you're moved far from home and warned that all connections with the past must be severed–if you hope to remain safe (and alive) and protect loved ones from potential danger. You're told there's no going back. Ever. Not for Grandma's funeral or your niece's wedding. The doctor and dentist you've trusted for years? He'll never know why you didn't keep your last appointment. Because for all intents and purposes, the old you is dead.

Sounds pretty bleak and lonely, doesn't it? That's because it is... and that's why inspectors go above and beyond the call of duty, serving as parent, sibling, friend, confidant, counselor. Available 24/7/365, they help witnesses get beyond the temptation to reach into the past–and save lives. (According to the U.S. Marshals Service, no witness *who has followed the rules* has ever been located, injured or killed by the parties they testified against.)

But what if, in a moment of weakness, a witness doesn't follow the rules? What if a child in protective custody unwittingly lets the cat out of the bag...and leads danger straight to her door?

That is the backdrop of the story you're about to read. I hope you'll enjoy this glimpse into the mysterious world of WITSEC, and that you'll write (www.loreelough.com) to share your thoughts on the light I attempted to shed on a sometimes dark and dangerous lifestyle.

Not to give anything away, but...here's to happy endings!

Loree

HARLEQUIN HEARTWARMING

# Loree Lough

## *Saving Alyssa*

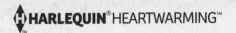

Recycling programs
for this product may
not exist in your area.

ISBN-13: 978-0-373-36667-5

SAVING ALYSSA

Copyright © 2014 by Loree Lough

This edition published by arrangement with Harlequin Books S.A.

For questions and comments about the quality of this book, please contact us at CustomerService@Harlequin.com.

® and TM are trademarks of Harlequin Enterprises Limited or its corporate affiliates. Trademarks indicated with ® are registered in the United States Patent and Trademark Office, the Canadian Trade Marks Office and in other countries.

Printed in U.S.A.

**HARLEQUIN®**
www.Harlequin.com

# LOREE LOUGH

Once upon a time, bestselling author Loree Lough sang for her supper. (That little corner in pubs reserved for "the piano lady"? Well, that's where she sat, strumming a Yamaha in cities all across the U.S.) Now and then, she blows the dust from her six-string to croon a tune or two, but mostly, she writes. With the release of this novel, she will have one hundred books on the shelves (fifteen bearing a Harlequin imprint), and 4.5 million in circulation. Her work has earned numerous industry accolades, movie options and four- and five-star reviews…but she's most proud of her "Readers' Choice" awards.

Loree and her husband split their time between a home near Baltimore and a cabin in the Alleghenies, where she continues to perfect her "identify the critter tracks" skills. A writer who believes in giving back, Loree donates a portion of her income to charity. (Complete list at Giving Back page, www.loreelough.com.) She loves hearing from readers and answers every letter personally. You can connect with her at Facebook, Twitter and Pinterest.

This book is dedicated to all WITSEC personnel, devoted to the protection of individuals and families for whom life in the shadows is a necessary way of life.

My heartfelt gratitude to the men and women of WITSEC who generously shared of their time, information and experiences, and made it possible for me to give readers a personal, accurate portrayal of life in the program. In order to protect each of them and the people in their care, I can't identify them by name, but they know who they are, and how thankful I am for all the help and friendship!

# CHAPTER ONE

"GIVE HER A couple of months," George Webster had said, "and she'll forget all about this. Kids are resilient."

Easy for him to say. The agent's little girl hadn't spent the past eighteen months being shuttled from one safe house to another in the dead of night. The agent's little girl hadn't been asked to trade her big, bright, once-happy home for a series of windowless dumps where gunshots, angry shouts and screaming sirens disturbed her sleep.

Nate stopped pacing and looked at his four-year-old daughter, Melissa. The flickering blue-green glow of the cheap alarm clock gave off just enough light to see her, lying spread-eagled in the narrow cot beside his. The soft, steady sound of her peaceful breaths reminded him of the many nights when, because he'd come home too late to tuck her in, he'd stood beside her bed, staring like a mute fool, thinking *perfection,* from the moment of her birth to this. Tears stung his eyes and a lump ached in his throat. Greed and arrogance were responsible for every wasted moment that could never be retrieved.

The clock on the battered nightstand said 10:15 p.m. In a little over twelve hours, he and Melissa would board a Baltimore-bound plane and begin the final leg of their slow passage into the unknown. "Don't think of it that way," Webster had said. "Think of it as leaving all the bad stuff behind. Focus on starting a whole new life in Maryland."

Easy for him to say, Nate thought again. But…something to hope for, anyway.

Hope. Pretty much all he had left, thanks to his own stupid choices. Choices that had brought them here.

Last night, when Webster had delivered the packet containing Nate's and Melissa's new identities, he'd also delivered what sounded to Nate like a well-rehearsed speech. He'd said he'd coached dozens of kids Melissa's age, and felt reasonably certain he could stress the importance of sticking to the program and keeping secrets, all without terrifying her.

Reasonably certain. Webster had said the same thing on the day of the trial, when Witness Security had moved Nate from the courthouse to the first of four safe houses by way of a long, meandering route. And it's what he'd said before each of three additional moves. The agency couldn't guarantee safe transport. Couldn't promise security, so what else *could* they say?

This time, at the conclusion of Webster's instructions, Nate had heard a worrisome, unspoken postscript: if the details traumatized Melissa, those consequences would be his fault, too.

The chirrup of his throw-away cell phone startled him, and he grabbed it before it could wake Melissa. The glow from the phone's display led him to the bathroom. Leaving the door slightly ajar, he flicked on the light.

"George," he whispered, squinting into the brightness, "what time is it?"

"Nearly 9:00 a.m."

Nate had spent hours, alternately pacing and staring at the jagged ceiling crack that jolted from corner to corner like a black lightning bolt. By his calculations, he'd dozed off at four, maybe four-fifteen. A good thing, he supposed, since he didn't know when he'd next fall asleep.

"So what's the plan?"

"I'll be there in half an hour, with breakfast. I'll have that little talk with Melissa while she's distracted by pancakes."

They hadn't eaten a meal—hadn't done *any-*

*thing* in public—since the trial. By now, the agent knew Melissa's preferences almost as well as her own dad did. And pancakes were her all-time favorite breakfast food.

"Unless there's traffic, I should be there by ten," George said, and hung up.

Nate showered and dressed, then sat on the edge of Melissa's cot. And as he'd done every morning since taking her from the only home she'd ever known, he sang her awake.

"Good morning, good morning, good morning…."

Long lashes fluttered as her lips formed a sweet smile. Stretching, she climbed into his lap. "Well," she said, "what are you waiting for? Let's sing the rest!"

Nate pressed a kiss to her temple, and they completed the song, together.

When they finished, she told him about the dreams she had had, another tradition that had started the morning after he had taken her from everything and everyone who meant anything to her. Melissa described how a talking ladybug had taken her for a ride, all the way around the world. And after that, she'd dreamed of a red-and-green parrot that sounded like George and told knock-knock jokes.

"Want to hear one?"

Even before he could answer, Melissa said, "Knock, knock."

"Who's there?"

"Boo."

"Boo who?"

"What are *you* cryin' about?"

Laughing, Nate hugged her, then covered her face with kisses.

"Daddy, stop. You're tickling my cheeks."

"Sorry, can't help myself."

"Knock, knock," she said again.

"Time for your bath," he interrupted. "George is on his way over with breakfast. You can tell both of us knock-knock jokes while we eat, okay?"

Melissa slipped on her Barbie slippers and headed to the bathroom. "Okay, Daddy."

It amazed him that she'd never pressed him for answers; surely she'd wondered why they'd been living in bleak, dark rooms all these months. Why the last home-cooked meal had been prepared on a hot plate. Why they hadn't visited grandparents or cousins, or talked to anyone on the phone except for George. What amazed him more was that she didn't seem to miss any of that. Not even her mother. All very normal, according to the agent.

Normal. Nate didn't think he could remember the definition of the word anymore, let alone experience the sensation.

"When you're all clean and shiny," he called to Melissa, "you can watch cartoons while we wait for George."

"I like George. He's nice. And funny."

Yeah. Hilarious. The agent was solely responsible for every inane riddle and groan-inducing knock-knock joke now stored in Melissa's subconscious. But at least he'd kept her laughing.

"Don't forget to brush your teeth."

"I won't."

As he packed their meager belongings, Nate heard the telltale splash that told him she still hadn't tired of the trick he'd taught her that first night away from home. If squeezing a wet bar of soap until it spewed into the air and landed with a plop could produce giggles after all they'd been through, it was worth the time and effort required to clean up the bathroom floor. Far more important than that, maybe George was right, and Melissa *would* adapt to their new life, quickly, and with no lasting aftereffects.

Nate folded the tiny pj's purchased during George's now-famous Fifteen Minute Walmart Expedition, and tucked them into the sparkly pink backpack that had replaced the purple one Melissa had carried to day care for two years. Using the list provided by Nate, George had also bought a week's worth of clothes and shoes for dad and daughter, puzzles, crayons and coloring books, two Barbies and assorted outfits for each. While adding the last items to her pack, Nate cringed, because later today, Melissa would lose her favorite doll, Cassie, which had been hand-sewn by her mother while pregnant.

He didn't have time for a lot of self-reproach, because George arrived just then with breakfast. Melissa loved the way the agent changed things up. Doughnuts one day, bagels and cream cheese the next, fast food from the local burger joint the day after that. Nate understood that the different types of food had nothing to do with surprising Melissa. Three meals daily, purchased from the same take-out place by a guy alone, would have sent up red flags.

Today, George produced pancakes from a big white bag. He opened foam containers and handed out plastic flatware, then dealt napkins as if he was playing cards, while Melissa shared last night's dreams, unwittingly providing the opening that allowed him to introduce her to her new name.

"You know how to play the name game?"

"I guess so," she said, pretending to feed her doll a bite of sausage.

"Excellent! Let's pretend your name is Alyssa, and my name is Mr. Poopie Pants, and your dad is—"

"Poopie?" she echoed, wide-eyed. "But...but that's a potty word!" She clucked her tongue. "You're lucky Mrs. Cameron isn't here. She makes everyone who says potty words stay inside when it's playtime." Melissa looked at Nate. "I know we're not allowed to go outside, so how will we teach George about potty words?"

"I think we can let him get away with it. Just this once." Melissa donned her but-that-isn't-fair! look so Nate added, "But only because he didn't know the rules." Nate shook a warning finger at George. "But next time, mister..."

The agent chuckled while Melissa thought about it.

Brow furrowed, she said, "Not even a time-out?"

"Not this time."

"Boy, are *you* lucky." A sly grin lifted one corner of her mouth. "Okay then, *Mr. Poopie Pants,* if my name is Alyssa, what is Daddy's new name?"

Present tense, he noted. And she'd said *new* name, not *pretend.* A lucky break? Or had she figured things out, all on her own? The latter, he hoped, because if she slipped up, even once, they could end up dead.

*Dead.*

The word caused an involuntary flinch. It didn't seem as if she'd noticed his movement, but just in case, he stuffed a huge bite of pancake into his mouth to hide it.

"The guy with the chipmunk cheeks, you mean? His new name is Noah. And you both get new last names, too. From now on, your name is Alyssa Preston."

"But why? Mommy told me that Melissa was her grandma's name. And that her grandma was her favorite person in the whole world... until I was born."

George scrubbed both hands over his face. If it was that tough answering a question he'd no doubt been asked before, Nate didn't know how he'd manage his own remorse for being the reason she was asking it in the first place.

"Well," the agent said, laying a big hand atop Melissa's, "you know why we don't go outside, right?"

She speared a bite of pancake and used it to draw figure eights in the syrup. Nate winced when she said, "Because it's dangerous, and we don't want to get hurt." She rested an elbow on the table, leaned her head on her palm. "But," she said, emphasizing the word, "I think it's a dumb rule."

"I know," George said. "But sometimes it's the dumb rules that keep us safe. One of the dumb rules is you can't use your old name anymore."

She sat up straighter. "Never?"

"Never, ever."

She put her fork on the napkin and leaned back in the chair. If she'd seemed sad or confused, Nate might have been able to ignore it. But she looked resigned to her fate, and that made him hang his head. Everything that had happened to her—her mother's murder, her own near kidnapping, living like an Old West outlaw...all because of him. *He* deserved to die for that, but she did not. Joining the WITSEC program didn't guarantee that, but, God willing, she'd never end up like Jillian.

George folded large-knuckled hands on the small table. "Think you're big enough to remember all that?"

Her brow puckered slightly as she said, "'Course I am. I'm *four*." She brushed blond bangs from her forehead and brightened slightly. "We learned about rhymes in school. Alyssa rhymes with Melissa. I can remember that." She pointed at Nate. "And Noah starts with an N, just like Nate." She shrugged. "Easy peasy."

George sent Nate a nod of approval, then fixed dark eyes on Melissa. "Your daddy wasn't kidding when he said you're smart for your age, was he?"

Yeah, his girl was smart, all right. Smart enough to pass for a first grader when she started school in the fall? Smart enough to maintain the charade, permanently? God help them if she wasn't.

His mind whirled with the memory of those final seconds in the courtroom: he'd just opened the big wooden doors when a loud, gruff voice had stopped him. "Nate…Nate Judson!" He'd turned, saw soon-to-be former Senator O'Malley straining against the deputies' grip. As the officers half shoved, half dragged him away, he had shouted, "You can run, but you can't hide!"

Nate groaned inwardly as George and Melissa swapped knock-knock jokes. He sipped coffee from a foam cup, remembering….

The deeper the prosecution dug, the more evidence they'd gathered on O'Malley. The stuff they'd coerced Nate into testifying about was just the tip of the proverbial iceberg. Even now, more than a year after agreeing to turn state's evidence, the senator's threat made his blood run cold, because despite a lack of evidence linking O'Malley to Jillian's murder, Nate knew the senator had ordered the hit. And if his hired goon hadn't coughed, alerting the school's staff, he would have succeeded in kidnapping Melissa, too. "Nobody turns on me and gets away with it," the senator had said.

George's voice broke into his thoughts, and Nate wrapped trembling hands tighter around his coffee cup as the agent asked Melissa, "So what's your new name again?"

"Alyssa Preston," she said, and spelled it.

He aimed a thumb in Nate's direction. "And he is…?"

"He's my daddy." Then she giggled. "I'm teasing you. His new name is Noah Preston."

George nodded in approval. "Here's a trick question. What's my new name?"

"That's easy. You're Mr. Poopie Pants."

Chuckling, George slapped his meaty thigh. "By Jove, I think she's got it!"

He wasn't smiling when he stood and looked at his watch. "Guess we'd better hit the road. We don't want to miss our flight."

Nate recalled the order of events George had outlined on the phone last night. Once his badge got them through security, they'd board the plane from the tarmac, rather than at the gate. To further confuse possible O'Malley disciples, they'd change planes in Detroit, and again in Philly before landing at the Baltimore airport.

Nate sipped coffee, wondering if their Baltimore-based sitter had stocked the apartment kitchen with real mugs, as promised. Over the past few weeks he'd spent enough time on the phone, and in Skype conversations with Maxine—aka Max—to know that she'd stocked the pantry and fridge, and added to the Walmart wardrobe George had provided. Everything they owned fit nicely in their backpacks, the only luggage they'd need between this dismal room and their new home in Ellicott City.

Nate slung his bag over one shoulder, helped Melissa into hers. She'd been a real trouper to this point, going along with every change, accepting every loss, for no reason other than that he'd given his word that things would get better soon. Would she feel that way after her favorite doll, Cassie, "disappeared"? Maybe. But just in case, he had an ace up his sleeve, an idea born as he'd tucked her in bed the night before last:

"Will Santa be able to find our new house?" she asked.

"Of course he will."

"But how will he get in? Does our new house have a chimney?"

Nate hadn't noticed a fireplace in the pictures Max had sent to his cell phone, but it was a hundred-year-old building.... "I'm not sure," he had said, "but even if it doesn't, we'll leave a door unlocked. You can tell him which one when you send him your wish list."

"I'm only writing one thing...*puppy!*"

His heart ached now, just remembering how excited she'd been when she'd said it. Nate hated to disappoint her, but what choice did he have? Dogs barked, relieved themselves outside, needed to be walked, and he couldn't afford the exposure. Maybe he'd surprise her with a kitten instead, and hope *it* would ease the pain of losing Cassie.

George opened the door as Nate exhaled a frustrated sigh. "Ready, cupcake?" he asked, tousling his daughter's hair.

She was on her feet and beside the agent in an eye blink. Fortunately, George was big enough to block the exit. Goose bumps formed on Nate's forearms. He needed to be on guard for that kind of thing from now on, because if she darted out of his sight, even for an instant...

A shiver snaked up his spine as she chattered excitedly about her first airplane ride, about meeting Max in person. Melissa didn't realize that Maxine Colson, like George, was a WIT-SEC agent. All she knew was that her Skype pal would meet them at the airport and deliver them to their new home. Max had helped Melissa find Baltimore on the map, taught her that the city was famous for the Orioles and the Ravens, steamed crabs and people who called each other "hon." Nate didn't know a whole lot more than that himself. But they had the rest of their lives to learn, together.

As she climbed into the backseat of George's boxy blue SUV, Melissa looked up at Nate. "Oh, Daddy...I mean, Mr. Preston? Can you belt Cassie in with me?"

She looked so proud about remembering his new name. Overwhelming sadness wrapped around him as he looked into her angelic face. "Sure thing," he said, tucking the doll under the belt. "Now you behave yourself, and listen to *Alyssa,* okay, Cassie?"

Nate slid into the passenger seat. Alyssa. Alyssa Preston. Would he ever get used to calling her that?

George got into the car, and as he inserted the key into the ignition, she said, "Oh no!"

The agent met her eyes in the rearview mirror. "What...did we forget something important?"

"Yes! Something *very* important! We forgot to give *Cassie* a new name!"

He swallowed hard, adjusted the Windsor knot of his rumpled blue tie. *"I only gave you one job to do,"* said the hard, silent gaze he aimed in Nate's direction. He'd stressed that, because of facial recognition software, Cassie, who was visible in nearly every family photo, could not go to Baltimore. So Nate had come up with a two-birds-with-one-stone plan: stuff Cassie into Melissa's backpack as they entered the terminal, and when she wasn't looking, leave the doll behind. A necessary evil to ensure his baby's safety. But he hadn't yet shared the idea with George.

"How about this," Melissa said. "Cassie has blue eyes like Mommy…."

The men exchanged a worried glance, because they knew where this was going. Knew other things, too. Things Melissa was far too young to understand. She would never again see her teacher and preschool classmates, beloved grandparents, aunts, uncles and cousins, or visit her mother's grave at the Rose Hill Cemetery. Because all ties to their old life were forbidden. Including Cassie.

"…so how about if I call her Jillian?"

That wouldn't work even if they didn't have to get rid of the easily identifiable doll. Melissa waited for the grown-ups in charge of her safety and her fate to respond. Instead, George fiddled with the radio dials as Nate looked for an imaginary something in the glove box. As a kid, he'd fallen from a tree, all the breath whooshing from his lungs in the hard landing. He felt that way right now.

George, having more experience with situations like this, regained his composure first. "Know what I wish?" he asked.

In the eighteen months since O'Malley's arrest, Nate had come to terms with his widowhood and had adjusted to life as a single dad. He more or less accepted the fact that because of his transgressions, he would never practice law again. When he learned that the marshals had built an entire livelihood for him around his questionable knowledge of tools, he figured he'd get used to that, too…thanks to George's savvy advice. How would he fare without the big-hearted agent to advise and reassure him?

"What do you wish?" Melissa asked.

"I wish you'd write to me, once you're all settled in your new place."

"Oh, I will. And you'll write back, won't you?"

"You bet I will." George winked. "Sure am gonna miss you, kiddo."

"Daddy says our new 'partment has a

sophie-bed. You could visit anytime you want."
She looked at Nate. "Right, Daddy?"

Oh, how he loved this kid! "George," he
said, "our sophie-bed is your sophie-bed."

Ten minutes into the half-hour drive to
O'Hare, Melissa dozed off.

"So you're comfortable, working with
Max?" George asked.

*Comfortable.* What a weird choice of words.
Nate pictured Agent Maxine Colson, who, after
hearing about the nightmares, hand-flapping
and stammering that plagued Melissa right
after her mother's death, had pulled strings
and called in favors. Not only had she secured
authorization to line up a child specialist, Max
had also gotten permission to Skype with Melissa during those critical in-between months,
easing the transition. During their often hours-
long daily sessions, she'd listened patiently as
Melissa recounted her days, recited entire plot
lines of cartoons and movies she'd watched,
and read *The Velveteen Rabbit*...seven times.
Melissa was comfortable with the pretty redhead, and that was good enough for Nate.
Still...

"I don't think I'll ever be comfortable with
a stranger again."

Nodding, the agent stared straight ahead.
"I hear ya. But Max is good people. I know,

'cause I worked with her before she transferred to the Baltimore office. She's great with kids, and keeps a secret better than a priest in the confessional. If you have problems, you can trust her with 'em."

Nate snorted.

"Cynic," George teased. "But mark my words, you'll change your mind about her."

His imagination? Or was there an unspoken *"People in your shoes always do"* at the end of George's statement? Not that it mattered. Nate had no intention of unburdening himself with the woman. As far as he was concerned, she had one purpose: to keep Melissa safe.

Correction. *Alyssa.* He'd better get used to calling her that. Better get used to referring to himself as Noah Preston, too. Nate Judson, former assistant district attorney for the city of Chicago, former husband of Jillian, former part-time law professor at the University of Illinois at Chicago, was as good as dead.

Yeah, he'd cooperate.

But he didn't have to like it.

# CHAPTER TWO

*Three years later...*

WALKING THE BROKEN mountain bike uphill would have been a challenge even without her sprained ankle. Billie hoped the owner of Ike's Bikes had earned his reputation as the guy who could fix anything, because the Cannondale had cost, used, almost as much as her four-cylinder pickup had, new.

She rolled the bike between two others in the rack—a McLaren Venge, easily eighteen thousand dollars, and the slightly more affordable Scott Spark Limited. After clicking her spokes lock into place, Billie noticed movement on the other side of the shop's floor-to-ceiling door. The owner of the Venge, she presumed, garbed head to toe in Gucci, just like her ex had worn.

A tinny bell announced her entrance, and Gucci waved. Billie pretended not to notice by sliding onto a stool at the counter and leafing through a dog-eared copy of *Bicycling Magazine.*

"Be right with you," called a DJ-deep voice from the back room.

Billie tensed. If the shop's regulars dressed like Gucci, could she afford to have Ike repair the Cannondale?

Another customer—a guy in threadbare jeans and a paint-spattered T-shirt—appeared from the back room, nodding a cordial hello to her, then Gucci, as he left the shop.

"Been riding long?" Gucci asked her.

"Not really."

And though she hadn't encouraged conversation, he launched into the story of how his first bike had been a Cannondale. A great way to break into the sport, he said, without breaking the bank. But Billie barely heard him because she was too busy remembering how she'd come into possession of hers: her obstetrician had recommended mountain biking as a great way to get back into shape, physically and emotionally, after Billie's baby was stillborn. Dr. Ryan had recently upgraded to a SuperSix, and made her a deal on the Cannondale she hadn't been able to refuse.

Gucci pointed. "So what happened to the ankle?"

"Tripped." He didn't need to know that she'd taken a curve too fast and skidded off the trail on Pennsylvania's Highland Plateau.

"Name's Jeff, by the way." He took a step closer, stuck out his right hand. "Jeff Graham."

"Billie," she said, shaking it. "Nice to meet you." She wasn't pleased to meet him, because his looks reminded her too much of her ex-husband, and triggered memories of the ugliness that had begun once he'd discovered her antibiotics had canceled out her birth control. Chuck had used the surprise pregnancy as an excuse to come clean about everything he'd been up to, including his affair with Amber. She hadn't been his first dalliance, and probably wouldn't be his last, but she'd do for now, because he didn't want kids, and neither did she. As if the awful truth hadn't hurt enough, he had accused Billie of getting pregnant on purpose, to trap him into staying.

"So I noticed you walked your bike here." Jeff nodded toward the rack out front. "You must live nearby."

She shook off the bad memory. "Couple of blocks."

"I live in Oella," he said, pointing east. "Rehabbed a hundred-year-old row house."

He wasn't guilty of anything, really, just making polite conversation, like any normal person. It wasn't his fault that she hadn't felt normal since Chuck had told her he was leaving, and that he refused to have anything to do with their child. Would he have stayed if he'd known the baby would die, even before she was born? Friends and family said they understood how losing her husband and child in the same calendar year could break her spirit. But that had been two whole years ago, they said; she'd healed physically, and it was long past time to get over it psychologically. Besides, what chance did she have of finding love or having another baby if she judged every man by Chuck's callous behavior?

Get over it, indeed. If they saw the way she reacted to baby food commercials, kids in playgrounds and moms pushing their babies in strollers, they'd know Billie felt anything but strong. At least, not strong enough to survive loss like that again.

"Took years," Jeff was saying, "but the place looks pretty good now, if I do say so myself."

She met his eyes, and decided it wouldn't kill her to at least be civil. "Sounds like a lot of work. And expense."

"I'll say! My wife thought I'd never finish. But I gave her my word that I'd be done before the baby was born. And I did. Now I'm working on an addition for the new baby."

Being sociable hadn't killed her, but now she was stuck passing time with this Jeff person, the total opposite of Chuck: married, with two children, and happy about it. Billie groaned inwardly, hoping he wouldn't whip out his wallet and show her a bunch of home-and-family photos.

She caught sight of herself in the big mirror behind the counter. It didn't take a genius to figure out that its purpose was to make the narrow shop appear wider. Too bad it couldn't give the illusion that she was something other than an ill-tempered, self-centered—

A small girl skipped out of the back room, singing "What a Wonderful World," as her shoulder-length ponytails bounced in sync with her stuffed bunny's floppy ears. When she spotted Jeff, she lit up as if Santa himself stood before her.

"Mr. Jeff!"

Hoisting her in his arms, he said, "How are you today?"

"Happy to see you." She looked behind him. "Where's baby Jeff?"

"Home with his mom. Nap time, y'know?"

"Now that I'm seven, Daddy says I don't have to take naps."

The baby Billie lost had been a girl....

Jeff put the child down as she reported, "Daddy said to tell you it'll take at least another hour before he can start on your bike. He's having troubles with that other one."

"No problem. Tell him I'll come back this afternoon."

As she ran off to deliver the message, Jeff shook his head. "She's a handful, that one. I'd invite her to my place, give her dad a break from the constant noise and motion, but he won't let her out of his sight." He glanced toward the back room. "My wife took it personally at first, and to be honest, so did I. Took us a while, but eventually we figured out that some single dads never trust anyone."

Billie had come here to drop off her broken bike, not to make friends or speculate about the shop owner's parenting and social skills.

The child returned to say, "If you're not in a hurry, Daddy wants to know if tomorrow morning would be okay with you."

Jeff patted the top of her head. "That's more than okay. In fact, it's better than okay. Looks like I'll see you in the morning, Alyssa m'dear."

Billie blinked back tears. The name on her daughter's angel-adorned tombstone at Philadelphia's Cedar Hill Cemetery was Ciara Marie, but Alyssa had been her second choice for girls' names.

Jeff paused at the door. "You might want to tell your dad there's another customer out here."

"Oh, he knows." She pointed at the camera high on the entry wall, hidden among cable housings and adjusting barrels. "When the other man saw her come in, he said, 'Whoa, she's pretty,' and Daddy said, 'Yes, she is.'"

Laughing, Jeff said, "They're both right." He opened the door partway. "Your dad must have gotten distracted, got busy with something and forgot she's here. Maybe you can tell him she sprained her ankle, and from the looks of it, ought to get home and prop it up."

Alyssa glanced at Billie's swollen, bandaged ankle. When she fixed her big blue eyes on her, the breath caught in Billie's throat. Would her little girl have been this stunning...if she'd lived?

Alyssa faced the back room and bellowed with a power that belied her size. "Daddy! *Daddy!* Mr. Jeff says come out and talk to this pretty lady about her *bye*-sickle because she has a big fat hurt ankle!"

Billie cringed as a dark-haired man emerged from the back room, wiping grimy hands on a grimier rag. "Who needs an intercom system with a human speaker on the premises?" He bent to kiss her forehead. "For a li'l bitty thing, you sure do make a lot of noise."

"Oh, Daddy, you *always* say that!"

The man smiled at Billie. "And yet she continues her quest to attempt to break the sound barrier."

The wide eyes narrowed slightly. "What's a sound barrier?"

He shot his daughter a wink. "It's just a fancy way of saying noisy."

She thought about it for a minute before asking if she could watch some television.

"The remote's on my desk. But you know the rules...."

She did her best to mimic her dad's baritone. "'The cartoon channel only, and if the volume goes over number twelve, off it goes!'"

Billie watched as his gaze followed Alyssa into the back room. He loved her. That much was clear. But something more glimmered in those black-lashed green eyes....

Jeff opened the bike shop's door all the way. "Catch you in the a.m., Noah." Eyes on Billie, he said, "Nice to meet you."

"Same here."

The little girl's father stepped closer. "Noah Preston," he said, "owner, repairman, candlestick maker. I'd shake your hand, but..." He showed her the rag again, then tipped his head toward the street. "That your Cannondale in the rack?"

Billie nodded, wondering why the sign out

front said Ike's Bikes if the man's name was
Noah.

"Bent the frame, eh?"

"'Fraid so."

"Saw you limping earlier, so sit tight while
I bring 'er inside for a closer look."

She reached into her pocket. "You'll need
this to unlock it," she said, dropping the key
into his upturned palm.

One of her twin brothers had been a marine,
and even after five years out of uniform, Troy
still wore his hair "high and tight." There was
something about his ramrod-straight stance
and no-nonsense word choices that told her he
hadn't always been a bicycle repairman. However, if the wavy, collar-length hair was any
indicator, Preston had not been a jarhead. No,
he had been something else. Billie had given
up her job as a flight attendant and enrolled in
law enforcement courses because Chuck didn't
like being alone, sometimes for days on end.
But he hadn't liked the long hours she spent
hitting the books, either, so she focused on web
design, and used study time to read mysteries
and thrillers. The fact that Preston managed
to keep an eye on Alyssa even as he unlocked
the bike and carried it inside made her think
maybe he'd been a cop. Had an on-the-job injury forced early retirement?

The bell above the door chimed as he el-
bowed his way back inside with her bike.
"Did I hear you telling Jeff that you walked
here with this thing?" He leaned it against the
counter, then squatted to give it a once-over.

"Um, yeah." She shrugged. "But only because I couldn't ride it from Tongue Row."

"Tongue Row? That's what, six, eight
blocks?" He stood, stepped behind the counter
and picked up a spiral notebook. "Between that
ankle and the bent frame, I'm surprised you
got here at all." He slid the notebook forward.
Plopped a ballpoint on the top page. "Name
and phone number," Preston said, "so I can call
you once I make a diagnosis. Please."

That slight hesitation before he tacked on the
courtesy reminded Billie of stories her mom
had told about the rude, bossy surgeons in the
O.R. Another scenario flickered in her imagination. But if Preston had been a doctor in his
pre-bike shop life, he could well afford a customer database. Unless he'd lost everything in
a malpractice suit.

"You have a computer, right?"

"Who doesn't?" His eyes narrowed slightly.
"How long have you lived in Ellicott City?"

"Just under a year." She met his steady gaze,
blink for blink. He'd responded to her ques-

tion, she noted, without really answering it. "And you?"

Preston shifted from one sneakered foot to the other. "A year, huh? Then you know how often we lose power around here. I like the added security of having customers' names written down in good old-fashioned black-and-white."

Another question unanswered, Billie thought, picking up the pen. She reminded herself that she'd come here to get her bike fixed, period. With any luck, she'd never need his services again.

He glanced toward the back of the shop, where Alyssa lay on her stomach in a beanbag chair large enough to accommodate her dad's muscular frame. He relaxed...but only slightly.

Oh, yeah. There was definitely something off about this guy.

She'd bet the Cannondale on it.

## CHAPTER THREE

NOAH LEANED BOTH elbows on the glass-topped counter, putting him at eye level with—he read what she'd written in the notebook—Billie Landon. Her real name, or was Billie short for something?

She slid the book back to him. "So eventually, you have to add this information to your database?"

"Yeah. Eventually." She had gorgeous eyes. Big. Bright. The color of rich black coffee. "But don't feel sorry for me."

"Sorry for you? Why would I feel sorry for you?"

Both her eyebrows had disappeared into thick, sleek bangs. Not brown. Not red. What *was* that color?

He cleared his throat. "Because," Noah began, "you're probably thinking if I had half a brain, I wouldn't duplicate my efforts."

The brows reappeared, in a frown. "That isn't what I was thinking."

Oh, but it was. In his district attorney days,

he'd interviewed enough victims and perps to recognize a distortion of the truth when he saw it.

She shrugged. "Word around town is that you're a magician when it comes to bike repair. No one mentioned your mind-reading talents."

He added quick-witted to the list. "No, not a mind reader." But he'd looked into enough lying eyes over the years to know a fib when he heard one. "You're right, though. My system means I have to do everything twice. But don't worry. I only do a couple dozen jobs a week, so there's no chance I'll get carpel tunnel."

A bold smile now, which only added to his suspicions about her. Why the flip-flopping emotions?

He took a half step closer, an interrogation tactic that sent a clear "I'm in charge" signal during his days as a district attorney. Noah didn't know which unnerved him more, the fact that his nearness didn't faze her, or that *her* nearness doubled his heartbeat. He straightened, took a step back. Crossed his arms over his chest. After three years, he should be comfortable with his single dad status. He'd cleaned up his act...too little, too late. But even if he were interested enough to pursue her, a wide gold band gleamed from the third finger of her left hand. Considering her injured foot, Noah wondered why her husband hadn't helped her deliver the bike. Was the guy married to his work, the way he himself had once been? Or a safety nut who didn't approve of mountain biking? Maybe there wasn't a spouse at all, and the ring served as a deterrent to unwanted flirtation.

"How long do you think it'll take to repair my bike? I have a race next weekend."

"On that ankle? You're kidding, right?"

She shot him a "who do you think you are?" look, and Noah supposed he had it coming. He moved to Billie's side of the counter again, crouched beside the Cannondale. "The fork is bent, and so's the down tube." Three years ago, if anyone had told him he could list bike parts, let alone repair them, he would have called them crazy. "If they won't hold a weld, I'll have to order new parts. Your chain is history, and I wouldn't put any confidence in this crank set, either."

Billie groaned softly. "In other words, I'm really *not* racing next Saturday."

"Well…" Noah stood up and, with one hand on the bike seat, said, "Not unless you believe in miracles?"

"Absolutely *not*."

She'd answered fast. Too fast. It made him

wonder what—or who—had turned her into such a pessimist.

"Do you need a deposit?" she asked.

Noah waved the offer away. "Nah." He picked up the notebook. "I know where you live. And I have the Cannondale as collateral."

Billie hopped down from the stool, wincing when she landed.

She'd walked the bike to his shop; going home the same way would cause further damage to her ankle.

"Tuesdays are slow," he began, "but even if they weren't, we're practically neighbors. I'll be leaving in a few minutes, so why not let me drive you home?"

Billie stiffened. "I appreciate the offer, but—"

"It looks like you stuffed a bowling ball into your sock. I'd bet *my* bike your doc told you to stay off it, keep it elevated. And iced down."

"As a matter of fact, he did." She exhaled a sigh of frustration. "So okay, I'll take you up on your offer. Thanks."

Noah had never been good at accepting help, either, and these past three years had only heightened his mistrust of people.

"My pickup is out back," he said, aiming a thumb over one shoulder. "Give me a minute to load Alyssa into her car seat, and I'll drive

around front so you won't have to traipse all
the way through the shop and into the side
alley."

By the time he turned off the TV, secured
Alyssa in her child safety seat—promising to
make her favorite for supper—then flipped the
store's Open sign to Closed, locked the door
and double-parked in front of the shop, fifteen
minutes had passed.

"Sorry, got a little waylaid," he said to Billie.
While she slid into the front seat, he checked
the locks on the Today's Specials bikes in the
rack outside the shop.

Alyssa leaned forward as far as the seat re-
straint would allow. "Does your ankle hurt
much?" he heard her ask.

Billie sat stiff and straight, facing forward,
even as he got into the driver's side, as if being
around his daughter was an imposition.

"No. Not much."

"I twisted my ankle once, jumping on my
bed. Is that what happened to you?"

"I fell off my bike."

"Oh. Did your elbows get all busted up,
too?"

"Broken," Noah corrected. He put the car
into gear. "Sounds more ladylike than busted."

"But…I'm just a kid. Why do I have to talk
like a lady?"

"Because I said so."

As he turned onto Main Street, his daughter said, "My name is Alyssa. What's yours?"

"Billie."

"But…but Billy is a *boy's* name."

"Only if you spell it *B-i-l-l-y*. I spell it *B-i-l-l-i-e*."

"There's a boy in my class," she said, "and his name is Billy— Daddy! Look!" She pointed across the street. "Isn't that little white dog the cutest thing ever!"

If he ever said yes to getting a dog, it sure wouldn't be a yippy ankle-biter like that one. "Uh-huh," he said. When he'd been forced to leave her favorite doll at the airport, Noah had soothed her tears by promising to replace it with a kitten. Mouser was nice enough, as cats go, but certainly not the in-your-face pup Alyssa had always dreamed about.

"If I had a dog," she said now, "it would be big, with a happy face. Like the one you had when you were a little boy, 'member, Daddy?"

"I sure do." How could he forget the gentle giant that had been more sibling than pet?

Alyssa giggled. "Tell Billie his name."

"Cash." He didn't know why, but he felt obliged to explain. "My dad named him Cash Money, because he'd been abused before we adopted him, and cost a fortune at the vet's."

Noah glanced over at her, and for a moment there she looked mildly interested. Then she pointed left, and he realized the route had captured her attention, not the story.

"You just passed my street," she said.

Now it was Noah's turn to groan, because it meant driving up to Hamilton Street to make a U-turn in the post office parking lot. Halfway there, traffic on Main Street slowed, then came to a grinding halt. While drivers around him raised their hands and muttered, Noah gripped the steering wheel until his knuckles ached. Trapped at a dead stop between parked cars and the constant flow of traffic heading east, he and Alyssa—and Billie, too—might as well have bull's-eyes painted on their foreheads.

He held his breath. Checked the side mirrors. Glanced over his shoulder, looking for *what,* he didn't know. Facing front again, he peered into the rearview mirror.

"What's wrong, Daddy? You look…scared."

"Nah. Just frustrated. You know how I get in traffic."

He watched the concern drain from his daughter's face, and just that fast, she was back on track.

"Oh, yes. Daddy hates traffic jams," she said to Billie. "Sometimes he even gets so mad about it that he says bad words!"

Billie chuckled quietly, then pursed her lips and looked out the passenger window. Noah shook his head. What a weird time to miss Jillian. On second thought, it wasn't weird at all. His wife had been so easygoing and easy to love. He didn't need an Einstein IQ to figure out why the few women who *had* inspired a second glance since her death had done so: they'd been gorgeous, smart and outgoing— just like Jillian. He blamed loneliness for his knee-jerk, momentary attraction to Billie back at the shop.

"Did your mom think you were going to be a boy?" Alyssa asked. "Is that why she named you Billie with an *i-e?*"

A second, then two passed before she answered. "My granddad's name is Bill."

Alyssa clapped her hands. "Oh, I get it! Your mom wanted to name you after him, but when a baby *girl* popped out, it was too late to pick a new name!"

"It's not my real name. It's just what everybody calls me."

If she didn't want to share the name printed on her birth certificate, that was okay with him.

Traffic eased up, and so did Noah's tension. They drove in silence for several blocks, until Alyssa noticed the Firehouse Museum. The next couple minutes were filled with what she remembered about its interior, where old firefighters' uniforms and helmets, tools and dozens of model-sized fire engines had been displayed behind red velvet ropes or inside glass-shelved cases.

"Have you been there, Billie?"

"No."

"Maybe we could go together."

Noah glanced over at Billie, whose eyes were wide with surprise…and indecision.

"The museum is open on Saturday. Can we go then, Daddy, and show Billie all the neat stuff inside?"

"We'll see."

Alyssa thought that over while Billie shot him a half smile that said "thanks." For sparing her from having to say no? Or for stalling the visit until she could walk around better?

"Oh! Daddy?"

Noah glanced at his daughter in the rearview mirror again.

"Do you mean we should wait until Billie's ankle is okay?"

He nodded. "That would be a good idea."

Alyssa leaned forward in her seat. "How long before it's better, Billie?"

The woman turned slightly, and only long

enough to say over her shoulder, "A week, maybe two."

"Don't worry." Alyssa smiled. "I'll think of something else. Something fun you can do sitting down."

For as long as Noah could remember, Alyssa had been a natural-born caretaker. He watched as her forefinger tapped her chin. He counted backward, waiting for her to come up with an idea for an outing that would allow Billie to participate while seated.

Ten, nine, eight—

"Do we still have that coupon from T-Bonz? The one that says 'Live Music on Saturdays'?"

Alyssa wanted a mom, like the other kids in her class. Noah got that. What he didn't get was why she saw mother potential in just about every female who crossed her path.

"The music doesn't start until eight o'clock," he told her, "and you're way too young to be up that late."

"It's just as well," Billie said. "I have a website to design for a client by Monday." She gestured. "There's my stree—"

Noah made the right turn onto Old Columbia Pike, eliminating the need for her to point it out. "I fiddled around with a website for the bike shop." He slowed the pickup, waiting for her to tell him which house was hers. "Put a day's work into a page, and gave up when I lost the whole thing with one keystroke."

Billie nodded. "Mistakes like that make up half of my business." She paused. "That's my place up ahead, right beside the jewelry shop. It says Hi Ho Silver on the sign. You can't miss it."

Noah braked and assessed the conditions of the road. Sharp curve. No shoulder. Two narrow lanes, and a sidewalk barely wider than the hallway between his kitchen and dining room. Even after all this time in Ellicott City, he disliked the inconvenience of having to drive through narrow alleyways to access his parking pad. Tongue Row—the road that passed a mere five feet from Billie's front door—left no room for slowing down, let alone parking long enough for her to exit safely. "Maybe I should drive around back, drop you off—"

"Thanks," she said, unbuckling her seat belt, "but there's no need to go to all that trouble. I won't get hit."

"But will *we?*" he asked, with a glance in the rearview mirror.

Billie peered over her shoulder. "Don't worry. If anyone rams you from behind, I'll be your witness." She got out of the truck. "Thanks for the ride. You have my number, so feel free to call whenever you've fixed the bike. Or…or you're interested in talking about a website."

She closed the door, and as he merged into traffic, Noah could see her in the side mirror, stooping to lift the doormat and retrieve her key. "Is she nuts?" he muttered. "Who does that anymore?" Evidently, she wasn't as suspicious of people as he first thought.

Alyssa turned and waved, and Noah saw Billie smile as she returned it.

"She's nice, isn't she, Daddy?"

"I guess."

"I wonder why she doesn't smile more. She's very pretty when she smiles, isn't she?"

"I guess," he repeated.

"Do you think she's as pretty as Mommy?"

"No way."

He pictured Jillian, tall, willowy, too girlie to test a mountain bike, let alone ride one hard enough to mess up an ankle.

Alyssa sighed quietly. "She reminds me of Mommy, kind of."

"She does? How so?"

"Mostly, the way she looks at me."

Noah might have asked what she meant, if Alyssa hadn't lifted her shoulders until they touched her earlobes, a sweet, dainty gesture that always made his heart thump with fatherly affection.

"I saw her looking at you that way, too," Alyssa said.

"She did?"

"Uh-huh. Did it make you think of Mommy, too?"

He hadn't noticed Billie looking at Alyssa in anything other than a polite, neighborly way. As for how she'd looked at him, impatience came to mind.

"Look there," he said, leaning closer to the windshield. "Emily is loose again."

Their neighbor's goose was a regular escape artist. One of these days she'd waddle into the road, and that would be the end of her…if the county didn't cite Meb for allowing her to violate the noise ordinance by honking at all hours. Noah parked on an angle, effectively blocking the alleyway as he dialed Meb's number.

"No answer," he said after seven rings. "You sit tight while I put Emily back into her pen." After pocketing his keys, he uncuffed his shirt-sleeves, then reached into the glove box and grabbed a pair of worn leather work gloves usually reserved for stacking wood in the back of the truck. Last time he'd tried to save Emily from getting run over by a car, she'd nearly blinded him with a flurry of fluttering wings. She'd bitten him, too, leaving nasty

bruises on his forearms. To add insult to injury, she infected him with a bad case of mites.
When Meb had found out about the mites, he
had brought Noah a giant bottle of Listerine.
"Shower, splash this on and take some antihis-
tamine," the farmer-turned-artist had said. The
home remedy had worked...after two miserable, itchy weeks. This time, Noah wasn't taking any chances.

It took nearly twenty minutes just to catch
her, and another ten to ease her into the wood-
and-wire pen Meb had built for her. After securing the latch, Noah noticed that Emily's
food bowl was empty, so he refilled it by pouring pellets through the mesh. The only human
allowed near the enclosure was Meb. The only
one allowed in the *yard* was Meb. To Noah's
knowledge, no one had ever tried to steal
the iron and steel sculptures that were Meb's
trademark...and his livelihood. And no wonder, with a crazy, biting, mite-infested goose
standing guard!

When he finished, Noah smacked the gloves
against his thigh, then peeled off his shirt and
dropped it into the nearest trash can. Better
to lose it than risk bringing parasites into the
apartment.

"So what are you in the mood for tonight,

kiddo?" he asked, parking the truck in its usual slot.

"We haven't had spaghetti in a long time. With meatballs, and garlic bread, too."

Her mom's favorite meal. "You got it, cupcake."

The moment they were inside, Alyssa grabbed her crayons and a stack of construction paper.

"I'll be in my room," she announced, "drawing a picture of Emily. I might need help, spelling some things for Meb."

"Soon as we finish eating. I'll call you when it's time to set the table, okay?"

He grabbed a T-shirt from his dresser drawer as she said, "Okay, Daddy."

While he filled the pasta pot with water, he thought about what Alyssa had said earlier, and tried to remember how Jillian had looked at him. Nothing came to mind. Not even with his eyes closed. Worse, he couldn't see her at all. Maxine, his Baltimore connection with the Marshals Service, had warned him about this three years ago, but he hadn't believed it.

"What kind of man shares years and has a child with a woman—causes her death—and can't raise a mental image of her?" he'd demanded.

"First of all," Max had said, "you didn't

cause Jillian's death. Senator O'Malley did. As for forgetting what she looks like? Trust me. It'll happen. And when it does, it will prove you're healing. Because you're normal."

If she thought a quote from some required psychology course would help alleviate the fear, she was dead wrong, and he'd told her so. Besides, how could a person who'd never lost a spouse know what was normal and what wasn't?

Much as Noah hated to admit it now, Max had been right about one thing: the day had come. She'd been off beam about that other thing, though, because he felt anything *but* normal. He could call her, put George's "she's a good listener" claims to the test...again.

Water from the tap overflowed the pot's rim, shaking Noah from his daze. He emptied half the water down the drain, then carried the pot to the stove. He turned the burner on high, thinking it probably wasn't a good idea to call Max. She knew every hideous detail of his past. That if he hadn't joined forces with the corrupt senator, it wouldn't have been necessary to choose between jail time and testifying against the man. If he hadn't testified, the accident intended for him wouldn't have killed Jillian, which prompted the decision to move from a fourteen-room house in Chicago's River North neighborhood to a four-room apartment above a bike shop, living under assumed names, afraid to get close to anyone for fear that what happened to Jillian might happen to Alyssa.

Yeah, Max knew the details of his story and accepted the facts without passing judgment. Not that she needed to…

Noah despised himself enough for both of them.

## CHAPTER FOUR

BILLIE SAT AT her desk, trying to get comfortable as she keyed in html code on a client's website. Not an easy feat with one foot propped on an open file drawer. She missed her exercise ball, but since the accident, she'd had to make do with her old, non-ergonomically correct chair. That alone, she thought, hobbling toward the kitchen, was incentive enough to keep the ankle iced and elevated, per doctor's orders.

The doorbell rang as she grabbed a fresh ice pack. According to the wall clock, it was nearly nine o'clock.

"What kind of nut drops by unannounced at this time of night?"

A peek through the front door's sidelights told her: Troy, the oldest of her twin brothers, dodging moths drawn by the porch light.

She threw open the door. "Holy smokes, Troy, what are *you* doing here?"

"I, ah…" He chuckled quietly. "Good to see you, too."

"Sorry. That didn't come out right at all." She wrapped him in a hug. "I'm just surprised to see you." Stepping aside, Billie waved him into the foyer and tried not to stare as he dragged a big, bulging suitcase inside. "Good grief. Is there a body in there, or are you planning a trip around the world?"

He looked at the bag and shrugged. "I kinda left in a hurry, and just jammed stuff in there."

"Uh-oh. What's up?"

"Can we talk about it later?"

"How much later?"

"Feed me, and maybe I'll feel like dredging up the bad news."

"Always the tough guy, huh?" Billie pointed toward the hall. "You know where to stow your gear." On the way to the guest room, he nodded toward the home office space she'd fashioned in one corner of the living room. "I'll stay out of your hair. Promise. You keep designing those websites as if I wasn't even here. This is temporary. I just need to get my head straight before I go ho—" He cleared his throat. "Before I go back…" he frowned slightly "…to Philly."

He'd started to say *home,* and changed his mind. That worried her almost as much as the notion that her big, rough-tough marine brother, who'd earned a Purple Heart and a Silver Star in Afghanistan, had come here to hide. But from what? She hobbled alongside him and pointed at the hideous black soft cast the E.R. doctor had prescribed. "I'd never admit it to anyone else, but my ankle is killing me." Silently, she acknowledged that if Noah Preston hadn't insisted on driving her home earlier, it would hurt a whole lot more.

"What did you do to yourself this time?"

"Took a curve too fast during a race," she said, limping along behind him. "You can have your Superman and Captain America. My hero is the tree that kept me from going over the edge."

He rolled the suitcase into the guest room's closet. "You've fixed the place up real nice. Hard to believe it's only been a year since you moved in," he said, glancing around. Then, pointing at her ankle, Troy said, "Let me guess. You're planning to go out again, next chance you get."

"Why wouldn't I? I love cycling." It had saved her, in more ways than one. But since Troy knew that almost as well as she did, Billie saw no need to remind him of those awful, scary months following the stillbirth.

"Maybe I'll get a bike and go with you, see if riding can fix what's wrong with my life, too."

The sadness in his voice wasn't lost on Billie.

"Another fight with Victoria?"

He only shook his head.

"You're way too good for her," Billie said. "I never understood what you saw in—"

"Do me a favor and drop it, okay?"

She took one look at his all-business expression and decided to press him for details later, after he'd had a meal and a good night's sleep. "You still driving that small convertible?"

"Yeah…."

"Then we're in luck. I traded my car for a small pickup, and it came with a double bike rack. I know where we can get you a great mountain bike, too…if Victoria hasn't talked you into another cruise or something."

"Billie, c'mon. Give it a rest, will ya? You don't hear me asking when you last talked to that idiot you married, or how you can afford this place after caving to avoid a confrontation with the jerk—who took way more than he deserved in the divorce settlement—if you ask me. Or if you regret giving up your job as a flight attendant just because Chuck the Pilot didn't like you being in the air when he wasn't." Her brother took a breath and plowed on. "Or if you're sorry you left Philly, where the baby is buried."

"Okay. All right. I get the message. I'm

sorry! If I'd known you would bring up every awful thing in my past, I never would have—"

"I'm the one who's sorry."

And he looked it.

"I have a good mind," she said, pretending to pout, "not to show you where the extra hangers and clean towels are."

Troy laughed halfheartedly. "You'd only be punishing yourself...." Wiggling his eyebrows, he said, "Now show me what you've done with the place since we moved you in."

Billie gave him a tour of the five-room cottage, and then headed to the kitchen to pour two glasses of iced tea. Troy carried the tumblers and followed her to the back deck, where she flopped onto a lounge chair.

"I can't believe how much you did in such a short time," her brother said. "The folks made it sound like you were living in an unfurnished shoebox." He sat on the other lounge chair. "If I could find a place like this, I might never go back."

Evidently, things with his fiancée were worse than Billie had thought. "I know you're vulnerable right now, so maybe this isn't the best time to tell you there are at least two houses for sale within walking distance."

He didn't comment, and instead gestured

to her small, fenced-in yard. "Did you plant all that stuff?"

"Artfully dodged, Jack Dawson," she teased. "And to answer your question, yes, I planted all that stuff. Gardening is way cheaper than a therapist."

Troy reached across the space between them and squeezed her hand. "I'm glad you're doing well. You had us worried there for a while."

"Us. What a laugh. I know the rest of the family meant well, but you were the only one who was really there for me after Chuck dumped me." She returned the squeeze. "And whether you like it or not, I intend to be there for you, too."

"I'm countin' on it." He leaned back, crossed one ankle over the other. "So are you seeing anybody?"

"Between the web design business and cycling, there isn't time for stuff like that," she answered. "Besides, I'm not exactly girlfriend material."

"Yet."

Billie only shrugged. Thankfully, he hadn't quoted their parents: "It's been two years, Billie. You need to get hold of yourself. Put Chuck in the past and move forward with your life."

She *had* moved forward. New home, new

job, new friends and hobbies. But she was far from ready to consider a new man in her life.

Troy stared up at the sky. "Yeah, this is great, all right."

His stomach rumbled, and he explained, "Like I said, I left in a hurry."

"What say I make us each a sandwich?"

Inside, he sat at the bar counter as she assembled the ingredients. "It's almost as if you knew I was coming," he noted.

"Don't flatter yourself. Ham and Swiss on rye toast is my favorite sandwich, too, remember."

They ate in a comfortable silence.

Billie thought of how their parents didn't seem to have any trouble airing their grievances. Clearly, it was a trait she and Troy hadn't inherited. He rarely talked about his overseas assignments, and even when he did, the discussions were tip of the iceberg, at best. Except for that night several months after the stillbirth, when he'd come to make sure she was all right. It had been the two-year anniversary of the roadside bomb that had wiped out all but four men in his unit.

"So how's the website business?"

"I'm doing well enough to keep the wolf from the door."

"I didn't see the Cannondale anywhere

around," he said. "Did you wreck it in the accident?"

"It's a little scratched and dented, but not totaled." She remembered all the repairs Noah had told her he'd make. "The guy at the bike shop might need to order parts, but," she said, pointing at the ankle, "I'm not going anywhere for a while, anyway. From the way he talked, it didn't sound expensive. At least, I hope it won't be. I hate to dip into the savings I've squirreled away for real emergencies."

"Real emergencies?"

"The furnace is on its last legs, and so's the water heater. And in a year or two, I'll probably need a new roof."

"Sounds like you're planning to make Ellicott City your permanent home."

Billie shrugged. "I guess I am." She looked around at the mismatched flea market lamps she'd rewired, the cushiony sofa she'd reupholstered, the glass-topped coffee table she'd made from an old wire spool. Billie didn't even care that "shabby chic" wasn't chic anymore, because piece by piece, she'd rebuilt her life, just as she'd rebuilt the bar counter in the kitchen.

"Mom won't be happy to hear you're not coming home. She figured you would…eventually."

"Soon as that twin of yours and his wife have a couple of kids, she'll have happier things to distract her. Besides, this is the last place Chuck will think to look for me."

"Todd and Dani aren't planning to have kids for another year or two. Besides," Troy added, "after accusing you of getting pregnant on purpose to justify cheating on you? Even Chuck isn't stupid enough to get in touch with you."

Billie harrumphed.

Her brother paused, then turned in his chair. "Whoa. Are you saying he *did?*"

"No. I haven't heard from him since the house sold. I just don't want him adding insult to injury by calling to say he sold all our furniture."

"Or worse," Troy added, "to announce that scuzzball he left you for is pregnant."

That hurt far worse than Billie cared to admit.

"I still can't believe he got more upset about losing your half of the house than about losing the baby."

Billie shook her head. "Why would that upset him? He never wanted her." Heart pounding with the bitter memory, she said, "He never believed she was his, anyway."

"That's bull. You know it, I know it and that no-good piece of garbage knows it."

"There's ice cream in the freezer," she said, interrupting his tirade. "What'll it be? Ice cream sandwich or chocolate marshmallow swirl?"

He glanced at the clock. "Ice cream. At ten-thirty. You're kidding, right?"

She started for the fridge. "If we're gonna be up all hours, rehashing our sad pasts, I want something to sweeten the atmosphere."

"Our sad pasts," he echoed. "If that means you expect me to spill my guts about what happened between Victoria and me…"

"I'm going to get it out of you sooner or later," Billie said matter-of-factly.

"You still a fan of the evening news?"

"Are you still a jarhead?"

She knew what he'd say, and Troy didn't disappoint: "Once a marine, always a marine."

But ten minutes into the late-night news, he was dozing, one arm crooked over his face as he sprawled on the couch. The scene reminded her of happier times with her twin brothers. "Lost my job," he said at last, without moving.

"No way. Why? Your boss loved you! I was there, remember, when he announced you were the new regional manager. Is he having money troubles?"

"No, he's doing great. I'm the one who's having troubles. Not money troubles, but…"

Troy levered himself up on one elbow. "I just couldn't live the lie anymore."

"What lie?"

"Don't get me wrong—I care about Victoria—but I'm not in love with her. I know you believe she thought of me as nothing more than a paycheck, but she's really a great gal, and deserves to be with someone who's crazy about her."

He sat up, leaned both elbows on his knees and clasped his hands in the space between. "So I sat her down and told her the truth, then gave the boss two weeks' notice. No big surprise...she gave me the weekend to clear out."

Billie sat beside him. "Why do I get the impression all of this happened a long time ago?"

"Not that long," he said dully. "Just two weeks."

"You left the house two weeks ago?"

He nodded.

"Troy! Where have you been staying all this time?" She gave his shoulder a sisterly punch. "And why didn't you call me!"

"I've been in a hotel. And don't give me that 'why didn't you go to Mom and Dad's' nonsense. You know the answer to that even better than I do." He heaved a deep sigh. "As for why I didn't call you, I could say it was because I didn't want to heap my troubles on top of yours, but that would be a lie. Truth is…I'm ashamed of myself."

"Why?"

"I let things go on way too long. I kept telling myself that once she got to know me—really know me—she'd break it off. Who knew she'd do the old head-over-heels thing?" He groaned quietly. "She deserves better. A whole lot better."

"So it's really over between you two?"

"Yeah." He hung his head and whispered, "Yeah, and it's best for Victoria."

For the first time since they'd entered adulthood, Billie felt more centered and mature than her big, rough-tough marine brother.

"Sorry I misjudged her," she admitted. "Sorry I wasn't there for you, too."

Billie slid an arm around his waist and simply held him, and after a moment, Troy disentangled himself and got to his feet.

"You sure it's okay if I crash here for a while?"

"Stay as long as you need to. Tomorrow I'll give you a copy of the front door key." She looked up at him. "Have you told Mom and Dad where you'll be?"

"I'll call them tomorrow."

Billie stood, too. "And what about Victoria? Does she know where you are?"

He nodded. "She's going to call once the house is sold." Troy gave a halfhearted chuckle. "Ironic, isn't it, since I only bought the place because she was so crazy about it."

It seemed to Billie he must have loved Victoria, at least at first.

"I guess she's taking a page from your book, Billie—sell, move forward, don't look back."

"And so should you. Whether you want to admit it or not, what you did was a gesture of love."

"How so?"

"Some guys might have waited until after the wedding, when a child or two might be involved. She's hurt now, but someday she'll realize how much more it would have hurt if you hadn't been honest."

"How'd you get so smart?"

"Runs in the family, I guess."

Troy yawned and stretched. "Well, I'm beat. Think I'll turn in."

"Good idea. You know what Mom says…."

"Things always look better in the morning," they said together.

Laughing, Billie gave him a shove. "See you tomorrow, then…y'big softie."

"Better watch it, tough girl. I still have fifty pounds and eleven inches on you."

At the guest room door, he kissed her forehead. "You're a lifesaver, kid."

"Guess that runs in the family, too."

Troy nodded.

"If you need anything," she said as his door swung closed, "make yourself at home."

"Thanks. I will."

The latch clicked as she whispered, "Sweet dreams."

## CHAPTER FIVE

"SWEET DREAMS," NOAH whispered, pulling Alyssa's door closed.

He headed for the kitchen, taking care to avoid the loud squeak just outside her room. Three years ago, she could sleep through her mother's book club meetings, his late-night phone calls, even thunderstorms. Since her mom's death, it seemed his daughter slept with one eye open and one ear cocked. He understood that, because Jillian's murder had all but turned him into an insomniac.

A gentle early autumn rain pecked the windows as he checked the back door, which had leaked like a sieve during the last downpour. So far, so good, he thought. But just to be safe, Noah tucked several towels near the threshold. Tomorrow, after dropping Alyssa off at school, he'd walk over to Kaplan's Hardware for weather stripping.

He grabbed a beer from the fridge, then popped a CD into the stereo and settled into his well-worn recliner. He dimmed all the lights except for the one beside his chair, and as Bonnie Raitt's haunting, husky voice filled the room, the mood was set.

Noah pried open the brass clasp on the manila envelope. Inside, three smaller envelopes held letters from his parents, his brother and sister.

A quiet knock at the French doors startled him. It didn't surprise him to see Max through the slight opening between the curtain panels. What did surprise him was that he hadn't heard her climb the long narrow staircase that led to the apartment.

When he opened the door, she pointed at the porch swing. "Oh, man, I've always wanted one of those! Is it new?"

"Yes and no. Taylor's was having a sidewalk sale, and Alyssa went crazy over it."

Max hung her leather jacket on the hall tree as he dropped the envelope onto the coffee table.

"And of course," she said, making herself comfortable, "you couldn't say no."

"I just popped a beer," he said. "Want one?"

She tucked long, copper-red curls behind her ears. "Sure. Why not. I'm off duty."

He went into the kitchen for a bottle, and when he returned, Max was admiring the porcelain-faced baby doll he'd bought on the same day as the swing.

"I don't remember seeing this before." She thanked him for the beer, then leaned the doll in the sofa's opposite corner.

The recliner creaked when he dropped onto its seat. "It kinda came with the swing."

Max took a swig, then shook her head.

"What?" Noah said.

"You'd better learn to say no, that's what, or that adorable kid of yours will be so spoiled by the time she's sixteen, you'll find yourself working a second job to pay for her pink Corvette. And a pony. And—"

"No way."

"You forget how long I've had this 'agent' gig, Preston. I've seen it before. That's how I know you'll be sorry if you don't soon get a handle on your yes-man tendencies."

He didn't want to talk about Alyssa, or how hard it was to deny her anything. The 9x12 envelope sat on the coffee table, and he was anxious to read the letters from his family.

Max followed his gaze and picked it up. "So my sources at the agency were right. You *did* get mail today." Fingering the envelope's flap, she added, "So what's up in the Windy City these days?"

"Don't know. I was just about to read the letters when you showed up."

In typical Max fashion, she gave an unlady-like snort. "Well, don't let me stop you." She toed off her high-heeled cowboy boots and propped both black-socked feet on the table. "Can't remember when I last heard a Bonnie Raitt tune. *Lord,* but that woman can sing!"

She leaned into the backrest and closed her eyes. "Well, what are you waiting for? Christmas?"

Noah sighed. The woman knew just about everything else about him. Why not add *Watch me fall apart...again* to the list?

His mom had stapled a newspaper clipping to her note, and he read the headline out loud. "Gina Judson Takes Six Blue Ribbons in Baking Category." Beneath it was a full-color photo of his mom, standing in front of the Du-Page County Fairgrounds entrance. "Man. I haven't seen that in years." He put the article on the coffee table, and while Max looked at it, he read his mom's letter. Amos Miller next door had finally chopped down the messy mimosa tree that stained his mom's prized brick driveway, she'd written, and the last of her tomatoes were ripening on the sunporch.

He could picture them, lined up in tidy rows on the glass-and-rattan table, could almost hear

his mom scolding his dad for swiping the rip-
est for a sandwich, instead of leaving it for her
famous tomato-watermelon salad.

"She has lovely handwriting," Max said
when he handed her the letter. "You just don't
see that anymore, what with email and texting
and social networking."

While she read, Noah opened Eddie's letter.
His brother, as usual, had started out by lam-
basting the Chicago Bears' coaching staff, and
went on to grouse that if the Cubs' manage-
ment had one functioning brain among them,
the team might actually get into the playoffs
at some point during his lifetime.

"Clearly," Max observed, "your mom focused all her 'neat penmanship' energy on
you, because Eddie's writing is horrible!" She
fanned herself with the pages. "Why doesn't
he type his letters on the computer, so people
who aren't hieroglyphics specialists can read
them?"

"Keep it up and I'll revoke your reading
privileges," Noah said wryly. "And to answer
your question, he writes because our mom in-
sists it's more personal."

And as he opened Grace's letter, Max zipped
her lip.

Noah's sister and her firefighter husband
still shared their sprawling rancher in Glen-

dale Heights, and her letter read like a to-do list for Stan. The porch needed a coat of paint, and the boxwood hedge hadn't been trimmed since last summer. Stan's excuse? That Eddie had borrowed the hedge trimmer and the paint sprayer, and as usual, hadn't returned either.

Noah hit Replay on the CD player while Max read Grace's letter. "Another beer?" he asked.

"Better not," she said. "How would it look if a cop stopped me on the way home?"

Noah tossed both bottles into the recycling bin.

"I'm wondering…do Grace and Stan have kids?" she asked.

"No, but not for a lack of trying. I'm wondering something, too."

Heavily mascaraed green eyes opened wide. "About?"

"You."

"Uh-oh…"

"You're great at what you do, there's no getting around that. But are all these questions you ask the result of careful training? Experience? Or were you just born nosy?"

Max rolled her eyes. "It's stuff like that makes me wish I'd set you up at the Comedy Club instead of this bike shop."

"Well, it's a natural question. You're too young to be so nosy."

"Now there's a backhanded compliment if ever I heard one!"

"So why aren't *you* married?"

Max sat up straighter. "Aren't you just full of questions tonight."

"Reading mail from my family makes me nostalgic. So shoot me."

"Can't. The agency makes me account for every bullet fired…."

"You're not getting off that easy," Noah said. "If you'd had a mind to, you probably could have been a model. So which is it—you're a workaholic or a man-hater?"

Max threw back her head and laughed. "Neither. I just don't believe in mixing business with pleasure, and all the good marshals are spoken for." She shrugged. "But you're a fine one to talk. Three years in the program, longer than that since your wife died…why are *you* still unattached?"

Noah frowned. "I can't believe you'd ask such a question." For one thing, Jillian didn't simply die, she'd been murdered. Even if his conscience allowed him to see other women, his fatherly instincts would never permit him to trust anyone to babysit Alyssa.

Max nodded. "Yeah, well, other people in

your situation manage it. At least they didn't become monks."

A stony silence descended. Max rolled her eyes, then asked, "So how's that li'l princess of yours?"

"Still a happy, well-adjusted kid," he said, nodding toward Alyssa's door. "Mostly thanks to you."

Max waved the compliment away. "Knock it off, will ya? You know how easily I blush."

"Yeah, well—"

"If you're about to go over that same old 'it's my fault' ground again, spare me, okay? Sit down. Read your dad's letter." Max paused, softened her tone. "I know you like to save his for last."

He couldn't deny that he'd gone down that road too many times to count. Couldn't deny that he enjoyed hearing his dad talk about the crazy antics of his microbiology and immunology graduate students. This time, however, the letter sounded more like an official report on Senator O'Malley and others affiliated with Noah's downfall.

"Listen to this," he said to Max. And then he read aloud, "'I can't prove it, of course, but rumors are circulating that indicate a certain slimeball is still cutting deals and calling the shots from his Stateville prison cell. But don't

worry. I'm keeping an ear to the ground.'"
Noah met Max's eyes. "What does he mean
by *that*?"

She sat up straighter, reached for the letter.
"Don't get your boxers in a knot. It's probably
nothing."

"No offence, but that's not much comfort.
Why do I get the feeling Alyssa is still in danger, even after three long—"

"Shh," the agent said, pointing at Alyssa's
door. "What if the kid hears you?" Max folded
his father's letter, returned it to its envelope.
"Okay if I take this back to the office?"

"Why? I thought you guys read every word
before the mail is delivered, so you can black
out every name and date."

"We do. But the letters pass through a lot of
hands between here and Chicago. I'd rather err
on the side of caution than take any chances."

"I know that Alyssa and I aren't the only
people you're assigned to, and that the letters
have to pass through three, sometimes four
post offices to throw off the bad guys."

"Hey, don't knock it," Max said. "It's working, isn't it?"

"So far. I guess. And that isn't much comfort, either." Noah inhaled a shaky breath, remembering the alarm in his father's letter.
"Sorry. I don't mean to sound like an ingrate.

I appreciate everything you and the agency have done for us."

Reaching across the space between them, Max gave his hand a gentle pat. "There's a 99 percent chance that what your dad heard is a rumor. The mad rantings of a foolish old convict, shooting off his mouth and thumping his chest to prove he's still a big shot." She held up a finger to silence Noah's protest. "But I'll look into it. You have my word on it."

The clock struck the half hour.

"Nine-thirty? How can that be?" Grunting and groaning, Max tugged her boots back on, then shrugged into her jacket. Almost as an afterthought, she gave Noah a hug.

"Relax," she said, patting the envelope in her pocket, "and let me take care of this. If there's anything to it, I'll let you know."

He locked up, then sat on the edge of his recliner and stared at the scuffed hardwood beneath his bare feet. He was tired. So tired of worrying that every stranger had been sent by O'Malley, to finish what he'd started. Tired of pretending this life they were living was normal.

Alyssa would be disappointed to learn they hadn't sent anything for her, so Noah stuffed the letters back into the manila envelope, sealed it and placed it in the lockbox hidden behind a row of ancient Reader's Digest books on the top shelf of the bookcase.

Noah held his head in his hands and tried to think of something about their world that wasn't a lie. When nothing came to mind, he slumped onto his chair and drove his fingers through his hair. Maybe when he answered the family's letters, he'd ask them not to write, at least not for a while. It was hard enough holding things together without their black-and-white reminders of what life was like compared to what it could have been: Alyssa sleeping in a tiny apartment above a bicycle shop, instead of her big sunny room in Chicago. A dad who sold bike chains and air pumps instead of putting bad guys into prison. A dad who had become one himself.

If she hadn't already lost so much, he might be tempted—

"Aw, don't cry, Daddy," his daughter said, climbing into his lap. Holding his face in her hands, she said, "I cry, too, when I miss Mommy. But everything is going to be okay. I promise."

Word for word what he'd said to her dozens of times over the years. But until she'd echoed the phrase, Noah hadn't realized he'd been crying.

He hugged her tight. Kissed her cheek. Buried his face in the crook of her neck and inhaled the scent of baby shampoo. She deserved better than this. Better than the self-pitying, self-centered coward he'd allowed himself to become.

"I'm okay," he lied. "Got something in my eye, is all."

She studied his face and, satisfied with his response, frowned slightly. "I just hate it when that happens. Do you want me to get the eyedrops?"

Standing, he hoisted her onto one hip and carried her back to her room.

"No, that's okay. But if whatever it is hasn't worked itself out soon, you can get the eyedrops, okay?"

"Okay," she said, as he tucked her in. "I like taking care of you."

Noah pressed a kiss to her forehead. "Sweet dreams," he said again, heading for the hallway.

She rolled onto her side and hugged her pillow tight as he turned out the light. He stood in the doorway for a moment, watching, listening, wanting nothing more than to be the father she deserved.

"Love you, Daddy,"

He could barely speak. "Love you, too, cupcake."

# CHAPTER SIX

"ARENT YOU GOING to answer the phone?" Troy asked, leaning over her desk.

The caller ID window read Unknown. Billie rarely answered calls she didn't recognize, and never picked up blocked, unknown or multiple zero numbers. "That's what voice mail is for," she told him.

"Hey. Billie. It's Noah Preston. From the bike shop?"

She grabbed the handset, hitting speakerphone without realizing it.

"Hi," she said. "I was beginning to think you'd had to send the bike back to the manufacturer or something."

"So you didn't get my message last week? About the parts that were on back order?"

"Oh. Yes, I did. I meant to call, but…" But between Troy and work, she'd forgotten to return the call. "Sorry. I meant to let you know there's no rush."

"Oh. Right. The ankle is still messed up, huh?"

"It's much better, but I won't be riding anytime soon."

"Bummer. Guess that means you'll miss the Tidewater race."

"Yeah. And the Pocono Challenge, too." She shook off the moment of self-pity. "But it's no big deal. There are a couple of races in October."

"Chambersburg?"

"Right. And Green Lane, Pennsylvania, too. But enough about that." She giggled, too long and too hard. Groaning inwardly, she said, "Any idea when the parts will be in?"

"Two, three days. But that's just one of the reasons I called today. Are you still interested in building a website for me?"

"Of course."

"Don't sound so eager," Troy whispered in the background. "He'll think you don't have any other clients!"

Frowning, she sent a "Shh" warning his way.

"I'm just wrapping up something for another client. How about if I stop by, spend an hour or so watching you work, see if I can get some ideas for your main page?"

Troy shook his head. Noah cleared his throat. "Well, how's tomorrow, say, after lunch?" She turned her back on her brother and clicked the speaker off. "Works for me. What time does Alyssa get home from school?"

"I pick her up at three-thirty."

Billie wondered why he didn't let her ride the bus like the rest of the kids in the neighborhood, then remembered the guy she'd met at the bike shop that day, who'd implied Noah gave a whole new meaning to the word *overprotective*.

"I'll see you between one and one-thirty," she said.

Billie hung up, then faced Troy. "Look. You've been a great houseguest, and I appreciate the way you fixed the deck door and reattached that loose gutter. And your chili recipe is to die for. To be honest, I wouldn't mind if you moved in here permanently...if you'd learn to keep your nose out of my business stuff."

"When you're right, you're right. It won't happen again." With one hand raised in the Scout salute, he said, "Sorry."

"No need for apologies," she told him, heading into her office nook. "As long as you stay out of my business."

Troy saluted. "Message sent and received."

Billie fired up the computer, clicked her most recent client's file and began adding photos to the About Us page.

"You can fool other people, kid, but you can't fool me."

She swiveled her desk chair to glare at her brother. "What's that supposed to mean?"

"You've been alone long enough. It's okay to like that guy. You know...*like* that guy."

"That guy is repairing my bike, so I'm his customer. If I'm lucky, that guy will like my website ideas, and he'll be my client. That's all there is to it, okay?"

"You're right. It's none of my business. It's just, well, your voice changed when you talked to him, so I figured maybe you were interested. Let me make it up to you. Pepperoni-mushroom pizza, or subs for supper?"

Billie did her best to dismiss his "your voice changed" comment. "Pizza sounds great." There'd be plenty of time to rehash the conversation later.

Troy went back to his online job search as she scanned the internet for other bicycle shops. She wanted to see what was missing from those websites and ensure Noah's site stood out from the others. It didn't take long to figure out what she'd change about the examples. Photos on the home page were too large, distracting from the business message. And either there were too many tabs, or those provided didn't perform a specific function.

She opened a blank page and began typing.

LANDON DESIGNS
WEBSITE PROPOSAL

CLIENT: NOAH PRESTON,
OWNER, IKE'S BIKES

In recent months, this shop has noticed an increase in competition in the Baltimore vicinity (see list of stores below). A website designed to serve existing patrons, while attracting new ones, will provide people with more accurate comparables. To effectively capture the market from its competitors, *Ike's Bikes* website design must implement a marketing strategy focused on this goal. This will start with a needs analysis session to identify the key elements of the site, different customer types and all necessary calls to action. The session will be followed with a content plan focused on specific goals, and will move into the design phase, which will include the following:

Billie paused and thought for a second before beginning to type a bulleted list of the pages she would include on Noah's site: Home, Types

of Bikes, Bike Parts, Rides/Events, Rentals/
Repairs and Contact Us. Each page would include a defining paragraph and photographs.

After supplying a list of similar shops in
the area, she printed the proposal onto Landon
Designs letterhead, slid it into a hunter-green
pocket folder, slapped her label on the cover
and set it aside. Tomorrow, when she visited
him at the shop, Billie would ask him to turn
on his computer so she could show him her
own business website. He would be impressed
by the number and variety of clients she'd ac-
quired since opening the doors to Landon
Designs three years earlier. Feeling suitably
prepared, she went back to updating another
client's site.

Hours later, she noticed the clock in the corner of her monitor. How could it be after midnight? Working the kinks out of her neck and
shoulders, she walked into the kitchen, and
was immediately greeted by a bold black message printed on the pizza box lid: "BUY A
TIMER," it said, "AND YOU WON'T GET
HEARTBURN FROM EATING COLD
PIZZA AT MIDNIGHT." And beneath it, a
smaller line that read, "Or make your brother
eat alone."

Poor Troy. She had been too caught up in
work to even notice the time. Billie grabbed a

slice of pizza and bit into the now congealed cheese. Not bad. She took another bite. She'd risk the heartburn.

BILLIE SHOULD HAVE taken Troy's advice. She'd tossed and turned all night, waking up and falling asleep more than a dozen times, thanks to dreams of those life-altering moments under the glaring delivery room lights.

She got up and trudged into the kitchen to start the coffeemaker, then grabbed Troy's sweatshirt jacket from the hook beside the door and carried a slice of pizza onto the deck. A light rain was falling, so she pulled up the jacket's hood. A motorcycle buzzed by out front, and on Main Street, the squealing brakes of a school bus pierced the otherwise quiet morning. It had rained hard last night and she inhaled the scents that rode the autumn breeze: of roses, planted all around the deck. Damp leaves, fluttering against the fence. Bud, her elderly neighbor, frying bacon. Her coffee, spewing into the carafe.

Leaning into the railing, Billie watched a chipmunk scamper through the mulch surrounding the sunflowers, its cheeks puffed to three times their normal size as it prepared for the winter. She loved it here, in this place she'd bought and paid for with her half of the settlement, arranged by Chuck's attorney.

An odd feeling engulfed her, something between resentment and melancholy. Even after all this time, Billie still didn't fully understand why her ex had left. She'd loved everything about being married, even the things that most women complained about, like socks on the floor and toothpaste tubes squeezed from the middle. Living alone all through college had taught her that she wasn't cut out for a solitary life, so having someone who shared her views on politics, menu changes at their favorite restaurant and what to save their money for had felt like a fairy tale come to life.

She frowned as the same old questions resurfaced.

If Chuck felt that strongly about not having kids, why hadn't he said so when she'd told him about her dream of having a big family? Had he expected her to change her mind once she saw how delightful her life could be with him at the center of it? If she hadn't pressed him to have a baby, would he have stayed? Would she have wanted him to…?

Bud's cat, Inky, padded up and wound figure eights around her ankles, alternately purring and meowing in the hope Billie would share a pepperoni slice. Stooping, she fed him a sliver of meat, then stroked his glossy fur. The coffeemaker hissed, signaling a full pot. She peeled off a tiny blob of mozzarella, and the cat licked it from her fingertip. "Life," she said, "is a little bit like you. Soft on the surface, rough and raspy when you look a little deeper."

"I hope writing greeting card verses isn't on your bucket list," Troy said, joining her on the deck, "because that was *awful*."

Meowing, Inky rubbed Troy's calf. "Sorry, pal," he said, hands extended. "I got nothin'." He met Billie's eyes. "And even if I did, I wouldn't give it to you, because as any sane person knows, if you feed a stray cat, it will keep coming back."

"Inky isn't a stray." Billie stood up. "He belongs to Bud."

As if on cue, Inky sauntered toward the corner of the yard, leaped onto a fence post and disappeared.

Troy nodded toward the half-eaten slice of pizza in Billie's hand. "That's a horrible breakfast. I'm telling Mom."

"Go ahead," she said, smirking, "and I'll tell her…" The joke fizzled even before she completed the thought. If he ever found out that she'd heard him crying himself to sleep, he'd be mortified.

He followed her into the kitchen. "Tell her what?"

She filled two mugs with coffee, buying time to think of something. "That you leave wet towels on the bed."

"You wouldn't."

"I could, so don't push your luck."

"So what time is your meeting with *Noah?*"

Her brother's sarcasm wasn't lost on her. But she needed to choose her words carefully, or risk heightening his belief that her interest in Noah was more than strictly business.

Pouring Lucky Charms into a bowl, Billie said, "Are these a regular item on your grocery list? Because I haven't had them since I was ten years old. Eight, even."

"Nice try, but I'm not that easily distracted. But don't worry. I know when to back off."

She didn't intend to give him a chance to prove it. Billie carried the cereal bowl to her room, and before closing the door, hollered, "I'm going to take a shower, so don't run the hot water, okay?"

When she returned to the kitchen, the note propped against the salt and pepper shakers on the table said, "Appointment with Realtor. Back by suppertime."

She'd known he wouldn't stay with her permanently, but this visible proof of it tugged at her heartstrings. Tossing the note into the trash can, Billie grabbed the file folder containing her proposal for Noah's website, locked up and headed toward Ike's Bikes. Her ankle hadn't felt this good since that day on the trail, and she decided to walk to the shop. While waiting to cross Main Street, she heard someone call her name. Turning, she saw her next-door neighbor jogging up behind her.

When he caught up, she said, "I'm not speaking to you, Bud Kirk. You made bacon and didn't invite me over."

"You smelled it, all the way from your place?"

"That's the price we pay for having back doors that are twenty feet apart."

"That, and a northerly wind."

"So how are things, Bud?"

"That's one of the reasons I'm glad I ran into you this morning." He looked uncharacteristically serious.

"I just thought you had a right to know…that young fella who's staying with you had company the other day. Tall, good-looking brunette."

"That young fella is my brother. Troy has had a run of bad luck lately, so he's staying with me until he can figure things out." She remembered the note Troy had left on the table this morning. "The woman is probably his real estate agent."

"Your brother. No kiddin'?" Bud took a moment to process the information. "Never would have guessed it. I didn't see any resemblance."

"People say that all the time," she agreed. "What was the other thing you wanted to tell me?"

"I'm having a little procedure next week, and wondered if you'd keep an eye on Inky for me, feed the fish, water the plants."

"What kind of procedure?"

"Doc wants to install a couple stents in me. Says it's no big deal…unless I don't cooperate." He winked. "That's why the bacon. My last hurrah, y'know?"

"I'm happy to take care of things for you."

A horn blared and a driver bellowed, "Yo! Buddy boy! How goes it!"

Billie didn't recognize the man, but Bud did. No surprise there. He knew just about everyone in town…and every bit of juicy gossip about them, too.

"It goes," Bud yelled back. He faced Billie again. "So where are you headed, all dressed up?"

She'd worn a simple coral sheath and matching sweater with black ballet flats. It must have been the silver hoop earrings and bracelet that made the outfit seem dressy. Either that or he'd grown accustomed to seeing her in jeans and khakis.

"I'm meeting with the owner of Ike's Bikes." She glanced across the street and saw Noah through the shop's huge window, leaning casually against the counter as he talked with a customer. "If it goes well, he'll hire me to design his website."

"Noah?" Bud shook his head and whistled low. "Now, there's one eccentric dude."

"What do you mean?"

"He can talk for half an hour straight without really saying anything. You know me— once a detective, always a detective. I looked him up to see if I could find out where he's from, what kind of work he did before moving here, what happened to his wife." Bud shook his head again. "Came up empty. It's like he didn't exist before coming to Ellicott City." Frowning, Billie's neighbor aimed a thick forefinger at her. "Just between you, me and the lamppost here, I'm guessing witness protection. But you keep that under your hat, you hear?"

Billie nodded. "Don't worry. My lips are sealed. I just want this job. If I get it, he'll be my hundredth client."

"What do you mean, if? You're the best in

the business, and half the shop owners on Main Street know it. And if Noah has talked to any of them—and I'm sure he has, if he's thinking about a website—he knows it, too."

Bud's bright blue eyes narrowed. "That's how he heard about you, right? From one of his neighbors?"

"Actually, we met when I walked my bike to his shop for repairs. When I told him what I do for a living, it didn't seem like he hadn't heard it before." She thought of everything the guy in Gucci clothes had said about Noah's overprotectiveness toward his little girl. Maybe Bud was on to something with his witness protection idea. "He seemed nice enough when he drove me home that day, so I wouldn't have to hike back up the hill."

Bud glanced at her ankle. "Ah, right. The Great Cannondale Fall." Then he met her eyes. "No need to look so worried. Just because a man keeps mostly to himself doesn't mean he's dangerous." Her neighbor nodded toward the shop. "And anyway, if the way he takes care of his little girl is any indicator, I'd have to say he's good people."

If that were true, why did he seem so secretive? And why did he only look relaxed and happy when Alyssa was around? "If you have time when you're through with him," Bud said, walking backward toward his house, "stop by and I'll show you where I keep Inky's stuff."

"Will do," she said. The light changed again, and Billie crossed the street as a customer exited the bike shop.

"Saw you talking to Bud," Noah said when she walked up to the counter. "From where I was standing, it looked like a pretty serious conversation."

"He's having surgery next week, asked me to take care of his cat while he's hospitalized."

"For what?"

"His doctor wants to insert stents in his heart."

"That's the last thing I'd expected you to say. Bud seems healthy as a horse. Jogs everywhere." Noah put down the wrench he'd been holding. "Plays a mean game of tennis, too."

Well now, that was odd. Bud hadn't mentioned playing tennis with the bike mechanic. "I believe it. He keeps a treadmill, a weight bench and an exercise bike—the kind with handlebars that move—in the middle of his living room."

She handed over the folder, and as Noah opened it, said, "That's just an overview, to give you an idea how I'll develop your site." Billie almost tacked on *if I get the job,* but thought better of it.

He gave the proposal a cursory glance and slid it back into its pocket. He'd told her that he'd given up trying to build his own site, due to negligible computer skills. Hopefully, she hadn't jumped the gun, drafting it without first discussing it with him in more detail

She pointed at the big PC in the corner. "Is it already on?"

"Yeah...."

Billie pulled up her website, and as Noah looked over her shoulder, she explained how she'd built the others in her portfolio. She noticed that he exuded a clean, crisp scent that reminded her of the white soap her grandmother had been so fond of. He took a half step back. "Impressive. But you don't have to sell me. Your reputation precedes you. I trust you to give me my money's worth."

Had one of their neighbors recommended her? Before she had a chance to ask which one, he picked up the wrench and walked to his workbench.

"When we spoke on the phone yesterday, you said something about watching me work. I don't get it, frankly, because really, there isn't much to see. I fix bikes. And sell them. But hey, it's your time."

"I know it seems odd," she said, following him past the twin rows of shiny new bikes that flanked the narrow aisle, the racks of cycling apparel and shoe displays. "But when I'm dealing with a service or a business that's new to me, watching helps me describe people's work ethic."

Using the wrench, he pointed at several packages on the bench. "Those are the parts for your bike. You're welcome to hang around while I install them, but if you nod off from boredom, don't say you weren't warned."

Warned, by a man who could very well be in hiding from a sinister past. A sense of unease settled around her as she tried to think up a reasonable excuse to leave.

Instead, she asked, "Do you ever rent bikes?"

"I keep a few that customers can borrow."

"What about races and rides? Do you keep up with organizers, and send flyers to your customers?"

"Not as often as I should, but yeah, I do that from time to time."

Billie jotted the information in her notebook. Good. She had already included those tabs in her proposal.

"Do you participate in the rides?"

"Can't," he said without looking up. "Alyssa doesn't ride."

Billie should have known. And the always-protective dad probably wouldn't consider hiring a sitter so that he could.

She looked around the shop, where brick walls and exposed overhead ductwork gave the place an industrial feel. There wasn't a single fingerprint on the glass-and-steel cabinets that housed tidy rows of goggles and sunglasses, gloves and mitts, bike locks and lights. Normally, orderliness calmed her. Today it did not, because in every mystery she'd read, the bad guys were obsessive, compulsive and dangerous.

"Thought you wanted to watch."

The suddenness of his question startled her. "I—I am watching."

"Uh-huh. Everything but the bike repair. Not that I blame you. But I told you this would be boring."

"Oh, trust me. I'm anything but bored."

One eyebrow quirked, and Billie would have sworn he'd ask for an explanation. Instead, Noah got back to work.

"There's a stereo in my office. I work faster to music. How 'bout sliding in a CD?"

A hint that she could leave? In one second, Billie considered doing just that. In the next, she decided against it. Maybe, with time and patience, she'd learn something about him that made sense.

It was easy, picking up on his cue, and just
as easy finding a CD, because he'd alphabet-
ized the cases. Billie chose an Eagles collection, popped it into the disk changer and
turned up the volume until the music reached
the speakers she'd seen out front.

On the way back to his workstation, Billie passed an apartment-sized kitchen that
boasted a fifties-style fridge and stove, and a
worn enamel sink, the obvious victim of one
too many scourings. On the chrome soap dish
beside the gooseneck faucet, she spotted a bar
of Ivory, the source of the clean, fresh scent
she'd inhaled earlier from Noah.

Across the room, he'd set up a play area for
Alyssa. An oversize leather beanbag chair.
A child-sized pink plastic kitchen. A stocky
shelving unit filled with books, stuffed animals and an assortment of Barbie dolls. And
under it all, a colorful patchwork rug to warm
the tile-over-concrete floor.

A strange, forlorn mood enveloped Billie as
she wondered if her own little girl would have
played with toys like these. And with it, sym-
pathy for the man who'd been forced by sad
circumstance to raise his child alone.

She slid onto the stool near his workbench,
wondering how he'd lost his wife.

"What are you," he mumbled around the mini flashlight between his teeth, "sixteen?"

Billie frowned slightly. "Um, what?"

He met her eyes long enough to say, "Turn down that music, will ya?" And focusing on the Cannondale again, he added, "Either that or grab my earplugs. I keep some in the top right-hand drawer of my desk, so I can concentrate when Alyssa is watching cartoons and I'm trying to balance the books."

Billie remembered her dad complaining when she or the twins turned the TV up too loudly. Rather than scold his daughter, Noah had found a way to deal with the noise. Yet another reason to like this quiet, sad-eyed man. "Wouldn't it be easier just to let her watch upstairs?"

He stopped working, leaned an elbow on a bent knee and looked at Billie for what seemed a full minute. "You're not the first to accuse me of being overprotective, and you won't be the last."

"Sorry," she said, backpedaling toward the office. "I'll just turn down the music."

Why did she care where he'd lived before moving to Maryland, or how he'd lost his wife? And what difference did it make if he spoiled his daughter or not?

It mattered, she acknowledged, because

she'd seen that sad-eyed, distant expression a hundred times…in her own mirror. Had she finally met someone who understood what loss could do to a person?

"Help yourself to a soda," he called out.

She was about to say, "Thanks, but no thanks," when he added, "Grab one for me while you're at it, will ya?" A second, perhaps two passed before he said, "Please?"

Billie was only too happy to oblige. She didn't understand why she felt an overpowering desire to take care of this man.

Their fingers touched briefly as she handed him the root beer, and when he held her gaze, she repressed the urge to finger-comb the lock of hair that had fallen over his eye. If she had any sense at all, she'd leave right now, before she did or said something she'd regret.

## CHAPTER SEVEN

"So how's it coming?" she asked Noah.

"I should be finished in—"

His cell phone rang, cutting him off. He answered, and Billie discovered something they had in common: a tendency to pace while on the phone. He stood near the store entrance, nodding and muttering something she couldn't make out from this distance. One thing was certain. The person on the other end hadn't delivered good news.

"It's Alyssa," he said, clicking off. "School nurse thinks she's coming down with something."

"Hope it isn't serious."

"Doesn't sound like it. But this time of year, her allergies make her miserable." He walked toward the back room. "The symptoms mimic a head cold, so even though she isn't contagious, it's better to err on the side of caution."

Billie followed, and watched him scrub all traces of the bike's grease and grime from his hands—and then from the bar of soap.

"I wonder if you'd do me a huge favor," he said over one shoulder, "and stick around until I get back with Alyssa. I'm expecting a delivery. One of those 'it goes back to the factory if you miss it' kinda things." Facing her, he dried his hands. "I know it's an imposition, so if you can't, I understand."

"It's not a problem." Any parent would look concerned after a call from the school nurse, but Noah looked *afraid,* and that didn't make sense. "It's what neighbors do, right?"

Her words did little to ease the fear in his eyes, heightening the need she felt to comfort him.

"I shouldn't be gone more than half an hour." He grabbed his keys and opened the door. "I owe ya one, kid," he said, and then he was gone.

Kid? Troy and Todd had called her kid for as long as she could remember. She didn't like thinking that, like her brothers, Noah saw her as someone to be protected. Didn't like it at all. Billie looked for something else to focus on. Such as how large the package might be, or where the delivery guy should put it. Noah hadn't told her what to do if any customers came into the shop, either.

The bell above the entrance chimed, and in walked Jeff Graham. He must have ridden his bike here, because today he wore moisture-wicking cycling gear instead of the head-to-toe Gucci garb he'd worn on the day they'd met.

"Billie, right?" he said.

"Right. I was here gathering information to develop a website for Noah when the school nurse called. He's expecting a delivery, and asked me to stick around until he got back."

"Ah."

He didn't have to say more; his knowing expression made it clear that he thought there was more to it than that. And it was her own fault for giving him more information than he'd asked for.

"Was he expecting you?"

Jeff shook his head. "No, I just stopped in to see if he had any elbow pads." He showed her his. "These are about shot."

He wasn't exaggerating. "I think he has some in the display case," she said, pointing.

And there it was again, that "something's going on" expression.

Jeff peered through the countertop. "Yeah. Those are perfect." He leaned a padded elbow on the glass. "How's the ankle?"

"Almost back to normal. Amazing what following doctor's orders—and having a sit-down job—will accomplish."

"Speaking of which, I should hook you up

with my wife. She writes articles, mostly, but her first novel is about to come out. Her agent and publisher have been bugging her to make a website, but with two kids underfoot, she hasn't had time."

Billie never went anywhere without business cards. Opening her purse, she took one out and handed it to him.

He gave it a passing glance and tucked it into a zippered pocket on the front of his shirt. "So tell me, what do you think of Noah, now that you know him better?"

"I don't know how to answer that, since I've only spent an hour or so, total, with him. He seems nice enough, I guess."

"You guess?" Jeff snapped his fingers. "Darn. I was hoping you could fill in some of the blanks."

He'd made several pointed observations about Noah's reserved and overprotective tendencies. Was he referring to those now?

"Blanks?"

Jeff straightened, tugged at the snug sleeves of his Lycra shirt. "Like how his wife died. Where he lived before moving to Maryland. What he did for a living before buying Ike's Bikes. Why he never lets that kid out of his sight, except when she's in school. I've been doing business with him for years, but I don't know any more about him now than when I first walked into this shop."

Bud had said pretty much the same thing. Proof that the article she'd read in *Cosmo,* claiming that men were every bit as nosy as women, had been correct? Or evidence that Noah had something to hide?

A knock at the back door interrupted the conversation.

Billie was halfway there when Jeff said, "So there really was a delivery."

She pretended not to hear him, mostly because she had no idea how to respond.

The delivery guy deposited a steamer trunk-sized carton near the back door, then thundered across the deck and down the wooden steps leading to Noah's parking pad. Billie returned to the front and tore a sheet of blank paper from Noah's spiral notebook.

"I'll leave a message here," she told Jeff, "for Noah to get in touch with you about the elbow pads."

Billie had no sooner started writing when she saw Noah come in through the back door, carrying his sleepy-eyed, yawning little girl.

"Ah," he said, putting Alyssa into her bean-bag chair. He popped a movie into the DVD player and added, "I see the package came while I was gone. Thanks for being here to sign for it." When he entered the shop moments later, he said, "She'll be asleep before the theme song ends."

That's when he noticed Jeff, leaning on the counter. The men exchanged a friendly greeting.

"She just saved you from losing a customer," Jeff said, nodding hello to Jeff. "I'd say you owe Billie, here, dinner out to show your appreciation."

She could feel Jeff's eyes on them, assessing the relationship as he waited for a response from Noah.

"That won't be necessary, " Billie said. "It's what any neighbor would do." She gestured toward Jeff. "Mr. Graham needs elbow pads, like the ones he's wearing."

"Mr. Graham?" Jeff echoed. "You make me sound like a doddering old man. Do me a favor. Call me Jeff, okay?"

Noah slapped a package of pads onto the counter as his cell phone rang. As soon as he answered it, his expression changed, and so did his tone of voice.

"You're kidding," he grated into the phone. "When?" Then, seeing Jeff and Billie watching him, he pressed the mute button. "I need to take this," he said, and hurried out the back door.

"See?" Jeff said. "Stuff like that makes me curious as all get-out."

"You know what happened to the cat...."

"What cat?" And then he nodded. "Oh. The one curiosity killed." Chuckling, he patted the seat of his bike pants. "Didn't bring my wallet," he said. "I just stopped in to see if Noah had some in stock. Just tell him to set those aside for me. I'll swing by here tomorrow and pick them up."

There wasn't a thing she could do out front, so Billie returned to the back room, where Alyssa drowsed in her chair. Billie knelt beside the child and placed a palm to her forehead.

"Well, you don't feel warm," she said. "That's a good thing."

"I hate it when Daddy does that."

"Does what?"

The girl pointed at Noah, visible through the glass patio door leading to the deck.

"Walks back and forth, back and forth. It reminds me of the way the lions and tigers walk back and forth in their cages at the zoo." She hugged her lop-eared bunny tighter. "And it makes me sad."

Billie hadn't wanted to like Noah, and didn't want to like his kid, either. "I pace when I'm on the phone, too. It's nothing to be sad about," she said, standing. "I'm sure it just means he's concentrating on a problem with an order, or trying not to lose his temper with a dissatisfied customer."

Alyssa studied her face for a moment, then looked back at the TV screen, where a passel of kids had gathered in Julie Andrews's big ornate bed.

"Do you cry at night, too?"

Cry at night...*too?* "What do you mean?"

"Sometimes Daddy does. He leaves his door open so he can hear me if *I* cry. But I don't. At least, not anymore." She met Billie's eyes. "You, too?"

"I suppose everyone cries themselves to sleep once in a while." Had Alyssa grown up, just enough to stop missing her mother? Was Noah still mourning his wife? Was *that* why he cried at night? If Alyssa could hear him from down the hall...

Billie shook off the sadness the questions roused. "What can I get for you? More juice? A snack? A book?"

When Alyssa met her eyes again, Billie wondered what the child had seen and survived, to explain the penetrating, too-old-for-her-age expression.

She held up her empty juice box, and as Billie took it, she said, "You're very pretty."

Billie was about to thank her when she

tacked on, "Not as pretty as my mommy, but very pretty."

"You know," Billie said, handing her a fresh juice box, "I feel the same way about my mom." As Alyssa unwrapped the tiny straw, she added, "So how do you like third grade?" She extended her hand, and Alyssa put the cellophane into it.

"It's okay, but I liked second grade better."

"Because there's less homework?"

"Oh, no. I like homework. But I liked Mrs. Kuchar better than Miss Woods."

"Oh?"

Frowning slightly, she sipped the juice. "Miss Woods is always in a hurry. I don't think she likes children all that much."

"What makes you say that?"

"She has *no* patience. We're seven," Alyssa said, "not fifteen. Sometimes we're loud, sometimes we're messy, sometimes we don't do what we're told the very first time."

"You're very perceptive," Billie admitted. Too perceptive, she thought, especially for one so young. According to Jeff, Noah rarely let Alyssa play with other kids, and even then, only when he supervised. So had she been born insightful, or had spending so many hours alone with Noah made her that way?

"My head hurts," Alyssa said. "I need an allergy pill. Could you get me one?"

The question took Billie off guard, and she said, "I think you need to wait for your dad to come back."

"Oh, don't worry. They aren't the kind of pills that come from the doctor. They're just the grocery store kind. Daddy won't mind if you give me one."

"Still...doling out medicine is his job."

Her lower lip began to tremble. "He would have given me one by now. But he's on the phone. Again. He could be out there for an hour. He does this all the time!" And then she started to cry.

Billie had always been a sucker for weeping children. Infants, toddlers, kindergarten kids... They were little for such a short time, and she couldn't stand to hear them suffer. It seemed a shame to let Alyssa get more upset, especially when it would only exacerbate her symptoms, and the problem could be solved so easily.

"Hold on a sec, sweetie. I'll ask your dad."

"Please don't interrupt him. He hates to be interrupted!"

Billie dismissed the child's protests. She couldn't imagine a father as indulgent as Noah making his daughter wait to take medication that would relieve her discomfort. Billie hurried to the back door and opened it a crack. Based solely on his angry expression, it wasn't a pleasant conversation. He stood still long enough to glance at her, and went back to pacing. Alyssa wasn't kidding when she'd said he didn't like interruptions. But what choice did she have?

"Alyssa says she has a headache," Billie whispered, "and that you won't mind if I give her an allergy pill."

He shot her an impatient frown, as if to say, "Can't you see I'm on the phone?"

Billie felt a tad angry herself. He hadn't been in there, listening to Alyssa cry. She stared him down and, in a louder voice, repeated, "She says you won't mind if I give her an allergy pill."

He rolled his eyes, then covered the mouthpiece. "Okay. Fine. Whatever."

She let the door close on its own. If the slam disturbed him, well, *okay, fine, whatever!* "You're in luck," she told Alyssa. "He said it's okay to give you a pill."

The little girl smiled. "They're on the top shelf of the cabinet above the sink," she said. "You're not tall enough to reach it. There's a stool beside the refrigerator."

Billie climbed up, and as she got hold of the small, rectangular box, Alyssa added, "I can't wait to get bigger. I can't even reach them when I use the stool!"

"Mmm-hmm," she said, distracted by the directions. One tablet every four to six hours for children twenty-three to thirty-six pounds. "Good grief," she grumbled. How were parents supposed to make a rational decision about dosage when it could come down to ounces?

"How much do you weigh, Alyssa?"

"Last time I saw Dr. Anderson, I was forty-one pounds. He doesn't know why I'm small for my age, because my mommy was very tall, and so's daddy."

Billie froze, remembering Jeff's earlier question about how Noah's wife had died.

Frowning, she popped one lavender tablet from its foil-and-plastic package and pictured her own mother...somewhat intrusive, slightly bossy, but always well-meaning. Crazy and juvenile as it seemed, Billie wished her mom could live forever, because life just wouldn't be the same without her. Would she feel this way if she'd lost her at age four?

"Do you have enough juice to wash it down?"

"Oh, I don't need to wash it down. They taste just like candy. I just chew them up!" As if to prove it, she did exactly that.

Billie put the package back where she'd

found it, returned the stool to its place beside the fridge, then glanced outside, where Noah was still pacing, still talking, still waving his free hand in the air, no doubt making some important point.

He sure was spending a lot of time out there, and for such an overprotective guy, he'd put an awful lot of trust in someone he barely knew. She thought of the lengthy to-do list on her desk at home. Client files to update. Invoices to send. Laundry to fold. And Troy's note had said he'd see her at suppertime.

"You said your dad leaves you alone a lot while he talks on the phone?"

"Yes," the little girl said, pouting. Julie Andrews was singing "The Lonely Goatherd" when Alyssa yawned. "And it makes me very sad," she mumbled as her eyes slowly closed.

Oh, to fall asleep that quickly and easily, Billie thought on her way back to the door. "Alyssa is sleeping," she said. After the way he'd dismissed her—like an errant child—she didn't care that he was in midsentence. "I'm leaving. I'll email you when your website is ready."

Half an hour later, she was chopping vegetables for the stew pot when her kitchen telephone rang.

"Alyssa tells me you gave her an allergy pill?"

"Well, yes, because—"

"Where do you get off, medicating my kid?"

"Excuse me?"

"How many did you give her?"

A demand, she noticed, not a question.

"Just one. I read the directions and—"

"But I'd already given her one! Do you know how close I came to rushing her to the E.R.? Lucky for you, she's just sleepy. But it could have been serious. A lot more serious. Next time you get it in your head to make decisions that involve my little girl, ask me first."

Alyssa's peculiar little smile made sense now. She'd said, in plain English, that the pills tasted like candy. If a sweet treat was what she wanted, why hadn't she just asked for one?

"If you'll recall," Billie told him, "I did ask your permission." Voice and hands shaking, she added, "And you said yes!"

The noise he made was as close to a growl as she'd ever heard from a human.

"Is *that* what you were talking about? Good grief, Billie, I was in the middle of a business conversation. You own your own company, so you should know that overlooking details can be costly. And anyway, can't you tell when someone is totally distracted?"

"Evidently," she said, pronouncing every syllable, "I can't." Anything she said now would only make her look guilty: she'd thought he *had* heard her question, and of course she knew how dangerous the double dose could have been. She was sorry, truly sorry about the misunderstanding, but *Alyssa* had known he'd already given her a pill. Why had she asked for another?

"I should have known better," Billie admitted. "I'm sorry. I really am. If you're still interested in having me build your website, you can email me. The address is in your spiral notebook."

With that, she hung up and went back to chopping vegetables. She was still at it when Troy joined her in the kitchen.

"Shoo-ee," he said as the knife flew, "what got *you* all riled up!"

"Who, not what," she said, sliding bite-sized potatoes and carrots from the cutting board to the stew pot. "If that jerk was half as smart as he *thinks* he is, he'd be dangerous."

The story spewed out, like steam from a pressure cooker, and when Billie finished, her brother said, "Wow."

"My sentiments, exactly. There's something off about that guy," she said, "and as soon as we're finished eating, I'm going to find out what."

"What do you mean, off?"

"Everything about him is a big fat secret. How his wife died. When he moved here. Where he came from and what he did for a living before. I haven't seen the apartment above his shop, but there are no pictures anywhere downstairs. Not in his little girl's play area, not on his desk, none, nada, zip. And you should see the way he hovers over Alyssa." Billie sprinkled salt and pepper into the stew and gave it a quick stir. "When he isn't completely ignoring her, that is. No wonder she sometimes behaves like a spoiled brat!"

"You can find anything with Google these days," Troy replied. "Criminal records, divorces, land purchases. I was in security, don't forget. I know how to dig stuff up, so if you want my help…"

"Thanks." Then she laughed. "Want to hear something funny? Bud thought you and I were living together."

"Well, we are. For now."

"Yeah, but he thought we were *living together*." She drew quote marks in the air. "And that you were cheating on me."

Troy laughed. "What! Who did he think I was cheating on you *with*?"

"Some brunette. I gave him the highlights of your situation and told him she's probably a Realtor." Billie rummaged in the drawer beneath the oven and found the lid for the pot. "Speaking of which, how did the meeting go?"

"You're right. Cynthia is my agent. Showed me three places today. One is right around the corner, literally. Great spot. The other one is okay. Just this side of the border between Ellicott City and Catonsville."

"Oella?"

"Yeah."

*That's where Jeff Graham lives,* Billie thought. Wouldn't it be ironic if those two ended up as neighbors!

"And the third house?"

"No way." He snorted. "I don't have the time, the money, the energy or the skills to make that dump livable."

"So your favorite is the one near here?"

"It's move-in ready."

"Then why even consider the other one?"

"Didn't know how you'd feel about me living practically on top of you, for one thing."

"You're practically living on top of me now, and I've enjoyed every minute. So what's the other thing?"

"Money. I can't make a move until the house in Philly sells."

"I have some savings. Use it now as your down payment, and repay me when your place sells."

"I couldn't ask you to do that."

"You didn't ask."

Troy stared at her for a long moment, then said, "You've got a heart of gold," and headed down the hall.

"Where are you going? Supper's almost ready."

"To Ike's Bikes, that's where."

"Troy...you had better be kidding...."

"Calm down. I'm not an idiot. I'm joking. But I'm no saint, either. If I thought for one minute you cared about him—and he hurt you—I'd have no problem making him sorry."

And Troy would, too, as evidenced by the tongue-lashing he'd given Chuck on the day of the divorce.

"Call me when supper's on the table. Meanwhile, I'll be in the living room, surfing the net for dirt on Noah Preston."

For a reason she couldn't explain, Billie hoped his search, like Bud's, would be futile.

## CHAPTER EIGHT

NOAH HAD READ half the newspaper before Max finally joined him in the living room.

"You were gone so long," he said drily, "I was considering charging you rent."

"Ingrate." She plopped onto the sofa. "I'll have you know she brushed her teeth, said her prayers, and now? She's fast asleep, so you're welcome."

Noah put down the newspaper. "You were in there an awfully long time…."

"Uh-huh. Talking about you…and the big spat with Billie."

"What spat? And who even uses that word anymore?"

"My sainted grandmother, whose shoes I hope to fill one day. And to answer your first question, Alyssa wasn't napping before dinner when you called Billie to give her a piece of your mind. As if you can afford to give even a sliver away."

"But…but Alyssa was asleep!"

"Not even close. The kid is miserable. Because she likes Billie. She thinks you like her, too. And now she's afraid you two will never get married, all on account of her fib."

"Married? Where'd she get a cockamamie idea like that?"

"Hey. Don't shoot the messenger. And who uses words like *that* one anymore?"

"Wait....on account of her fib?"

"That business about the allergy pill and how she didn't tell Billie you'd already given her one." Max explained how Alyssa had wanted something sugary, and because the candy jar was empty, she'd hoped the medication would satisfy her sweet tooth.

Noah heaved a heavy sigh. "I took one of those things once. They taste awful. Why would she want two?"

"Because she's seven?"

He drove a hand through his hair. "So why, when I gave Billie what for, did she not defend herself?"

"If I know you, you didn't give her a chance."

"I don't remember much about the conversation, except that she hung up on me. If she was so innocent, why would she do that?"

"Oh, I dunno. Maybe because you can be intimidating when you want to be?"

"I hope you aren't calling me a bully, be-cause—"

"Spare me," Max said. "I know you better than just about anybody." She sat back, fiddled with the throw pillow she'd pulled onto her lap. "Remember a couple months ago when you asked me why I'm still single?"

He nodded. "You blamed the job. Long hours. Sometimes dangerous situations." But even as he said it, Noah had a feeling Max was about to tell him the real reason.

"None of that would matter, if I could find the right man. Instead of guys like you, who think they have all the answers, for everybody, all the time."

He could recite the list of his failings and flaws, but she'd heard them all before…and diffused them, one by one.

"News flash, Preston. You don't have all the answers."

"I never said I did."

Max got up and crossed the room, placed her palms on the arms of his chair and gave it a shake. "You feel something for that woman. Don't bother to deny it, because Alyssa is a sharp kid. If she got it into her head that Billie is mother material, it's because you've been sending subliminal messages." The agent shook the chair again before straightening. "Go ahead, tell me I'm wrong!"

"Jeez, Max. The truth is I barely know her.

I'm working on her bike. She might build me a website, and—"

Max dropped onto the sofa again. "What do you mean, might?"

"Well, like I said, she hung up on me."

The woman hid behind her hands. "I don't know whether you're more exasperating than dense or the other way around." She came out of hiding. "Did you see samples of her work?"

"Yeah…"

"Is she any good?"

"I guess…"

"Then hire her. And don't look at me that way—it really *is* that simple. She's a professional. If she wants your business, she'll overlook your little temper tantrum. And as you get to know her better, you'll figure out if what you feel for her is something worth pursuing or not."

"What if I considered all of that?"

"Did you?"

"No, but if I had, I might have come to the conclusion that it would be selfish, starting something with her that I can't finish."

"Why can't you?"

Noah threw his hands in the air. "You of all people know why!"

"I've said it before, I'll say it again. Other people in your situation found ways to live normal lives. If that's what you want, you'll find a way to get it."

Noah sighed. "Talk about exasperating."

"Somebody has to keep you straight." Max pointed at the phone. "Call her."

"It's nine o'clock."

"She's a businesswoman. Believe me, she's awake and working."

"I'll call her in the morning."

"Chicken."

When Max was right, she was right. "I need to sleep on it," he hedged, "so I won't put my foot in my mouth again."

The agent got up and grabbed her jacket. "You'll do what you want—you always do."

And when she was wrong, she was wrong. He hadn't done anything he wanted to do since agreeing to testify against O'Malley.

"My advice?" she said. "The longer you put it off, the harder it'll be."

Nodding, Noah walked her to the door. "I'll think about it."

"I've worked with a lot of guys in this program who were built to live alone." She jabbed a forefinger into his chest. "You, my friend, are not one of them."

"Yeah, well, that's the price to pay for living a lie."

"Oh, give me a break. I'll bet full disclosure

causes more divorces than anything else. Even
if you had a normal history, you wouldn't tell
Billie *every*thing. And she won't tell you all the
details about her past, either. Get over yourself.
You like her. Admit it. Give her a call." Max
gestured toward the living room behind him.
"You're safe here, so take a chance at happiness,
why don't you?"

"I'll think about it," he said again.

"You know I'm right."

He was fortunate to have a friend like Max,
and would have told her so...if she hadn't
closed the door in his face.

Noah locked up and returned to the living
room. Another glance at his watch told
him only five minutes had passed since he'd
last checked the time. He wanted to call Billie
and apologize, but not now, and not without
a plan. Remote in hand, he turned on the
TV and closed his eyes. With any luck, a few
ideas would percolate while he listened to
some inane sitcom.

The wall clock said two-fifteen when he
woke with a stiff neck.

Noah got up, stretching as he walked into
the kitchen, and put on a pot of coffee. He'd
been down this sleepless road enough times to
know that going to bed now would be pointless.
He'd only toss and turn, fighting the desire to

watch the flickering digits on the clock count the minutes until the alarm buzzed. When the coffee finished perking, he'd carry a mug to his desk, put in an order for bike chains, trail pedals, crank tools and tire pumps. Then he'd balance the business checkbook and reconcile his personal bank accounts, too. Because few things annoyed him more than wasting time.

Half an hour later, with the Ike's Bikes books in order, Noah blew a stream of air through his teeth as he focused on his personal account. He was the only one writing checks to pay the water, phone and internet, cable and electric bills. He used a calculator, there were no outstanding checks and he'd compared his totals to the bank's four times. The numbers ought to match, instead of being off by five cents.

Noah realized he had no one but himself to blame for his rising frustration. If he had confidence in anyone other than himself, he would have hired an accountant to take care of the bookwork.

But if he didn't trust the bank, why would he trust a CPA? Mistrust had permeated every area of his life. It's what made him think Billie might have deliberately double-dosed Alyssa. But Max didn't do things halfway, and according to her investigation, Billie had no connection to O'Malley. Noah didn't feel bad about jumping to conclusions, about jumping all over *her*. It's what people did when fear. dogged their heels. If he had the chance to do things over again, he wouldn't change a thing. Because what if he'd been on target?

The bike shop provided well for him and Alyssa, so he didn't really need to increase business with a website. But he'd let himself get sucked in by that lost, lonely look in Billie's eyes, a look he saw every time he glanced in the mirror. Now that the wheels were in motion, it provided a perfect excuse to call her, start a dialogue and hopefully mend the fences he'd destroyed.

He got up to refill his mug.

"Daddy?"

He lurched. "Good grief, Alyssa, you scared me half to death."

She stood in the middle of the kitchen, hugging herself, one bare foot atop the other, pigtails and Barbie nightie askew.

Crouching, he took her in his arms. "You're cold," he said, kissing her cheek. "What are you doing up at this hour?"

"I heard something. And then I smelled coffee." She bracketed his face with small, chilly hands. "What are *you* doing up?"

Standing, he hoisted her onto one hip. "Couldn't sleep, thinking about all the work I forgot to do yesterday." He carried her to her room. "What's your excuse?"

"I couldn't sleep, either."

Noah gently deposited her on the bed. "Still stuffy-nosed, huh?"

"No." She sat cross-legged and tucked her hands under her behind. "I feel bad that I got Billie in trouble."

"Yeah," he said, sitting on the edge of the mattress, "about that…"

Curly wisps had escaped her ponytails, and he tucked them behind her ears. He'd planned to keep her home from school tomorrow, so it wasn't critical that she get right back to sleep.

"We talked about how dangerous it is to take medicine when you don't need it. That's why I keep it way up high, out of your reach, remember?"

She nodded.

"And you remembered that I had already given you an allergy pill, right?"

"Um-hmm."

"Then why did you trick Billie into giving you another one?"

She flopped back on her pillow and crooked an arm over her face. "To see if she was patient."

He waited, hoping Alyssa would explain on her own.

"I really like her, and I think she'd be a good mom. So it was like a test, to see if she'd get mad over nothing, like my teacher, or if she'd be nice, like Mommy was."

Noah's heartbeat doubled. He knew how much Alyssa wanted to be like the other kids in her class. How could he not, when she ended every bedtime prayer with a special request for a mother?

"So was Billie patient and nice?"

"Yes." Alyssa got onto her knees, then sat back on her heels. "I don't think she knows it yet, but she would make a great mom."

His daughter, the armchair shrink.

"How do you know?"

Alyssa climbed into his lap. "I just do." She linked her arms around his neck. "I like her, and I think you like her, too."

He remembered that Max had said he must have sent subliminal messages, cues that his ever-alert daughter picked up. In truth, he *did* like Billie. Enough to trust her with his well-guarded secret? *Get a grip,* he thought as Alyssa yawned.

"Okay," he said, helping her under the covers, "time for you to get to sleep, missy."

"Are you going to sleep, too?"

The castle-shaped purple clock on her bedside table said ten to four. His own alarm automatically went off every day at six. "I'm gonna try."

She rolled onto her side, yawning again as she hugged her pillow and favorite stuffed bunny. "Bet I'll be asleep before you are."

He turned off the nightstand lamp. "We'll just see about that."

"If I win, will you make pancakes for breakfast?"

Noah kissed the tip of her nose. "Sure. And if I win, what will you make me?"

Alyssa thought about that for a moment. "I'll make you call Billie," she said around yet another yawn, "so I can tell her I'm sorry!"

# CHAPTER NINE

*Stateville Correctional Facility*

THE CELL DOOR slid open and the guard peered over O'Malley's shoulder. "What's that, a novel?"

O'Malley clicked Save and put the PC into sleep mode. "Autobiography," he said, getting to his feet. "Not that it's any of your business." He smiled to take the edge off his brusque statement, because Parker was the only guard at The Ville who treated him with even a modicum of respect.

"So what brings you to my humble abode today, Gus?"

"You've been summoned."

He could recite a hundred things he hated about Stateville, right off the top of his head: the thin, narrow cot. The cold walls. The non-stop noise. Ghastly food. High on the list was the rule that said any clown who passed the check-in criteria could visit him, whether he wanted to see them or not. Which simpleton would he have to put up with today? The frumpy broad whose only claim to fame was the true crime books she'd written about prisoners? His idiot lawyer? Hopefully not his wife, because conjugal visits were never *conjugal,* thanks to her nonstop nagging and carping.

The unmistakable sound of handcuffs and leg irons echoed in the small space as a second guard, Will Rayford, joined them in the cell.

"What's this all about?" O'Malley demanded as Rayford slapped on the cuffs.

"The warden didn't say," Parker answered.

Rayford stooped to snap on the leg irons.

"The warden? But…but what does he want?"

"Didn't say," Parker repeated.

Rayford linked his wrists, ankles and waist together.

"There must be some mistake. Warden Josephs and I have an understanding."

"Yeah, yeah," Rayford said, leading O'Malley from his cell…

…like a dog on a leash. Anger sluiced through his veins. Josephs had a lot of explaining to do, and he'd better have a very good explanation for putting him through this degrading treatment.

"Step it up," Rayford ordered. "I got better things to do than babysit some whiny hotshot."

O'Malley got the guard's meaning. From day one, he'd been assigned segregated housing in a private cell. He ate alone, exercised alone, showered alone, because the state feared he wouldn't last ten minutes in general population. Much as he'd enjoyed the perks of his senate office—rubbing elbows with movers and shakers in D.C., invitations to celebrities' homes and red carpet events—he didn't mind his current near-solitary status.

The warden liked to think he'd been instrumental in the decision to keep O'Malley out of the reach of inmates he'd sentenced when he'd been a judge, and O'Malley had no reason to tell him otherwise. Hopefully, that wouldn't change today.

It was a long walk from his cell to Josephs's office. He broke into a slow jog, thinking to turn it into a mini workout.

"Look at him go," Rayford said, laughing. "He's in pretty good shape…for an old guy."

O'Malley was itching to turn around, see if Parker was laughing at him, too. But what did he care? He had nearly three and a half years to serve and saw no point in making trouble that could add to his sentence.

The guards walked slightly behind him, one on either side, talking. Parker had bought his son a puppy. Rayford's daughter would graduate high school in a few months. All their talk of home and hearth made his blood boil, thinking of all he'd missed, thanks to Nate Judson... or whatever name he was going by these days. WITSEC wasn't invincible. Like every other government agency, it was rife with employees looking to make a quick buck. His people hadn't found one yet, but O'Malley knew it was only a matter of time. Sooner or later, he'd catch a lucky break. And when he did—

"Where's Patsy?" Parker said when they entered the warden's outer office.

"Don't know, but if she ever retires, I want her job. She's away from her receptionist desk more than she's at it," Rayford observed.

"Well, the door's open," Parker said, "and that means he's in there."

Snickering like a teenager, Rayford said, "Maybe Patsy's in there with him. Sure would explain why she gets away with murder."

Parker knocked and the warden said, "Come in."

O'Malley would recognize that nasal whine anywhere, and it was enough to heighten his bad mood by several degrees. *Better pull yourself together,* he thought as Parker nudged him through the door. *You can't afford to rile the man.*

"'Morning, Hank," Josephs said without looking up. "Have a seat."

Rayford led O'Malley to one of the two big leather chairs that faced the desk.

The warden had been reading his file. O'Malley knew, because he saw his name on the front. Josephs scribbled something on the top sheet and closed the cover.

The chains clanked as O'Malley raised his hands. "What's all this about, Warden? Shackles? *Really?*"

The man thanked the guards and sent them on their way, and when the door closed behind them, Josephs leaned forward and propped his fingertips together under his chin.

"I've been hearing some disturbing things about you, Hank. Things that forced me to re-evaluate your position here at Stateville."

O'Malley did his best to look unruffled. He'd likened dealing with people in here to encounters with wild animals: if they smelled fear, you didn't stand a chance.

"Disturbing things?" he said, laughing softly. "There are 168 hours in a week, and I'm alone for 150 of them. What kind of trouble can a guy like me cause in that much time?" He lifted his hands again, gave the chains a deliberate shake to prove his point.

"You have a computer in your cell...complete with internet access. And I arranged for you to have a cell phone, so you could keep in touch with your family." Josephs leaned back in his chair. "Seems you've been doing more than that—a whole lot more—and I can't allow it to continue."

Losing the cell phone wouldn't be pleasant, but losing internet access would seriously thwart his abilities to stay in touch with his men. *Wild animals,* he reminded himself. *Stay calm.* "Ford. Buddy. I—"

"Don't call me by my first name. If anyone heard you..." He ran a finger under his collar, then aimed it at O'Malley. "Let's get one thing straight right up front, Hank. I am *not* your buddy."

A vein throbbed in the warden's left temple and his face had turned bloodred. Beads of perspiration had formed on his forehead, and if he clasped his hands any tighter, he'd cut off all circulation to his fingers. What had he heard, O'Malley wondered, to rile him to this degree?

Might as well go for broke, he thought. He was chained up like one of the murderers or rapists Josephs usually dealt with. How much worse could things get?

"I'll save us both a lot of time. Might even save you having a heart attack or stroke," he said, smirking. "You owe me, Josephs. Owe me big, and we both know it. So let's stop playing games, shall we? Whatever you heard, no matter how *disturbing* it might be, we can handle it…if we keep our cool."

"Is that a fact? You can quash all the rumors about how you're running an illegal organization out there—" he pointed toward the window "—from in here?"

Somebody on O'Malley's payroll had been talking. When he found out who, he'd—

"Word about your activities reached the governor's office, you fool. He came down on me, hard. Naturally, I told him everything he'd heard was speculation and innuendo. I promised to get to the bottom of it, and assured him I'd take care of things."

A moment ticked silently by as the threat hung between them like a gritty spiderweb.

"Take care of things? What does *that* mean?"

"It means now that it has come down to a choice between protecting you and ensuring my career…" He raised his shoulders and extended both hands, palms up.

"You're in no position to throw me under the bus, *Ford.* One phone call and I can destroy you." O'Malley hoped he hadn't just given the warden the reason he was looking for to take his cell phone. Frustrated, furious and feeling desperate, he gave the chains a quick jerk, smiling a little when the rattle made Josephs lurch. "But I'd much rather break your spindly little neck."

"You asked earlier why the restraints were necessary, and now you know."

"Wait. No," he said, trying to make light of the threat. "I didn't mean anything by that. I'm confused. And upset. You would be, too, in my place." A burst of nervous laughter escaped his lips. "C'mon, now. You know me. You don't really believe I'm capable of actual violence, like some common criminal, do you?"

"I hate to rain on your pity party, O'Malley, but you *are* a common criminal."

Josephs reiterated the 78-month sentence, meted out by a federal judge as the penalty for ten counts of financial corruption, misappropriation of campaign funds, perjury, obstruction of justice, voter fraud and half a dozen other things unearthed by the prosecutor, thanks to that turncoat, Nate Judson.

"You got too full of yourself, as my daddy used to say," the warden continued, "and I'm afraid you've left me no alternative."

O'Malley wanted to ask for an explanation, but didn't. If he put his questions into words, and his voice shook the way his hands were shaking, Josephs would see his weakness, and use it to his advantage.

"You know, you *do* look a bit baffled, so allow me to clarify things for you." Josephs leaned back again, and this time casually propped both feet on his desk. "Parker and Rayford are in your 'pay to stay' cell," he said, linking his fingers behind his neck, "packing your meager possessions as we speak. When they're finished, they'll come back here and escort you to your new cell and make the necessary introductions."

O'Malley's heart thumped wildly, his hands grew clammy and he could barely swallow past the dry lump in his throat. For the first time in a long time, he was afraid. *Really* afraid.

"Warden. You can't do this. Before I ran for office, I was a judge. I put hundreds of those guys out there *into* this place. I wouldn't last until dinnertime."

The warden smiled. "When I set you up in your cushy little cell in minimum security, we had an unwritten contract of sorts. You wouldn't call attention to yourself, and I'd look the other way while you played Big Man Off Campus. But you violated that agreement. Made the staff question my authority. Worse, made the *governor* question my authority. You of all people should understand why I can't allow this to continue. Because what do you get if your people don't respect you? I'll tell you what you get. Anarchy, that's what. And in a place like this, that means war. Literally."

A little black box on his desk buzzed, and he hit a button.

"Yes, Patsy?"

"Mr. Parker and Mr. Rayford are here, Warden."

"See how well people function when they respect their boss?" He leaned nearer the intercom. "Send them in, dear."

Seconds later, Rayford unfastened the clip that held O'Malley's chains to the floor.

"On your feet, Hank," he said, helping him up.

Parker, standing at attention in the doorway, met O'Malley's eyes, and he knew in an instant that the man felt sorry for him. He'd seen a lot of emotions on the guard's faces…anger, hatred, fear, repulsion…but never pity.

"I'll come see you in a day or two," Josephs said.

"I won't last a day or two, and you know it."

A nonchalant shrug was the warden's only response.

He wouldn't be here if Nate Judson had been a man of his word, O'Malley thought. If he hadn't turned state's evidence to save his own skin. The man had taken everything—his senate seat, his home in Chicago's Gold Coast neighborhood, the trust of his wife and the respect of his kids. Hatred didn't begin to define what Hank felt.

He'd just returned a novel to the prison library, a story centering around a protagonist being stalked by a ruthless assassin. O'Malley identified with the hit man, and when he got out of this place, he wouldn't rest until he found Nate Judson. He had an important decision to make between now and then: Kill Judson immediately after the daughter, or let him spend the rest of his miserable life knowing his disloyalty had cost his wife and daughter their lives?

## CHAPTER TEN

IT WAS BARELY eight when the phone rang, and when she saw Noah's name in the caller ID window, Billie groaned. "Did you think of something you forgot to berate me about yesterday?" she said aloud. Because if that's why he'd called, he was in for a rude awakening. She'd looked forward to designing website number one hundred, but she wasn't desperate enough to put up with his guff.

Billie all but barked hello into the mouthpiece.

"Hi, Billie. This is me. Alyssa Preston. My daddy is Noah, from the bike shop."

*You mean Alyssa, the little girl whose lie cost me a client?*

"How are you?"

"I'm fine. How are you?"

"Never better," she fibbed. "What can I do for you?"

"Well...I was just wondering...if I could come over to your house?"

Her brother padded into the room in white

socks, a camouflage T-shirt and plaid pajama bottoms, looking like a high school boy instead of a thirty-year-old retired marine.

"Who's that?" he asked around a yawn.

Billie covered the mouthpiece and whispered, "Alyssa Preston."

Troy frowned. "What does that jerk's troublemaking brat want at this hour?"

Billie frowned, too, and waved him away. "Alyssa, is there something I can help you with over the phone? To, ah, to save your dad coming all the way over here?"

"No, thank you. I should do this in person. Besides, it isn't very far. Just point two miles from my house. I know, because I looked it up online."

Billie had been trapped in uncomfortable social situations before, but never by a third grader. "So how are you feeling today?"

"You already asked me that. I'm fine, remember, so don't worry. You won't catch anything from being around me."

Something told her the sooner she agreed to the visit, the better. "Okay, then, come on over."

"Daddy says we can't stay long because he has to open the store at ten o'clock today," Alyssa said, and hung up without another word.

Billie stared at the silent receiver for a second before replacing it on the cradle.

"Better get dressed, brother dear. Company's coming."

"I don't have anywhere to go or anyone to impress." He picked up a cookie and took a bite, then looked down at his clothes. "Why? Will my mismatched getup embarrass you?"

She shrugged and started a fresh pot of coffee. "No, but it might inspire a volley of little-girl questions."

"I think I have a pretty good idea what kind of craziness to expect from a seven-year-old girl."

The front bell rang and he followed her to the foyer. "Man. They're here already?"

"Apparently," she said, opening the door.

"I like your doorbell, Billie. It's fun." Alyssa twisted the brass key and laughed when it emitted a tinny sound.

Noah grasped her hand. "That's enough, okay?"

As they entered the tiny foyer, he said, "Thanks for letting us stop by so early."

His expression reminded Billie of the way Chuck had looked that morning she'd asked if he'd been keeping something from her. Did Noah really think the in-person approach would make it easier to hear he didn't want to hire her?

Troy peeked around the kitchen door. "There's fresh coffee and straight-from-the-oven cookies in here, in case anyone's interested."

Had he lost his mind? Not five minutes ago he'd called Noah a jerk and Alyssa a trouble-making brat!

"Thanks," Noah said, "but I've already had my three-cup quota for the day."

Alyssa glanced up at him, then looked at Billie. "He drank three *pots*," she said, "because he didn't sleep well last night."

Eyes closed, Noah tilted his face toward the ceiling. Summoning patience? Billie wondered. Or searching his mind for a phrase to counter hers?

"I made snickerdoodles yesterday," Billie told the girl.

"What are snickerdoodles?"

Troy stepped into the hall. "What are snickerdoodles! Only *the* best cookies on the planet!"

Alyssa pressed up against Noah as Billie said, "That's my brother Troy. He's staying with me for a while."

"Nice to meet you," Noah said.

"Same here." Hands on his knees, Troy bent

at the waist to make himself child-sized. "How 'bout I introduce you to the best treat you ever tasted while your dad and Billie talk?"

"No, thank you," she said, grabbing Noah's hand. "I'm the one who wants to talk to Billie."

Billie met Noah's eyes. "Really?"

"Well, yeah. She has something she wants to say. And then so do I."

Troy held out a hand to Alyssa. "Do you like milk with your cookies?"

She looked up at Noah again, and when he nodded, she put her hand into Troy's. "Just one cookie, though, okay?" Noah cautioned.

"Okay, Daddy," she said as Troy led her into the kitchen. "After my cookie, is that when I should say what we practiced?"

"That'll be fine."

Billie couldn't imagine what Alyssa had come here to say, but if it had anything to do with that dreaded allergy pill, she didn't intend to let Noah browbeat her a second time. She took a deep breath.

"I guess it's fate that you're here, so I can tell you in person what I should have said...."

His brow furrowed slightly.

"I'm sorry about the allergy pill."

"You didn't know I'd already given her one."

Billie didn't really *need* Noah as a client, but the money would have definitely come in handy, especially if Troy took her up on her offer of a loan.

"That's no excuse," she said. "You were right. I should have realized you weren't focused on my question."

He studied her face for a second. "Still, I overreacted. Big-time. You didn't deserve that, especially after the way you minded the shop while I picked Alyssa up at school, and hung around while I blasted that supplier."

"I'm confused. Aren't you here to say no thanks on the website?"

"The opposite, actually." He gestured toward the computer in the corner of her living room. "Is that my site on the screen?"

She followed his gaze. "No, but I can pull it up in just a second." Restless and unable to sleep, she'd worked on it last night, thinking it would be easy enough to change the header. He wasn't the only bike shop in town, after all. Billie led him to the alcove she'd turned into her office. "Make yourself comfortable," she said, removing the throw pillow from the wingback chair beside her desk. Then, facing the PC, she tilted the monitor so Noah could see it, and clicked through his site, tab by tab.

He pointed at the headline banner, where she'd typed in big bold Times Roman font SHOP EXTERIOR.

"I don't have any pictures of the store."

"No problem. I have a great camera." Billie sat back. "Do you have any suggestions? Questions?"

"We can do this whole thing without any photographs of Alyssa or me, though, right?"

What a strange question. But if Bud was right, and they were in the witness protection service… "Sure, if that's what you prefer."

His lips formed a grim line as he said, "It is."

"And this tab about experience and years in the business? How can we emphasize that I know what I'm doing without revealing that I have only a little more than three years' experience?"

People were always saying that her face was an open book, so Billie focused on the monitor, to keep him from reading it now.

"If it's there, people want details. If it isn't, they usually don't notice. At least, they don't point it out. That's been my experience, anyway. So it's best to delete it."

"That makes sense. Thanks." He got to his feet, slid a checkbook from his shirt pocket. "Your proposal didn't mention a deposit. How much do I owe you?"

She waved the offer away. "I'll invoice you

when the site is finished and approved, right before it goes live."

He repocketed the checkbook. "Part of me is looking forward to that…and part of me dreads it."

"Dread? That's an odd way to describe the results of more business and more income!" She punctuated the comment with a too loud, too long laugh that made her blush.

"More money would be nice. More attention…" he shrugged "…I could live without."

Billie didn't know how to react to that. "You're sure you don't want some coffee?"

"I'm sure." He held out his hand. "Good doing business with you, Billie."

She wasn't prepared for the strength and warmth of his handshake. "I'll probably have things wrapped up in a week or so."

"No hurry," he said, releasing her hand. "Guess I'd better get in there before Alyssa talks your brother's ears off. Besides, by now she's probably dying to deliver her speech. She worked on it all morning."

All morning? It wasn't even nine o'clock yet!

When they walked into the kitchen, Troy said, "There they are. See? I told you it wouldn't be much longer."

Immediately, Alyssa blurted, "I'm very sorry that I fibbed about the pill, Billie. And

I'm sorry that I got you in trouble with Daddy. I promise never to do it again."

A strange sensation spiraled in Billie's heart. She should have tried harder to dislike this child. Maybe then she wouldn't want to hug her. "I'm the grown-up," she began, "so I should have known better."

It seemed the most natural thing in the world to pluck a napkin from the basket on the bar counter, cup Alyssa's chin in her palm and gently brush cookie crumbs from her chin. So natural that it scared Billie, and dredged up the familiar sorrow, born when she had buried her own little girl.

She backed away slowly, and tossing the napkin into the trash, said, "Then we're even. I won't give you any more medicine, and you won't say you want some when you'd really rather have candy. Deal?" She held up a hand, traffic cop style, and waited.

Beaming, the girl gave her a high five. "Deal."

Troy reached into the drawer behind him and retrieved Billie's camera. "If this isn't a Kodak moment," he said, "I don't know what is. C'mon, you two. Let's get a picture for the kid's scrapbook."

Noah stepped between his daughter and Billie's brother. His posture, his voice, his facial expression shouted "No!" A tense moment passed, and then he relaxed. But not much.

"I hate to break up the party," he said, "but Alyssa has some homework to do, and I have a store to run."

He faced Billie. "Again, thanks for letting us stop by so early, and on such short notice." He took Alyssa's hand and led her to the foyer. "Let me know if I can do anything to help with the website."

Billie and Troy followed, stood side by side as he opened the door.

"Thank you for the cookies," Alyssa said to Troy. "And for the new knock-knock jokes."

"You're welcome. Enjoy your day off."

After they'd gone, Troy put the camera back into the kitchen drawer. "I thought you were making mountains out of molehills, but I stand corrected. There is something off about that guy." Grabbing a stack of snickerdoodles, he headed for his laptop in the living room. "And this time, I'm going to find out what."

## *CHAPTER ELEVEN*

ALYSSA HAD CLIMBED onto his big rolling chair. At first, she'd bent over the desk, muttering as her pencil scratched on the paper, filling the fat blue lines with words like *grab* and *band* and *flat*. She'd spent the past few minutes, though, spinning and singing, "Round, round, I get around, wa-ooh, wa-ooh-ooh-ooh-ooh-ooh."

"I need to limit your time with that Beach Boys CD," Noah said, squirting oil onto the squeaking cabinet hinge. "Having trouble with spelling a word, cupcake?"

"Just the extra-credit one," she said, grabbing the edge of the desk.

"Do you remember how to sound it out?"

She exhaled a sigh of frustration and, retrieving the pencil, made the hard *G* sound, followed by *R,* then *A.*

Noah gave the hinge another squirt. "How many letters in the extra-credit word?"

He could hear the pencil point tap-tap-tapping as she counted.

"Seven."

"That's a long, hard word…for third grade."

"Oh, it isn't hard. I can spell it. I just don't want to."

And then it hit him: the word was *grandma*.

Back in Chicago, they'd lived fifteen minutes east of Jillian's mother. Half an hour in the other direction put them at his mom's. Weekends, holidays and summer vacations had included lots of family activities, most involving the grandparents. And Alyssa, who'd been four when he'd taken her from them, remembered it all. There was a time when he'd looked down his nose at people who said, "If I could live that part of my life over again, I'd live it differently…." The mind-set was pointless at best, he'd thought, narcissistic at worst. Well, he didn't feel that way anymore.

He put down the oil can and went to her. Crouching in front of the chair, he held her beautiful little face in his hands. "I'm sorry, sweetheart."

She met his gaze, looking innocent and wise beyond her years at the same time. Common sense told him he could never give back all he'd taken from her, not even if he lived three lifetimes. But at the moment, Noah felt anything but sensible.

"You worked real hard on the rest of the list, so I think you can skip the extra-credit word."

Her eyes widened, and so did her smile. "Really?"

"Really."

"Whew," she said, shoulders sagging. "That's a relief. For a minute there, I thought you and me were gonna have another one of *those*."

"One of what?"

"You know. Those nights where I say something about Mommy or Gran or Pop," she began, bobbing her head, "and it makes you sad, and then *I* get sad, and then you feel bad…." She sighed.

Yeah, he knew, all right. Those nights weren't happening as often as they once had. But they happened. As recently as Mother's Day, when a commercial had appeared on TV, and Alyssa had said she wished the two of them could have shopped for a heart-shaped pendant for *her* mom. It had hit him like a roundhouse punch to the gut, and he'd locked himself in the bathroom to get hold of himself.

When he had emerged ten minutes later, and Alyssa had seen his red-rimmed eyes, she'd known he'd been in there blubbering like a baby. And when she'd hugged him, tiny hands patting his back as she'd said, "It's okay,

Daddy. It's going to be all right, I promise," he'd almost lost it all over again.

The bell above the entry door jangled, and he straightened. "How would you feel about driving over to Ledo's for supper?"

"I'd say *let's!*"

"Then it's a date."

A husky female voice called, "Anybody home?"

"It's Max!" Alyssa said.

"Hey, short stuff. Why aren't you in school?" She held up a palm. "Whoa. You're not gonna sneeze and make me sick, are ya?"

"No, I'm not sick. Me and Daddy couldn't sleep, on account of I took two allergy pills instead of one. So he let me stay home so I could take some naps."

Hands on her hips, Max looked at Noah. "What's this? You overdosed your kid?"

"It wasn't Daddy's fault. He gave me a pill, but I wanted candy. So I didn't tell that to Billie, and asked her to give me another one."

"Billie. Here. Doling out meds to your kid. Unsupervised."

She knew very well what had happened, but Max was Max, and he knew better than to point it out. She adopted a tough New York cop voice and crossed her arms over her chest.

"Why, I oughta cuff the both of yas—you

an' this Billie character—an' throw yas in the slammer."

Alyssa looked from Max to Noah and back again, and satisfied that the adults were joking, giggled.

"We're going to Ledo's for pizza," she said. "Would you like to come, too?"

Max's job with the U.S. Marshals Service wasn't common knowledge; rather than risk being recognized by someone who might connect her to the witness protection program, they could never be seen in public together. She'd purchased a ten-speed and car carrier at Walmart for the sole purpose of having a legitimate excuse to visit Ike's Bikes.

"Wish I could, but my boss will have a fit if he sees me out having fun when I should be working."

"We could order a pizza instead."

Max tugged gently at Alyssa's ponytail. "Tell you what, if it isn't too late when I get all my reports turned in, I'll be back, and we'll do that. Deal?"

"That's exactly what Billie said when we were at her house, right before we high-fived!"

"Far be it from me to be outdone by a… by a Billie!" Max gave Alyssa's little palm a gentle slap, then looked at Noah. "I have news for you."

The agent stopped by often, always with no warning whatever. Occasionally, she delivered a message that got stuck between post offices when the Marshals Service didn't have time for in-person deliveries. More often than not, though, the sole purpose of her visits was to see how things were going.

Noah tensed, and studied her face for signs that O'Malley had found them. No...she didn't look anxious, and didn't seem to be in a hurry to get them out of here and on to a new location. And since she hadn't suggested they talk in private, away from Alyssa's tender ears, he relaxed a little.

"If you ever get tired of marshaling, I'm pretty sure you could find work in Hollywood, teaching screenwriters how to build suspense into movie scenes."

"And if spinning bike wheels ever gets too boring, you might consider stand-up comedy." She rolled her eyes. "On second thought, maybe not."

"Max..." He held out his hands in a gesture of silent supplication. "You're killin' me here."

"Okay. I've had my fun. Now it's your turn to have some." She lowered her voice, to keep Alyssa from hearing. "O'Malley was moved into the general population."

If not for Max, Noah wouldn't know anything about the senator. Phone calls could be traced and internet trails could be followed… straight to his door. If O'Malley had lost the safe haven of his Pay to Stay single cell, he wouldn't last long.

Noah glanced at Alyssa, preoccupied by a blue jay splashing in the birdbath out back.

"How long ago?"

"Just happened." One eyebrow rose slowly. "I know what you're thinking, but don't get your hopes up just yet. O'Malley reminds me of the giant squids I read about in *Smithsonian*—huge, powerful, dangerous predators, with forty-foot tentacles covered by sharp-toothed suckers. They've been around since… since forever, because they sit quietly in the dark until—"

"See? I was right. You were born for Hollywood." It was a good thing that Alyssa was watching the bird, because a description like that might give her nightmares. It might give *him* nightmares. "I don't buy it. No one has ever seen one."

"Alive… Scientists have studied the ones that washed ashore, dead, or got tangled up in fishermen's nets." Max put her hands on her hips. "So, smart guy, they do exist. But that isn't my point. My point is it's way too soon to let your guard down. O'Malley is like that sea beast. He still has friends in high places on the outside. Who knows what strings he could pull? We're not out of the woods...yet."

She went to the window, spent a few minutes whispering with Alyssa about the strange and sometimes comical habits of birds, then came back toward him.

"Thanks for the update, Max."

"My pleasure. You can rest easy about Billie and her brother, too. They're okay."

It didn't surprise him that she'd had them checked out. She'd run his neighbors, Alyssa's teachers and all his customers through the Marshals' database. It had always been a relief, hearing the people he and Alyssa were interacting with wouldn't harm them, but never more than this time.

Before he could fully accept what he'd just acknowledged, Max said, "I saw you coming out of her house this morning." She lowered her voice to add, "If you want to keep up this 'it's strictly business' facade, you'd better do a better job of controlling your facial muscles."

Noah didn't know what to say, so he shrugged.

"I know, I know," she said, and began counting on her fingers. "You don't think you're ready for a relationship, that even if you were, you're not good enough for you-know-who.

Yeah, okay, so you were a workaholic, made some mistakes—big ones. But, Noah, you paid for them. You aren't that guy anymore. I know, because I've walked that rocky road, right alongside you."

Noah rubbed his chin. "Here's something I never told you, something that might finally change your mind about me—or at least about whether or not I'm entitled to a regular life." He made sure Alyssa wasn't listening, and continued.

"A few months before Jillian's murder, we left Alyssa with my mom and went out to dinner. No special reason. Jillian just wanted some time alone."

He remembered the way she had looked that night, cheeks flushed from too much wine, eyes glittering in the candlelight.

"She asked me if I loved her. Not one of those 'stroke my ego' things you women are famous for... Jill honestly didn't know. That wasn't on her. It was on *me*. I'd spent so many years putting career advancement ahead of everything else that I forgot what was important."

"But that night, you reassured her."

"Yeah, I did, because despite my conceit and self-centeredness, she was the love of my life. Every promotion and award I earned were more hers than mine. Because—to cite a tired old cliché—she held down the fort while I did it all."

"You were lucky. I'll give you that." The agent paused, stared hard at him. "But so was Jillian."

Max opened the door. "See ya, kiddo," she hollered to Alyssa. Then, facing him, she said, "There are no parallels, you know, between her and Billie."

And then she left him to think about her parting comment.

## CHAPTER TWELVE

NOAH JOCKEYED JEFF'S Venge onto the repair stand and inspected the bike's pulleys. The teeth were worn down, keeping them from spinning freely. "Yep," he said to himself, "gonna need to replace those."

As he assembled his tools, Noah pictured Billie's tiny house. It wasn't large by anyone's standards, but she had made the most of every square inch, filling the rooms with comfortable old furnishings that reminded him of his grandmother's house.

It had been nearly a week since Noah and Alyssa had paid Billie the impromptu visit. He remembered how she'd welcomed them with genuine warmth, despite the early hour, then patiently explained the objective of each website page. Pleasant as they were, those things hadn't kept him up nights. Nor had the scent of fresh-baked cookies, or the yellow sweater that brought out the green flecks in her dark eyes. The scene he couldn't shake had happened so quickly; he would have missed it if he'd blinked: Billie, tenderly brushing crumbs from Alyssa's face in a gesture he could only call motherly, and it set his heart to beating double time.

Any day now, she'd call to let him know the website was ready for his final approval, and when she did, he'd have to go back there, to the place that made him feel—for the first time since leaving Chicago—*at home*. And Noah didn't know how he felt about that.

It seemed easier to focus on those tense moments when her brother had picked up a camera and aimed it at Alyssa. Since leaving Chicago, Noah had done everything humanly possible to ensure there would be no photographs of her, anywhere. Other kids her age had stacked up three years of school photos. Alyssa did not, because he'd kept her home on picture day. It was the only way to ensure facial recognition software wouldn't lead one of O'Malley's henchmen to their door.

Noah couldn't apologize for his brusque behavior and hasty departure without explaining why he'd behaved like a paranoid lunatic. And yet, for the first time since entering the WITSEC program, that's exactly what he wanted to do. He heard his little girl singing in the back room. The thumps and bumps accompanying her solo told him she was dancing, too.

"Alyssa, you're supposed to be doing your homework, remember?"

He heard silence, then, "Yes, Daddy."

"When you're finished, we'll walk across the street and get some ice cream, okay?"

Her "Okay, Daddy" harmonized with the bell above the entry door. Deidre O'Toole was the last person he expected to see in his bike shop. The article he had read in the *Howard County Times* highlighting her Little Theater stated that the former Broadway star was sixty-five years old. He'd never been a math whiz, but even Noah knew she couldn't have worked with stars like Ethel Merman and Carol Channing unless she was in her late seventies.

"Noah Preston, you handsome devil," she gushed, "just the man I wanted to see."

"Got a hankering to buy a bicycle?"

"Handsome and funny, too? If you tell me you're on the Forbes 500 list, I'll leave that old husband of mine and we'll run away together." She threw back her head and laughed.

Noah wiped his hands on a cleaning rag. "Sorry, looks like you're stuck with Felix. I'm so poor that church mice put money in the collection basket for me."

"I do love a man with a sense of humor," she said, winking. And then, with a flourish of her great black cape, she hiked up her skirt and climbed onto the counter stool.

"I'm here to offer that beautiful child of yours the lead in my next production. I've looked and looked, and you know me…why settle for second best when you don't have to?"

Noah swallowed. His daughter's love of music was rivaled only by her talent for memorization, something Deidre must have figured out as Alyssa sang her way past the theater as they walked to the hardware store. But what Noah knew even better than Deidre was that a good memory also helped her keep details of her new life straight. Her old life was precisely why the audition could never happen.

"Where is she? I'd love to break the news myself."

"Doing homework." He took a deep breath. Noah liked the woman—everyone did—but if it came to a choice between disappointing her and risking a photograph falling into the wrong hands… "I appreciate the offer, but we're not interested."

"What?"

"Sorry."

"What can I say to change your mind?"

"Nothing. But we'll buy tickets."

Alyssa stepped up beside him. "Hello, Miss

O'Toole." She looked up at Noah. "Are you talking about *Snow White?*"

"No, hon," Deidre said, "we're talking about *Annie*. It's the next play I'm producing, and I need someone just like you for the lead role."

Alyssa's eyes widened as Noah's heart thundered.

"But I don't have curly red hair."

"No biggie. We'd get you a wig."

"I don't have little black shoes or a red dress, either." She frowned. "Well, I *have* black shoes, only I grew a lot since first grade and Daddy hasn't had time to get new ones for me."

Deidre fluttered a long-taloned hand, setting half a dozen bangle bracelets to jangling. "Don't you worry about any of that. I'll see to it you have everything you need."

Alyssa clasped her hands and tucked them under her chin, trembling with excitement. "Oh, Daddy," she said, looking up at him, "could I be Annie? Could I, *please?*"

He'd been clenching his jaw so tightly that his teeth ached. How could Deidre put him in this position?

"I'm sure every little girl in town wants to be Annie," he said, openly glaring at Deidre. Thankfully, she got the message.

"It's not like playing pretend," Deidre said to Alyssa. "Starring in a play is a lot of hard work. You'd have to practice for hours, every single day, whether you feel like it or not."

"How many?"

Deidre rubbed her chin. "Oh, I don't know... three or four hours, I guess."

Noah watched as Alyssa's eyebrows drew together and her lips formed a thin line. Then she held both forefingers aloft. The first time she'd done it, she'd still been in diapers, inspiring Jillian to say, "Looks like she just gave birth to an idea!"

His daughter looked up at him now. "How long is four hours?"

"About as long as it takes to watch *The Sound of Music* twice."

The birthing-an-idea expression returned, but only for a moment.

"There are a lot of other kids in *Annie,* because they're in a..." She looked up at Noah once more. "What's that place called where kids hafta live when they don't have a mom *or* a dad?"

"Orphanage."

"Yes, that's it." She faced Deidre again. "Would I have to work that long if I was one of the kids in the orphanage?"

"No," Deidre said. "No, you wouldn't."

"Good. Because *The Sound of Music* is a

long movie." She paused, then said, "Would I have to try out for one of the orphan parts?"

"Yes, yes, of course you would."

*Not if I have anything to say about it,* Noah thought.

"Auditions begin soon," Deidre said as they walked her to the door. From the sidewalk, she said, "I'll make sure you get a flyer."

*And I'll make sure Alyssa never sees it.* But Noah knew as well as everyone else on Main Street that Deidre was accustomed to getting her way. Maybe just this once, he could relax the rules a bit. It had been three years, after all, without a single incident.

Father and daughter stood side by side, watching their famous neighbor cross the street, and when she disappeared into the Little Theater on the Corner, Alyssa took his hand and skipped all the way to the back room, singing, "I'm going to play an orphan, I'm going to play an orphan!"

He hated to disappoint her, but what choice did he have? "Time to get busy on that homework, cupcake."

"Okay, Daddy." She sat at her worktable, then said, "You know what?"

"What."

"I love you to the moon and the stars, and more than anything in the Milky Way!"

He recited his portion of their mantra. "And I love you to every continent, to the bottom of the sea and around the equator ten times."

Noah went back to work on the Venge, and with every pull on the crescent wrench, counted the things he'd left in Chicago: his wife's grave. His family. The career that afforded him a big house and status cars. He couldn't believe any of that had ever mattered, because the most important thing in his world was humming "Tomorrow."

He tightened the pulley's hex-head bolt with a force that matched his anxiety. An ugly thought roiled in his head. It wasn't easy, admitting that the raw, unbridled hatred that put it there also put him on a par with O'Malley. One day soon, he hoped, Max would stop by to tell him that former senator Hank O'Malley was dead.

## CHAPTER THIRTEEN

"WELL, THIS IS a nice surprise!"

Instantly, Billie recognized her mom's not-so-subtle hint that she didn't call often enough.

"Just giving you and Dad a heads-up. I can't come to Philly this weekend, after all."

"Mary Margaret Elizabeth Landon, you had *better* have a good excuse."

"Remember Bud, my next-door neighbor? He's having surgery tomorrow, and since he doesn't have any family, I promised to take care of his place and his cat while he's in the hospital."

"That's my Billie, always looking out for *other* people."

Her mother's sarcasm inspired a soft groan. What would her mom say if Billie admitted that she'd offered to look after Bud once he went home, too?

"Who's looking after your business while you're looking after Inky?"

"Believe it or not, Mom, I can walk and

chew gum at the same time. As long as I have electricity to run my laptop, I can work."

"You'll wear yourself to a frazzle, make yourself sick."

"Don't worry, I bought a baby monitor, so I can sleep in my own bed *and* make sure Inky is okay."

Her mom sighed. "Well, I suppose we can do this weekend thing anytime."

"Actually, I was wondering how you and Dad would feel about spending Thanksgiving here. I'll invite Todd and Dani, too. It'll be a little crowded, but we manage at Gramps's cabin, and it's even smaller than my place."

"That might be fun, and who knows? Troy might have a place of his own by then, and some of us could stay over there."

"If you tell him I said this, I'll deny it. But I sort of hope he won't find anything, at least until after Christmas. I really enjoy having him here."

"I hate to say I told you so, but if you'd stayed in Philadelphia, you'd have no reason to miss your family."

Well, *that* hadn't gone as expected. The two of them had been over this ground so many times, Billie had lost count.

"Oh, dear!" her mom said. "There's someone at the door. Can I call you later?"

Saved by the bell, Billie thought. "Sure. Love you, Mom."

She hung up and called the next number on her list. A weird little buzz of disappointment went through her when he didn't pick up.

"Hi, Noah," she told the machine, "it's Billie Landon. I got your email and loved your suggestions. If you'd rather see the changes in person, let me know so we can schedule something. Otherwise, just shoot me an approval in your reply and I'll make it official."

She'd barely hung up when the phone rang again.

"Billie, m'darlin', how are things on your side of the fence?"

"Things smell like bacon. I thought your doctor told you that's off-limits from now on."

"That's kind of why I'm calling. Doc's nurse just phoned to say I need to be at the hospital by seven tomorrow for all the pre-op stuff. I know you said you'd drive me, but I can take a cab. Hopkins is a good thirty-minute drive. And it'll be rush hour, meaning—"

"I'm driving you. Got it?"

"Then have dinner with me tonight. We'll make it a big one. And early. My last hoorah, since I can't eat after midnight."

Billie thought back to yesterday. After showing her where he kept Inky's food and litter, and how much to feed the fish, Bud had handed her a legal-sized envelope that read To Be Opened in the Event My Doc Was a Quack. She would never admit it, but the minute she'd gotten home, Billie had opened it… and found Bud's will. How ironic that someone she barely knew trusted her more than the man she'd married had.

Billie swallowed. "How about if we celebrate after your doctor gives you a clean bill of health?"

Bud agreed, then they chatted about the weather forecast, the latest gas prices, the accident that blew out the traffic light at the corner of Old Columbia Pike and Main Street, and finally agreed to leave for the hospital at five-thirty the next morning.

Afterward, Billie spent the day cleaning and doing laundry, making calls and answering emails so things wouldn't pile up while she was looking after Bud.

It was nearly three when she answered a third call.

"Sorry to be such a pain," Noah said, "but I can't get your email to download. Is it okay if I stop by after I pick Alyssa up at school?"

She pictured his clunky PC and enormous monitor, and put part of the blame there.

"I'll be here all day," she said, "so come over anytime."

They arrived an hour later, and once Noah got Alyssa started on her homework, he and Billie sat at her desk.

"Was this here the other day?" He picked up a framed photo of Billie in a flight attendant's uniform.

"Yeah, but it was probably hidden behind a stack of work."

"Cute," he said, putting it back. "So web design wasn't your first career."

A statement, she noticed, not a question. It wasn't a stretch to assume he was only being polite, because a guy who didn't talk about himself didn't really want much information from others. "Bet it was a hoot, traveling the world for free."

"Not really," she said, pulling up his website. "You're usually not in a place long enough to see much more than the inside of a hotel room."

She'd left her desk drawer open, and followed his gaze to the picture of her and Chuck, standing side by side in the cockpit of a 747.

"Your ex?"

She closed the drawer. "'Fraid so."

Noah didn't respond right away, but when he did, Billie didn't know what to make of it.

"His loss."

That's what her friends and family said. How long before she believed it, too?

Pointing, she drew his attention to the monitor. After loading his main page, she reduced its size and pulled up a competitor's site. Tab by tab, she explained why his worked and the other one didn't.

"I don't know what to say, except wow. It's terrific."

His expression went from something akin to approval to baffled.

"What's wrong?"

"Nothing. It's great. But…" He met her eyes. "I just hope I won't be sorry."

"Why would you be sorry?"

"I could use the extra cash. With the economy in the shape it is, who couldn't, right? But I like not having to rush, and it's great having plenty of time for Alyssa. I'm not sure I want that to change, even for more money in my wallet."

"You're giving me way too much credit. You'll see some new business—how much, I can't say—but if I were you, I wouldn't put a down payment on a yacht just yet."

Noah produced a check and she tucked it under her mouse pad.

"I'd offer you coffee," she said as they

walked toward Alyssa, "but it's been on the burner since breakfast."

"I never touch the stuff after lunchtime, any—"

One look at his face told her why he'd stopped talking so suddenly.

There sat Alyssa amid an assortment of loose photos: Billie and her brothers as kids in front of a Christmas tree; her parents on their wedding day; Great-grandpa Landon on the hood of his shiny black Buick; the house Billie had shared with Chuck. The picture Alyssa held took her breath away. Billie had almost forgotten taking one of her baby's grave. Almost.

"Alyssa!"

The girl jumped at Noah's stern voice, which startled Billie, too.

"What do you think you're doing?"

"My knee bumped the box, and it fell off the shelf."

Billie dropped to her knees and, hands shaking, started gathering snapshots of her life.

"It's my fault," she said. "That shelf is no place for family photos. I should have put them into albums years ago."

Alyssa looked relieved, but Noah did not.

"You know better than to snoop through other people's things," he said. "We're going

to have to talk about this when we get home,
young lady."

The girl's eyes filled with tears. Her lower
lip trembled, too.

"I'm sorry, Daddy."

"It isn't me who deserves the apology."

Big, damp eyes locked on Billie's face. "I'm
sorry, Billie. I didn't mean to snoop."

"Oh, don't cry, sweetie. It was an accident.
That box falls off the shelf every time I vac-
uum."

Alyssa had no sooner dried her eyes on the
hem of her shirt than Noah took her by the
hand and led her to the foyer.

"Noah. Really. It's okay." Billie stood between them and the door. "No harm, no foul,
y'know?"

"Don't worry. I don't believe in spankings."
He fixed his impatient stare on Alyssa's face.
"But we *are* going to talk about a punishment."

"The shoebox slid off the shelf. A few pictures fell out. I'm sure it wasn't deliberate."

"Look, I appreciate your concern, but drop
it, okay?"

Drop it? How could she do that, with Noah
looking so annoyed and Alyssa looking so
worried? Billie had never expected to feel anything but grudgingly tolerant of the girl, because for years she'd soothed the ache of losing

the baby by telling herself that she didn't like kids, anyway. They were noisy. Sticky. Demanding. Rude. But this one, with her big eyes and bubbly personality, had exposed the lie.

"You're her dad," Billie stated. "And you know what's best."

If he hadn't looked so smug when she said it, Billie might not have felt it necessary to add, "Just don't go *too* hard on her, okay?"

He opened the door. "You're a great web designer, and I'll bet you were a dynamite flight attendant, too. But unless you can show me a certificate that proves you're qualified to analyze me or my daughter…"

In other words, Billie thought, butt out.

She gripped the doorknob so tightly her knuckles ached. "Your site is live now, but I can make changes anytime. Call me if you see anything you'd like tweaked," she said, and closed the door.

Nothing about him made sense. Troy had been a security specialist in Philadelphia, yet he hadn't been able to roust out one iota of information about Noah—not even after calling in a few favors from former coworkers. Who lives thirty-some years without leaving *some* kind of a paper trail?

## CHAPTER FOURTEEN

"YOU KNOW WHY you're in trouble, right?"

"Because I was snooping?"

"I thought the box fell, accidently."

Alyssa tucked in one corner of her mouth. "So when are we going back to Billie's house, so I can say I'm sorry *again?*"

Noah replayed those final five minutes at her place and grimaced inwardly. Everything he'd said and done had been uncalled for. Picturing her as she came to Alyssa's defense put a smile in place of the grimace: spine stiff, shoulders back, hands on hips and chin up, she'd stared him down...right up until the moment when she thought her attitude might affect the way he'd punish Alyssa.

"We'll give her a couple of days." The truth? *He* needed the time to come up with a good excuse to call.

Alyssa plopped back onto her pillow and flapped her covers. "I think she'd make a great mom." Her nose wrinkled. "Wonder why she doesn't have a husband and kids."

"Good question." Because Billie *would* make a great mom.

Noah listened to Alyssa's prayers and tucked her in, then left the door open a crack so the glow from the night-light in the hall could filter into her room. After settling into his recliner, he picked up the latest issue of *Bicycling* and flipped to the feature article, a story about the rise and fall of a cycling legend. Noah had read only a few paragraphs when a soft knock interrupted him.

The only time Max dropped in at this hour was when she had something to tell him that Alyssa shouldn't hear. Hopefully, the purpose of this visit was to tell him that Hank O'Malley would no longer be a problem.

But it was Troy Landon on the small landing, not Max. Had he come to read him the riot act for upsetting his little sister?

Noah opened the door. "Hey, Troy. How goes it?"

"It goes. I know it's late, and to be honest, Billie would have my head on a plate if she knew I was here."

"Soda? Beer?" Noah asked, closing the door.

"I'm good, but thanks."

The men sat facing one another in the living room, and Troy was the first to speak.

"I understand you had a little run-in with my sister today."

Noah didn't know what to say. First of all, it wasn't exactly a run-in....

"I'm sorry if she's upset. Alyssa and I were talking earlier about going back over there, setting things straight."

Troy leaned back, rested an arm on the sofa cushions. "Here's the thing about Billie—and if you tell her what I'm about to say, I'll—"

"Don't worry. I'm a great secret keeper."

Troy's eyes narrowed slightly, and he opened his mouth as if to ask what that meant. He propped an ankle on a knee instead, and said, "She's still mourning her baby, see, so she has...let's call them *issues*. She says the reason she avoids kids is because they always have runny noses and dirty fingernails." He inspected his own nails, then added, "But she isn't fooling anybody. All she ever wanted was to grow up, get married and have kids."

"Miscarriage?"

"Stillbirth," Troy said matter-of-factly. "She bounced back physically—thanks to the Cannondale—but for a long time, we didn't know if she'd ever recover emotionally. And that idiot she married didn't help matters."

Noah was curious about her ex, and wanted to hear what had ended the marriage. But the less he knew about Billie, the easier it would be to keep her at arm's length.

"Understood." He paused, then changed the subject. "How's the house hunting going?"

"Good. Found three properties I like. My place in Pennsylvania is on the market. With any luck, it'll sell fast so I won't have to take Billie up on her offer."

Her offer? To become her permanent roommate, Noah wondered, or loan him the down payment for one of the houses he'd seen? But those weren't the questions he wanted to ask. Why was Troy here? That's what he really wanted to know.

"So what brings you here, Troy?"

"Covering my bases, mostly. I'm guessing you have a wide variety of customers. Maybe somebody in the security business. One who mentioned a job opening."

For all he knew, Billie's brother was an ex-con. Troy's brow furrowed as he picked absently at a loose thread on his sock. "Don't know how much Billie told you, but my plan is to make Ellicott City my home base." He put both feet on the floor, as if preparing to stand. "So if you hear of anything—doesn't have to be security-related—let me know?"

Billie hadn't told him anything. No surprise

there. But Noah didn't see any reason to take it out on her brother.

"Actually, I do know a guy." Noah told him about Jeff, who owned a company that installed and repaired security systems. If Troy wasn't on the up-and-up, Jeff would find out during the interview process. "Last time he was in, he mentioned that he'd just lost his regional manager."

Troy leaned forward, clearly interested in the news. "Commercial or residential?"

"Both. I think. Want me to give him a call?"

"Hey. Sure. Thanks, man."

Noah opened his cell phone and scrolled to Jeff's number.

Troy laughed nervously. "Whoa. I didn't mean right now!"

"Relax. He's a night owl, like me."

Noah called and Jeff picked up right away. "This better be good, Preston. I'm in the middle of *Moby Dick*."

"What? You didn't read that in high school?"

"Not unless Cliff Notes count."

"How does a lazy guy like you end up running one of the biggest security firms in the mid-Atlantic?"

"By realizing at a very tender age that math would open more doors than classic literature.

But enough about me. What do you want at nine-thirty on a Friday night?"

"Remember Billie, the woman with the sprained ankle you met at the shop? The one who built my website?"

"Sounds to me like you're getting real cozy, not that I blame you. Besides, I remember the way you were looking at her. Not that I blame you for that, either."

First Max, now Jeff? If Noah knew what was good for him, he'd put more effort into a deadpan expression when he was around Billie.

"So anyway," he continued, "her brother is moving from Philly to Baltimore, and he's looking for a job in your field."

"If he's okay with running up and down I-95 every week, I want to talk to him."

"He's sitting right here. I'll put him on and you two can hammer out the details."

Noah handed Troy the phone and gave a thumbs-up.

In the kitchen, he uncapped a beer and took a swig, and leaning against the counter, visualized one of the photographs Alyssa had found: a white marble angel, cradling an infant. At the angel's feet, a brass plaque that was too fuzzy to read. According to Troy, losing the baby had been hard on Billie. From that, Noah could only assume the blowup between her and "her idiot husband" had been enormous. Why else would she have left that beautiful, well-tended grave behind?

What had brought her to Baltimore, of all places? Certainly not her job. With a business like that, she could work anywhere, as long as she had a power source and internet access. And why settle down in one of Maryland's oldest neighborhoods, instead of a modern house like he had seen in a photo she'd held just a second or two longer than all the rest, as she put them back in the box?

Troy joined him in the kitchen, smiling as he handed back the phone. "You have another one of those?" he asked, pointing at the beer.

"Help yourself," Noah said, using the bottle to gesture toward the fridge. "Things went well with Jeff, I take it."

"We're meeting tomorrow so I can sign an employment contract." Troy chuckled and popped the top off the beer. "Mr. Security Expert checked me out while we were talking, so I don't need to update my résumé or fill out an application." Billie's brother took a swallow of his beer, then leaned forward and clinked the bottle against Noah's. "I owe you big-time, dude. *Big*-time."

"Hey. I made a phone call. The rest is on you. Remember that, if things don't work out."

By eleven o'clock, there were six empties lined up on Noah's kitchen counter. He hadn't talked that much, all at one time, since leaving Chicago. In the hour and a half since the call to Jeff had ended, they had discussed sports, the weather, taxes…

…and Billie.

"I've known her all her life, and I can tell when she likes somebody. Trust me, man. She. Likes. You."

To be honest, Noah liked her, too.

Troy went home at eleven-thirty, leaving Noah to face an unsettling fact.

Everyone, it seemed, thought he and Billie ought to be together.

Everyone, that is, except Noah.

## CHAPTER FIFTEEN

TROY PADDED INTO the living room and immediately stretched out on the couch.

"So how's Bud?"

"Fine. Great, actually. Surgery went quicker than anyone expected. He was in and out of the O.R. in just a few hours. When I left him last night, he was sitting up and flirting with the nurses. I'm heading over to see him this afternoon. Want to come with me?"

Troy gave the thumbs-up sign. "That's a good sign. And yeah, I might just do that."

"Men," she said, clucking her tongue. "Where were you until all hours of the night?" She spun her desk chair to face him.

"At Noah's."

She saved her file and went to sit across from him. "No way."

"Why is that so hard to believe? He's a nice guy, I'm a nice guy." Troy sat up. "Case closed. Besides, your wannabe boyfriend got me a job."

"Wannabe…" Billie shook her head. "I

barely know him. And neither does anyone else on the planet, if the information available about him online is any indicator. Which, as you know, is nothing."

"I looked you up, just for fun. Except for your business stuff, there's nothing about you online, either. Same goes for mom. And Dani. And just about everyone else we know."

Billie caught herself staring, and closed her mouth. "Why would you look up our mother? And our sister-in-law?"

"It was a test. To prove that not everyone has a paper trail. From everything I've seen, Noah is clean."

"Well. That's good news, I suppose. Especially for Alyssa's sake." Would have been better news, if Noah really was her boyfriend.... "But wait a minute. Did I hear you say just now that he got you a job?"

Nodding, Troy said, "Jeff Graham, a customer of his, owns Graham Security Systems. Has offices all up and down the East Coast, along with a couple dozen franchises. My job will be to visit the cities where the franchise owners are, helping the new ones get set up and troubleshooting the existing ones."

"Sounds like you'll be on the road a lot."

"Two, maybe three days a week. But everything is within driving distance. And Jeff will provide a car, a cell phone and a company credit card."

"I can't believe it."

"Why? I told you…Noah's a good guy."

"That isn't what I meant. You came here, hat in hand, without a job or a home to speak of, and in just under a month you're a big shot? I don't get it."

He stretched pretend suspenders. "That's what clean livin' will get you, little sister."

"If clean living is the criteria," Billie sniffed, "I should be queen of the world."

"I don't want to hear it. Happiness is right around the corner. Literally. It's your choice to pass it by."

She didn't want to justify her reasons for staying a safe distance from Noah Preston. Mostly, because Billie didn't understand them herself.

"Tell me more about your job."

Troy explained that his first trip would include visits to Virginia Beach, Newark and Dover, where franchisees were installing surveillance equipment and alarm systems in beachfront condo lobbies, strip malls and office buildings.

"Basically," he said, "they're introductory. Jeff is having business cards printed up, ordering the phone and lining up the credit card."

His cell phone beeped, signaling a text message.

"Well, I'll be," he said, reading it. "It's from my real estate agent in Philly." He looked at Billie. "Victoria is going to buy the house, after all. And she's paying more than the asking price. Which means I'll have enough to put the down payment on that sweet little place up the street from you. See what clean living will get you?"

Billie sat beside him and wrapped him in a hug. "Congratulations, big brother. I'm happy for you."

As if to punctuate her good wishes, his phone rang.

"Oh, good grief!" she said. "If that's more good news, I'll eat my hat!"

"You aren't wearing a hat," he pointed out.

His teasing grin vanished when he read the caller ID window. "Oh, no," he groaned. "Victoria. Here's hoping she hasn't changed her mind."

While he took the call, Billie went back to her desk and made a note to thank Noah. She hadn't seen Troy this happy in years. Maybe she'd make lasagna. Or a pot roast. Steaks on the grill. And invite him and Alyssa—and the Grahams, of course—to help celebrate Troy's good news.

Her own phone rang, startling her so badly that she nearly upended her coffee. She didn't recognize the number, and said a coolly professional hello.

"Hey, Billie, it's Jeff Graham. The guy from the bike shop."

Troy's new boss…

"Well, hi. Did you ever pick up your elbow pads?"

"As a matter of fact, I did. That's kind of why I'm calling."

He told her that there was a two-day ride the following weekend, and he'd bought a block of tickets for some employees, but a few couldn't make it. He was calling, he explained, to invite her and Troy to join him and his family, along with Noah and Alyssa.

"Good way for us to get better acquainted," he said, "and it's a great package, if you like camping. We'll ride some of the Appalachian Trail, and along the Lehigh River. Kelly—she's my wife—is looking forward to some photo ops, since we'll see some canal locks and waterfalls, and ride through a couple of covered bridges. Leave it to her to parlay this into an article assignment."

A corporate mogul who wore Gucci and rode a Venge, plus did his own construction and liked camping. *What are the odds?* Billie thought.

"It sounds great," she told him. "I never had the chance to ride in the Greenbrier event after the ankle healed up. One thing after another, you know?"

"Just so you know…we aren't doing the whole fancy bed-and-breakfast part of the trip, though, so if you're opposed to roughing it, this might not be your thing." He hesitated. "Do you have a tent?"

"As a matter of fact, I do. Haven't had much occasion to use it lately, however."

"Sleeping bag? Camp gear?"

"Yes." She laughed quietly. "I have some freeze-dried trail food left from the last trip. And if I do say so myself, I make a mean campfire bean soup."

"Great. Kelly's looking forward to meeting you. She's starting to make notes for her website, so hopefully, she won't monopolize your weekend, talking business."

"No problem, even if she does. I like my job!"

Her excitement must have been palpable and visible, because when she joined Troy in the living room, he said, "Wow. Look at you. Who *was* that?"

"Believe it or not, it was Jeff Graham. You and I are invited to a trail ride next weekend."

"Are you going?"

"Only if you are."

"Don't have a bike. Can't afford a fancy schmantzy Cannondale, like yours. Don't have a tent or any other camping equipment, for that matter."

"You know as well as I do that if my doctor hadn't been upgrading, I'd be riding something from Walmart instead of my fancy schmantzy Cannondale."

Her brother laughed.

"Talk to your new best friend," she continued. "If Noah can't make you a deal, maybe he'll rent you a bike. You won't need a tent. I have one that sleeps four. Two sleeping bags, too. All you'll need to worry about is getting a backpack and some all-weather clothes. You know, case it rains." She did a little dance. "I'm kind of psyched. This will be my first time out since I messed up the Cannondale!"

"Communing with nature might be just what the doctor ordered."

She sat beside him. "What did Victoria want?"

"Money."

"Money? But the town house was yours. You bought it. You made the payments. She changed her mind? She doesn't want to buy it?"

"She wants me to reimburse her for the curtains she bought and hung in the family room. And the towels she put in the bathroom. Something about the bedding for the guest room...." He grimaced. "Considering what happened, I offered to send her a dollar check. And she cried. Said she can't believe it came to this." He punctuated the statement with a heavy sigh. "Frankly, neither can I."

Billie gave his hand a gentle squeeze. "I'm sorry, Troy. But look on the bright side. You have a new job, and soon you'll have a new home."

His expression grew thoughtful, his voice softer as he said, "Yeah. True." He faced her to add, "I have to admit, I didn't figure your wannabe boyfriend for the rugged outdoors type."

She withdrew her hand. "Will you please stop calling him that!"

"What would you prefer I call him, then?"

"A client. A neighbor. Anything but boyfriend. It sounds so...so junior high. And inaccurate," she quickly added. Because he hadn't shown the slightest interest in her as anything other than what came with their professional association.

"Okay," Troy murmured, retreating to the kitchen, "whatever you say."

She could hear him rummaging in the fridge

as a strange question echoed in her head: What if Noah really *was* interested in something more?

THE FLICKERING OF the campfire cast an eerie glow to the tent's interior. Troy, unaccustomed to cycling more than a few blocks, had fallen asleep almost before he finished zipping his sleeping bag. And since he'd turned in first, he'd chosen the space in back so Billie wouldn't have to crawl over him when she got tired.

She'd sat outside, listening to Jeff and Kelly talk about their months in Alaska before the kids came along. Jeff held them all spellbound with their grizzly bear encounter, and made her laugh with the story of life in an igloo. Eventually, though, even they had turned in, and Billie had followed, though she wasn't the least bit sleepy. Troy would be very happy, she knew, working with this warm, outgoing man.

She'd made sure to set up the tent so that the door faced downwind. Even so, the vent flaps rattled with every gust of the chilly October breeze. Troy's snoring, the creaking of the trees, even the pop and snap of the fire kept her from falling asleep. When had she last felt this keyed up? she wondered. And when no answer materialized, even *that* kept her awake.

Billie blamed her disquiet on the nature of the trip—slower paced and more crowded than she was accustomed to. Perhaps that's why it seemed as though every time she looked up, she'd caught Noah staring at her.

As if on cue, she heard his voice, deep as a DJ's, murmuring something to Alyssa from the tent beside hers. The child had never been camping before, so it was no surprise that she was afraid. Billie remembered her first night in the woods, when every cricket chirp and owl hoot had set her heart to hammering.

When Noah's quiet reassurances failed to soothe Alyssa, he began to sing. Billie had heard "Dream a Little Dream of Me" before, but it had never sounded like that.

Billie closed her eyes, imagined herself nestled in the crook of his arm as his breath puffed gently against her cheek, and felt herself relax.

He had the most perfectly shaped lips she'd ever seen. Would they feel as soft, pressed to hers, as they looked?

Billie's eyes snapped open and she stifled a gasp. Oh, she'd never get to sleep now!

Slowly, she unzipped the sleeping bag and turned it into a blanket. Dragging it behind her, she crawled out of the tent. Outside, she draped it around her shoulders. Grabbing a long stick, she poked at the fire, waking an explosion of sparks that winked at the darkness before disappearing. She jabbed it again, squinting as smoke rolled from the coals, rose up and twisted itself into an opalescent braid that spiraled toward the treetops.

Raw, blue-white heat radiated from the fire's core, pulsing and throbbing like a heartbeat. She put the stick down, closed her eyes and inhaled the musky-sweet scent of charred wood and heat.

"I thought I heard someone out here," Noah whispered.

"Couldn't sleep," she said, "and the fire always makes me drowsy."

He sat down beside her.

Though Billie stared into the flames, she sensed that he was gazing at her. She pulled the sleeping bag tighter around her.

He picked up the stick. "It's freezing out here. Wonder what the temperature is?"

"Forty? Forty-five?"

"Maybe." Noah scooted closer. "I'm cold." He grabbed a corner of her sleeping bag and covered himself, too.

"Wow. You weren't exaggerating. You *are* cold."

"Doesn't make much sense wasting a lie on something that trivial."

"Ah. So you prefer to lie about big important things, then."

He made a halfhearted attempt at a laugh, but he wasn't smiling when he looked over at her. "No one tells the truth all the time."

She had to agree. Billie had stretched the truth plenty of times. Little things, like misrepresentations that saved her from childhood punishments, and flattering friends who'd survived horrible haircuts. And serious things, like letting her family think she'd recovered from losing the baby, long before she had. Telling Bud he looked wonderful, fresh off the ventilator. And then there were the big bold lies she told herself: that she didn't like kids and never wanted any of her own.

"Warm enough?" he asked.

She nodded. "And you?"

He nodded, too.

"Think Alyssa will want to do anything like this again?" Billie asked.

"Sure. She's having a ball."

"Really? It didn't sound that way, a few minutes ago."

"She'll get used to the night noises."

"I suppose," Billie said.

"You suppose? Did she say something to you when you guys went looking for firewood?"

"No. It's just…" Why waste a lie on mediocre stuff? "Tent walls don't exactly offer much privacy. I heard her crying." *Heard you singing to her, too....*

"Oh. That." He faced the fire again. "She had a nightmare about her mom. Happens sometimes when she's overtired."

If Noah wanted Billie to know how his wife had died—and why it caused Alyssa's recurring nightmares—he'd tell her.

"You have a very pleasant singing voice."

He dipped his head. "Aw, man.... Sorry. I thought I was being quiet."

"No need to apologize. You have a really good voice."

Billie held her breath, waiting for a response. But the only thing she heard was her own pulse, drumming in her ears. She leaned forward to find out why he'd grown so quiet all of a sudden. Instead, she found out that a dimple formed in his right cheek when he smiled. His two-day growth of whiskers reminded her of nearly every male actor between the ages of eighteen and eighty. Billie had never found that look particularly attractive. Until now.

He shifted slightly, and when he did, the length of his thigh pressed against hers. The wind kicked up again, sending a blast of cold air into their cocoon. Was it instinct that caused him to lean closer still, seeking warmth?

Something was happening here. Billie couldn't put a name to it, because she'd never experienced anything like it before. She blamed the night. The scent of charred wood. Quiet snores and sleepy grunts coming from the tents all around them. The haunting one-note of an owl, perched in a nearby tree. And in the distance, the mournful wail of a train whistle.

A log broke apart in the fire with a hollow *whoosh,* startling her and sending sparks skyward like a red-orange fountain. The embers flickered and flashed, then faded as they rained back to earth.

The sleeping bag slid from their shoulders when he leaned closer still. "If you're the type who screams, this would be the time to do it."

"Why would I scream?"

"Because," he whispered, "if you don't, I'm going to kiss you."

## CHAPTER SIXTEEN

*JUST KISS HER,* he thought, instead of staring into her big, long-lashed eyes, which glittered in the firelight. *Just kiss her, and find out for yourself if her lips feel as soft as they look.*

When Billie closed her eyes, he felt as though she'd slammed a door in his face. She rested her forehead on his shoulder for a moment, then got to her feet.

"See you in a few hours," she said, giving the sleeping bag a quick shake.

As she disappeared into her tent, he turned and stared into the fire. It was just as well that he hadn't kissed her. Starting something he couldn't finish would have been thoughtless and reckless, completely unfair to Billie, who'd already experienced her fair share of heartache and loss.

Still…regret hammered at him. He tried to ignore it. Tried to explain it away. *It's just loneliness talking,* he told himself. But women weren't the only ones who longed for the warmth of an embrace, who wanted to love and be loved.

"Daddy?"

Starting something with Billie wouldn't be fair to Alyssa, who so desperately wanted a mother's love.

When he crept into the tent, she levered herself up on one elbow.

"Where were you?" she said. "I woke up and you were gone, and I couldn't see anything because my flashlight is busted!" She gave it a shake, as if to prove it wasn't working.

"Broken," he corrected, taking it from her. "And I was right outside, talking with Billie." He unzipped his pack, glad he'd had the good sense to toss in a couple batteries at the last minute. Locating the AAs, he replaced the dead ones in Alyssa's flashlight.

"Okay, cupcake," he said, handing it back, "you're all set."

She tested it…on, off, on again. "All fixed. Thanks." She gave it a final click and scooted deeper into the sleeping bag. "You're the best daddy in the whole world."

"And you're the best little girl." He climbed into his own bag. "Try to get some sleep. The sun will be up before you know it."

She rolled onto her side, facing him. "What were you and Billie talking about?"

Noah chuckled. "The weather, the elements…"

Yawning, Alyssa said, "Sounds boring."

It might have been, with anyone else.

Her eyes fluttered closed. "Love you," she murmured, around another yawn.

"Love you, too," he said, giving in to drowsiness.

Noah woke to the scent of coffee, and heard Billie teaching Troy how to take apart and pack up their four-man tent, in the same gentle voice that had reassured Alyssa after the box of photos had spilled across her living room rug.

He stretched, feeling reenergized. That surprised him, because he hadn't expected deep, dreamless sleep. Any other night, he would have tossed and turned, counting all the reasons it had been a mistake to kiss her. Correction—to almost kiss her. He rolled out of the sleeping bag and admitted it didn't matter if their lips had touched or not, because that moment was fused in his memory. A good thing, since it could never happen again.

When he exited his tent, he saw a circle of cyclists twenty or so yards away, and though she stood with her back to him, Noah easily picked Billie out of the small crowd. She was the smallest adult in the group, for one thing, with energetic hand gestures emphasizing every word. What might it feel like, he wondered, to have those hands on *his* face the way they'd been on Alyssa's that day...?

He helped himself to a cup of coffee, and continued to watch her through the steaming curlicues. With the exception of Troy, every man in the group—married or single—laughed a little longer and louder at whatever joke she'd told. One of the things Noah liked most about Billie was that she seemed not to notice. Or if she did, dismissed it as unimportant, unlike nearly every other woman he'd known.

He heard Alyssa moving around in the tent, and ducked inside to check on her.

"Look," she said, arms akimbo, "I'm all dressed and ready to ride!"

"Good girl. Ready to brush your teeth?"

She nodded.

"And comb your hair?"

Another nod. "What a kid," he said, returning her high five. "Hungry?"

"Oh, yes. Very. Do you think they have pancakes?"

He took her hand. "Let's find out."

Outside, Alyssa looked around the campsite. "Where's Billie?"

Noah looked for the Orioles baseball cap or the too-big orange sweatshirt that should have made her easy to spot. Why hadn't he noticed before that the space beside his tent was empty? Could she and Troy have policed their area and hit the trail in the short time he was inside with Alyssa? He knew that people often acted as scouts on trail rides, to report sights and activities that might be of interest to the cyclists, but she hadn't said anything about it earlier. He shrugged off his disappointment by telling himself he'd run into her at lunchtime.

He didn't see her again until everyone gathered around the extra-long passenger van Jeff had rented to make the two-hour trip home easier for the kids. One by one, the adults loaded backpacks and bikes into the pull-behind covered trailer. Another note of disappointment chimed in his head when Billie got into the van and moved to the back.

Alyssa tugged on his hand. "Do you think we'll be home in time for rehearsal?"

"Maybe." He sounded distracted, even to himself. Noah cleared his throat and met her eyes. "If we don't run into a traffic jam, I'm sure you'll make it in time."

"I know all my lines. I mostly just need to learn how to say them."

She probably meant lyrics, not lines.

"Miss Deidre says Molly is a big responsibility, and that's why it's important not to miss rehearsals."

Wait a minute...wasn't Molly the youngest orphan, the one who interacted directly with Annie?

"You have *lines?*"

"Well, of course. Molly and Annie are good friends!"

Alyssa studied his face, and quickly figured out that he didn't have a clue what was going on at the Little Theater.

"Oh, no." She slapped a palm to her forehead. "You forgot, didn't you?"

Absentmindedness would have been easier to own up to than ignorance. "Forgot what?"

"The permission form? *Remember?*"

A flash of memory took him back to a night last week, when he'd spent half an hour on the phone trying to correct an erroneous charge on his credit card statement. The customer service rep had been right in the middle of identifying the problem when Alyssa handed him a sheet of paper. Thinking it was a field trip permission slip for school, he'd signed, telling himself he'd examine it later...right before reiterating the Don't Interrupt When Daddy's on the Phone lecture. But soon after hanging up, she'd fallen and skinned her knee, prompting the Don't Run in the House speech, instead.

And until this moment, he'd forgotten all about that form.

"I get to sing in four songs now," she announced proudly, "and I have twenty-three lines. Miss Deidre says they're all *very* important to the play."

Noah grazed a knuckle over her cheek. "I'm really proud of you, cupcake." How would he tell her he'd made a mistake, agreeing she could perform in the first place?

She darted toward the van and quickly disappeared inside.

"Hold on a minute," he said, following. "What's the hurry?"

"Billie promised to save us a seat."

He looked for validation from Billie, but she was facing the back of the vehicle, talking to Jeff and his family, who were sitting side by side on the long rear bench.

Alyssa sat to Billie's right and patted the empty space beside her. "Quick," she said as Billie scooted closer to the window, "before somebody else gets it!"

It would be a tight fit, but Noah sat down, anyway. He withdrew his cell phone and typed a reminder into the notes area: "Call Max re: Play." Maybe she'd agree that letting Alyssa perform was too risky, and maybe she'd say he was just being paranoid. Again. Pretending he hadn't already made one of the biggest mistakes of his life wouldn't be tough.

He glanced at Billie, whose cheeks were rosy-red from riding in the chilly wind. She whipped off the baseball cap and stuffed it into a zippered jacket pocket.

Pretending he wasn't falling for her would be tougher still.

For most of the day, Billie had managed to avoid him. Even now, she'd managed to avoid direct eye contact. But she couldn't focus on the Grahams for the entire drive home.

She rarely went anywhere without carrying a few business cards. Taking one from a pocket in her jacket, she handed it to Kelly.

"If you get a chance in the next day or two, shoot me an email with that list of ideas you were telling me about on the trail. I have two sites to update, but they won't take long."

Speaking of taking long…Billie had a feeling the two-hour drive back to Ellicott City would feel more like ten. Why had she offered to save Noah and Alyssa seats?

Because Alyssa had asked her to, that's why.

"I don't know anyone very well," the girl had said. Billie had pointed out that she knew Troy, but Alyssa had said that didn't count, because Troy was a *boy*. She knew Jeff and Kelly and the Graham kids, too. But the Grahams were too old to have anything in common with her and their children were too young to be any fun.

"Are you mad at me because I lied about the allergy pill?" Alyssa had asked.

"That's ancient history," Billie had assured her.

"Because I spilled your pictures?"

"That was an accident. Could have happened to anyone."

"So if you aren't mad, why don't you want to sit with me?" she had asked, clearly puzzled.

It wasn't Alyssa's fault that Billie had developed a ridiculous, unexplainable high-school-type crush on Noah. But she couldn't very well admit that, so had agreed to save them both a seat. Now, as Noah thumbed through messages on his cell phone, Billie admitted he could never be more than a neighbor and client. Was he remembering their near-kiss and thinking the same thing? Was that why he seemed so uncomfortable?

"So," she said to Alyssa, "where were you guys all day?"

"Trying to catch up," the child said. "You guys are way faster than us."

Billie slid an arm around her. "Well, when you get a little bigger, and learn how to ride a big bike, I have a feeling you're going to be some serious competition."

"Do you really think so?"

"Oh, I know so."

Alyssa leaned her head on Billie's shoulder...and promptly fell asleep.

Noah put his phone away and said, "She's never done that with anyone before."

He'd slid down in the seat, closed his eyes and crossed both arms over his chest, so Billie couldn't tell if that was a good thing or a bad thing.

"She likes you," he said. "More importantly, she trusts you."

"Really?"

But Noah didn't answer, because he was dozing off, as well. With any luck, they'd both sleep all the way home, saving her from having to deal with the unsettling fact that she liked Alyssa. Far more than was healthy, considering everything the child had been through. Much as it pained Billie to admit it, she liked Noah, too, even though he'd done everything but hang a sign in the bike shop window, a big red circle with a diagonal line crossing out the word *Relationship*.

"She trusts you," Noah had said.

If only *he* trusted her enough to fill in the blanks of his history.

So where did that leave Billie?

On a minibus with a man and a child who seemed to want a loving family as much as she did.

So why was the child the only one honest enough to admit it?

## CHAPTER SEVENTEEN

WHEN SHE'D MOVED to town last summer, Billie hadn't known how serious Ellicott City residents were about celebrating autumn. From the wine tour early in October to the harvest festival and midnight tours of 1770s haunted houses later in the month, the calendar swelled with activities that attracted tourists from all over the country. Because she'd been new to town, she hadn't participated. But this year, Billie hoped to enjoy a few of the events she'd read about in the *Howard County Times*.

According to the articles, doctors and teachers and ordinary citizens claimed to have seen spirits and apparitions lurking in the attics and alleyways. It surprised her that Bud, who'd lived here for decades, had never taken the haunted tour. "Never had time," he'd said. "If it wasn't work getting in the way, it was something else." Such as a fourteen-year-old son who'd died of leukemia, and a brokenhearted wife who'd grieved herself to death.

Bud's life hadn't been easy, but as he often

said, "Self-pity is an ugly, selfish emotion."
Billie not only admired his determination
to squeeze every drop of joy from each day,
but wanted to emulate the man she'd come to
think of as an elderly uncle. The new mind-set
changed so many things. If not for Bud, who
knows how much time she might have wasted,
wishing for things she couldn't have, regretting
choices that brought her nothing but misery?
Billie hadn't been this happy or satisfied with
life in years, and she wanted to do something
to show her appreciation.

Before his surgery, they'd talked about
celebrating his health and her new client by
signing up for one of the ghost tours. He was
doing great, post-surgery, but not great enough
to walk the cobbled streets of Ellicott City.
His birthday was coming up, though, so why
not pick up a card and the fixins for a home-
cooked meal from Yates Grocery...directly
across the street from Ike's Bikes.

Billie could see Noah over there, unpacking a shipment of cycling shoes, then stacking
them along the back wall. She considered of-
fering to give him a hand, and decided against
it. Since the camping trip, he had called only
twice. He'd been friendly enough, asking
her to add links to his website, and yet he'd
seemed...distant. She blamed the kiss they'd

almost shared. If it scared him half as much as it had scared her, no wonder he was working hard to appear detached and uninterested! And it was just as well, because neither of them were in any condition emotionally to get involved.

Oddly, she found herself missing his bright, energetic little girl, who despite a seemingly endless cache of riddles and jokes, looked every bit the sad-eyed orphan she'd soon play in Deidre's production of *Annie*. Alyssa called every day. Conversations that started with questions like "Can I wear a flowery shirt with a plaid skirt?" and "Do you think Daddy will let me get my ears pierced?" always led to child-friendly snack recipes or something a kid in her class did. The better Billie got to know Alyssa, the more stupid her "I don't like kids, I don't want kids" attitude seemed.

Last Halloween, she'd watched the constant stream of children march up one side of Main Street and down the other, their trick-or-treat bags bulging as shopkeepers, restaurant owners and even the staff at the B&O Railroad Museum handed out candy and trinkets. This year, if Noah would let her, she and Alyssa would be part of that parade.

Home again, Billie signed Bud's card, tucked

an invitation to dinner inside and slid it into the matching envelope.

"It's not my birthday," Troy said, reading over her shoulder.

"It isn't?" Billie thumped the heel of her hand against her forehead and feigned shock. "I've already mailed Todd's card. He'll think I've lost my mind."

"*You're* a card. Seriously. Who's it for?"

"Bud, next door. Saturday's his birthday."

"Speaking of Saturday, my real estate agent rigged a special weekend meeting at the title company." He wiggled his eyebrows. "This time next week, you'll have your guest room back."

Billie sighed. "I'm torn.... Happy for you, of course, but I'm kinda sorry you're leaving. I like having you around."

"I'll be right around the corner. Want to see the place?"

"Now?"

"Sure. Why not?"

"But if you don't settle until Saturday, how will we get in?"

"I watched the agent punch in the code on the lockbox."

"You're sure it's okay?"

"Why wouldn't it be? Nobody lives there, and it isn't like we're burglars or vandals.

They cashed my earnest money check, so it's as good as mine."

"I suppose," Billie said.

And half an hour later, they were standing on his deck, looking out over the small backyard, when Troy said, "Well?"

"It's perfect for you. Not too big, not too small, easy to maintain—a good thing, since you'll be on the road a lot."

He led the way to the front door, and while he locked up, Billie said, "Have you told the folks?"

"Yeah…."

"Well, don't keep me in suspense! What did they say?"

"Dad seemed pleased, but Mom…" Troy shook his head. "I'm surprised she hasn't called you, tried to enlist you in the Get Troy Back to Philly campaign."

"Oh, she won't do that," Billie said wryly. "She thinks if I hadn't made it so easy for you to stay, you would have gone home, patched things up with Victoria, and she'd be well on her way to her two-point-two grandchildren by now instead of changing your address in her little purple phone book."

They started walking back to Billie's.

"Two-point-two grandkids, huh?"

"It's a start."

"Well," Troy said, "I guess Todd and Dani better get a move on." He pocketed one hand, rested the other on Billie's shoulder. "And speaking of moving…will you help me figure out where to put the furniture?"

"You know I will. Have you already arranged a moving van?"

"No need to. I sold Victoria the place, furnished."

"But your clothes…"

"Mom and Dad will bring them down when they come for Thanksgiving."

"Good grief. I nearly forgot."

"Can you believe Todd and Dani got away with skipping it this year? Next chance I get, I need to have a heart-to-heart with that twin of mine, find out how he talked Mom into putting her stamp of approval on their combination second honeymoon, business trip. Smart choice, especially since it saves us driving to Philly."

"With all the move-in stuff going on and a new job, I hear ya."

Troy frowned. "Why do I hear a *but* in that statement?"

"I'm just now wondering why Mom agreed so easily. She loves making Thanksgiving dinner."

He looked guilty and shrugged. Meaning

he'd promised their mom could prepare the feast here, in Ellicott City.

"My kitchen or yours?"

"Ah-h-h…"

Billie pictured her kitchen as it would look on Thanksgiving morning—steaming pots on all the burners, every utensil and mixing bowl piled in the sink—and sighed.

"I have a favor to ask Noah," he said, opening the door.

"A favor? But you barely know—"

Alyssa rushed up and made the "shh!" sign. "We have to be quiet," she said, pointing toward the back room. "Daddy's sleeping."

"At four-thirty in the afternoon?" Billie asked.

"He had a headache and a stomachache."

"Uh-oh," Troy said. "Hope he didn't pick up the bug that's been going around."

"I'm not asleep," Noah called out, "and yeah, I picked up something."

"Sorry," Troy said.

"Me, too," Billie added.

"Not as sorry as me, I'll bet," Alyssa whispered. "He's too sick to take me to rehearsal tonight."

"That's no problem. I'll take you," Billie offered. It had been a knee-jerk reaction to Alyssa's disappointment, which instantly vanished.

"Really? You will?"

"Sure." She remembered the allergy pill fiasco and quickly added, "If it's okay with your dad."

The three of them started toward the back room, waiting for a response. Billie was beginning to think Noah had dozed off when he appeared in the doorway, dark circles under his eyes, and said, "You're sure? You don't mind?"

What she minded was how quickly she'd volunteered to take his place. What she minded was how she must look to him now, jumping into the mommy role without even being asked. But Alyssa was waiting for confirmation.

"It'll be fun," Billie said. "And a good chance to visit with Deidre. I haven't seen her in ages."

"It's a school night, so straight home afterward, okay?"

Alyssa nodded, and Billie asked, "What time does rehearsal start?"

"Six-thirty," Noah answered.

The clock behind the cash register read four forty-five. "Straight there and back," Billie echoed, "and if it's all right with you, I'll take her to my house and fix her some supper first."

He groaned. "Please. Don't mention food."

Troy said, "Dude. What are you doing down

here? Shouldn't you be upstairs in your apartment, sleeping?"

"Probably. I'll head up as soon as you guys leave."

"Before we go," Troy said, "I have a favor to ask you."

"Long as it isn't food related, I'm all ears."

"I just bought the house up the street," Troy explained, "and I need to hit the discount stores for pots and dishes and towels and stuff. Think maybe I could borrow your truck?"

Noah leaned against the doorjamb and ran a hand through already-rumpled hair. "When do you need it?"

"Just a couple of hours on Saturday. Move-in date is two weeks from now, but I have permission to store a few things over there before settlement."

"No problem. If I'm feeling human by then, I'll give you a hand."

"I'll owe ya one, pal."

Billie wondered why neither of them had given a thought to Alyssa. She might enjoy shopping for flatware and dishes, but where would she stay while the guys hefted the boxes into Troy's house?

"Better grab a jacket," she told the little girl. "It might be chilly when we walk home."

"I'll get some scrunchies, too, in case Miss

Deidre wants my hair up." She started for the stairs, and hesitated on the bottom step. "Do you know how to make braids?"

"Yes…."

Half an hour later, while Troy served up leftover lasagna, Billie stood behind Alyssa, weaving her shining blond waves into two tidy braids. Their walk to the theater was slowed by neighbors who'd stepped outside their shops to bring sale items inside for the night. They chatted about everything from taxes to the weather to which little girl would win the Prettiest Actress title—not that looks were what mattered onstage—so it was no surprise when Alyssa said, "Don't you just love living here, Billie? Everyone is so nice!"

*From the mouths of babes…* The shopkeepers were friendly. They were right, too, she thought as the children performed. Alyssa was by far one of the cutest children in the cast. One of the most talented, too, which made her wonder why she hadn't been awarded the lead role.

Rehearsal ended promptly at seven forty-five, and as the kids waited for their parents to pick them up, Billie chatted with Deidre, whose enthusiasm about the production was contagious.

Her exuberance fizzled slightly as she said,

"Don't breathe a word of this, but I think it's going to be a dynamite show, even though I had to settle for second best as Annie."

"Second best?"

"I wanted Alyssa to play that part. Just look at her," Deidre said, pointing.

Sure enough, the girl stood center stage, singing "Tomorrow" at the top of her lungs… and looking every bit like a star.

"She's perfect for the role. But Noah…" Deidre clucked her tongue, and with an exaggerated sigh, said, "That man takes overprotective to a ridiculous extreme."

And then, in typical Deidre fashion, she left Billie alone, going to greet the mother of one of her actors at the other side of the stage.

Billie waved Alyssa closer. "I know we told your dad we wouldn't take any detours, but I have some homemade chicken soup in the freezer. How about if we stop by my house again, just long enough to get it?"

"Oh, that's a great idea, Billie. He couldn't eat anything all day. He's probably starving by now."

Based on how he'd sounded earlier, it wasn't likely. Hopefully, he'd picked up a twenty-four hour bug, and he'd feel more like eating tomorrow.

"Before we go, do you want to hear me sing 'It's a Hard Knock Life'?"

"I'd love that!"

Alyssa sang her part and Annie's, and danced the steps, too. She faced stage right, stage left, spun in a circle and snapped her fingers.

The a cappella performance was so engaging that Billie barely noticed that on the other side of the stage, another little orphan was putting on a similar show for her mom.

"Hold still, honey," the woman said, "so I can take a picture to share with Grandma and Grandpa in Chicago!"

## CHAPTER EIGHTEEN

"DARN. I WAS hoping to get your answering machine."

Noah listened to the quiet hiss of Billie's voice on the other end of the phone, and thought maybe they'd been disconnected.

"Well, that's a first," she said. "I'm so very sorry to disappoint you. Would you like me to hang up so you can call back and leave a message?"

Noah wondered if growing up with two brothers made her impervious to insensitive remarks, or if she'd been born a good sport. Either way, it felt good to know she wouldn't hold his feet to the fire.

He took a breath and started over. "Troy said you were going with him to the settlement this morning. Took me by surprise, that's all, when you answered."

"Settlement was postponed. Something about a missing page from the title search. So what can I do for you, Mr. Tact?"

So much for thinking she'd let him off the

hook. "I'm having trouble pulling up some pages of my website, and hoped you could show me what I'm doing wrong." He filled the brief pause with a qualifier: "Not now, of course. Just whenever you get a minute."

"I could come over later today."

"That would be great!"

"How are you feeling this morning?"

"Tired, but I'm okay. I don't think I'm contagious, if that's what you're worried about."

"If I was worried about that, I wouldn't have spent hours with Alyssa…who spent hours with you while you were sick."

Noah winced. She was probably wondering if he was born a jerk, or if he worked at it.

"That soup was fantastic," he said, hoping to change the subject. "Thanks, and for tucking Alyssa in, too. I didn't even hear you guys come in."

"We put a lot of effort into being quiet."

"I appreciate it. And the way you cleaned up the kitchen, too."

"Just something to do to pass the time until she fell asleep. The way you hover over her, I knew you wouldn't want her running around unsupervised."

Hover? Oh, Max would love that one!

"Anyway," Billie said. "I'll see you later."

And hung up the phone.

Noah stared at the receiver for a second before returning it to the cradle. "See," he told it, "this is why I wanted to leave a message. No groveling required."

He felt as if he'd been hit by a bus, and didn't know whether to blame a twenty-four hour bug or the convenience store hot dog he'd eaten for lunch. Either way, he shouldn't have taken his bad mood out on Billie. It wasn't her fault that being around her felt…weird; she hadn't initiated the kiss, but it *was* her fault that every time he'd seen her since, he wanted to do it again.

Saturday was the shop's busiest day, but he didn't care. Noah left the Closed sign facing the street and went upstairs. He found Alyssa in the kitchen, leafing through a catalog of Halloween costumes.

When she looked up at him, he wasn't sure how to define her expression. Boredom? Uncertainty? And then it hit him: resignation.

"I know, I know. It isn't safe to go trick-or-treating, but could I still get a costume? Please? So I could wear it to the Day of the Worlds parade at school?"

"Day of the what?"

"Worlds," she repeated. "I heard the teachers talking in the hall. Their bosses said it can't be a costume parade or a Halloween party because it wouldn't be fair to the kids who don't believe stuff like that." She shrugged and went back to looking at the Snow White outfit. "So it's called World Day so the kids who aren't allowed to do those kind of things can march around with us."

Halloween had been one of Noah's favorite days when he was a boy. Pulling crazy outfits together from clothes in the rag bag and his grandmother's attic had been almost as much fun as yelling "Trick or treat!" at every neighbor's door. He felt a little sorry for Alyssa, who would never experience any of that. Changing the name to World Day made sense because the world was an entirely different place now. Still, the day just wasn't as much fun anymore.

"I think you'll look real pretty as Snow White," he said, looking at the costume she'd pointed out.

She hopped down from her chair and put the catalog on his desk. "You should order it tonight, so it gets here in plenty of time." Then she headed for the living room.

"I think you must have left your manners at school." She looked a little puzzled until he said, "Don't I get a please or thank you?"

"Please and thank you for ordering the costume tonight. Can I watch some TV now?"

Her attitude was disappointing, but he

wasn't in a mood to lecture her. "Sorry, kiddo," he said instead. "No TV. You were supposed to clean your room, and you didn't."

Her shoulders drooped in a full-body pout, and she trudged in that direction. "Fine. I'll do it now," she snapped.

"Hey. Get back here, missy."

She huffed and puffed, then stood before him and stared at the floor.

"Sulking is against Preston House rules. You know that. So what's with the big frown?"

"I don't want to clean my room. My friend Sheila doesn't have to clean her room. And neither does Molly or Emily."

Noah stood back and crossed his arms over his chest. "Oh, really. Who cleans their rooms?"

"Their mothers do it. Their mothers do *everything*."

Translation: she didn't have a mother. And if he had anything to say about it, she'd never find out *why*. He could let his guilt dictate his decisions, let it goad him into giving in to her every whim—and guarantee she'd become a self-centered, spoiled brat.

He leaned forward and pressed a kiss to her cheek, then gently turned her around. "Call me when your room looks shipshape."

She was a good kid, and so far, hadn't

learned how to hold a grudge. He always felt bad when he was forced to hold her feet to the fire. Tonight, after he tucked her in, he would get online and try to order the costume.

She deserved more, a whole lot more, but in their circumstances, Noah was limited as to what he could give her. Couldn't even let her go trick-or-treating, like other kids. It wasn't likely anyone would recognize her, but he couldn't take that chance.

So he'd come up with a next best thing. In years past, kids had come to Main Street from Annapolis, Baltimore City, even as far away as Frederick to take part in the annual trick-or-treat event. Alyssa enjoyed standing at the door of their shop, playing hostess as she dropped candy into tote bags and plastic pumpkins. She'd never complained, but he could tell that she would much rather *get* treats than give them, so he'd promised to give her a nickel for every one she shared, and encouraged her to contribute the money to the children's center at Johns Hopkins.

But in a few short years, she wouldn't even want to go trick-or-treating. How would he feel when that time came, and he had to admit she'd missed out on yet another childhood memory because of the lifestyle made necessary by his past mistakes?

"Somebody's at the back porch," Alyssa said, breaking into his thoughts.

It surprised him to see Billie here already. "Come on in," he said, opening the door.

She said a cursory thanks and headed straight for Alyssa.

"Found some cool scrunchies," she said. "They're tiny, and perfect for braids."

While they inspected the colorful blobs of material, Noah closed the door and stepped into the kitchen. He poured himself a cup of coffee and hoped it wasn't too soon after his stomach bug…and wondered how to put a stop to the growing affection between Billie and his daughter. His girl wanted a mom, and his neighbor seemed to fit the bill. But according to Troy, she had emotional baggage, and Noah couldn't take the chance that her issues might spill on to Alyssa.

He heard his daughter say, "Are you here to fix the computer?"

Noah carried his mug into the living room as Billie asked, "What's wrong with it?"

"I can't watch my movies on it anymore."

"Yes, you can," he said, "if you know the password." He looked at Billie. "Lots of weird stuff out there. I don't want her stumbling into any of it, accidently."

Alyssa started to protest, until Billie said,

"That's a great idea. It only takes a few seconds for your dad to type in the code."

He raised his mug, more to thank her for backing him up than to invite her to join him.

"I'd love some," she said. And while he went and poured her a cup, she asked, "So what's up with your website?"

"I'm having trouble accessing the comments page."

"Well, we have to do something about that," she said, heading back to the living room. "Who knows how many potential customers might have asked for your advice!"

Billie sat in his big desk chair, which made her look even smaller than her five-foot-two-inch height. "Pull up a chair," she told him, "and let's see if we can solve this little mystery."

Her fingers flew over the keyboard, and as pages popped up on the screen, she slid the mouse around on its pad. A moment later, his website's comments page appeared.

"I don't get it. I goofed around with it for half an hour last night, and it wouldn't open for me."

"Maybe that's the problem. Computers resent being goofed around with."

Billie stood and gestured for him to take her place in the chair, then knelt beside the desk.

She was a good teacher, and patiently walked him through the steps, then made him repeat them without her help. "By Jove," he said when the third try produced the right results, "I think I've got it."

Alyssa joined them and put her catalog on his desk. "Since you know how to use the internet now, can we order my costume?"

His satisfaction disappeared, and in its place, doubt. But Billie wasn't having it. With that same patient, gentle voice, she taught him how to find the company's website, fill in the form and place the order. Within seconds, his email alert pinged, confirming that it had gone through.

"Well, cupcake, looks like your costume will arrive..." he read the message aloud "'...in five working days.'"

"Yay! Thanks, Billie!"

"Don't thank me," she said. "Your dad is the one paying for the costume!"

"Thanks, Dad."

He didn't know which hurt more, her lack of enthusiasm or the fact that she'd called him Dad instead of Daddy.

"I wish I could go from house to house," Alyssa said, "like all the other kids. So everybody could see my pretty costume."

"They'll see it," he told her, "when they trick-or-treat here at the shop."

Billie's eyebrows disappeared under her bangs and her eyes widened. For a moment he wished he could read minds, because he'd love to know what was going on in that quick-witted head of hers.

"How about you go put your new scrunchies where they belong?" she said to Alyssa.

Instantly, his daughter agreed.

When she was out of earshot, Billie said, "I'm guessing she stays here, handing out candy, because you can't be in two places at one time."

She hadn't phrased it as a question, and yet Noah felt obliged to explain. "Yeah. That pretty much covers it."

"That's a shame. Some of my best child-hood memories center around trick-or-treating with my brothers and a big pack of neighbor-hood kids."

"Yeah," he said again, "same here. Maybe you could take her."

He couldn't believe he'd said the words out loud. Evidently, the suggestion surprised Bil-lie, too.

"Me?"

"You're going to think I'm a greedy, ungrateful pig," he said, "asking another favor of you."

"Another favor?"

"You took her to rehearsal, remember? And again, thanks for the chicken soup, by the way. It really hit the spot. Might even have been what helped me turn the corner."

"Oh. That. No big deal. I was happy to do it."

He didn't need mind-reading talents to know she meant every word, and her sincerity stirred something in his heart. Something he hadn't experienced in a long, long time.

"She's only gone door-to-door once," he said, mostly to distract himself from the feeling, "but she was just two at the time and doesn't remember it. Jillian dressed her up like a little lamb."

"Aw, I'll bet she looked adorable."

She had. Not long ago, the image would have really hurt. Circumstance had put him in the peculiar position of giving Alyssa a great memory…and he wouldn't be there to share it if Billie took her trick-or-treating. Noah honestly didn't know which hurt more.

Alyssa joined them as Billie said, "What if I mind the shop while you take her?"

"Take me where?"

Billie understood, really understood. Did

she realize that with her thoughtful offer, she'd made it tougher to stay away from her?

"Take you trick-or-treating," Billie said.

"But...but who will give the children their candy?"

"I will," she answered.

Alyssa looked at Noah. "Really?"

"Really."

He'd seen that look before. Any second now, she'd launch herself into Billie's arms to demonstrate her gratitude. Having been on the receiving end of an exuberant Alyssa hug, he knew it could knock a woman Billie's size on her keester. Bending at the waist, he whispered, "Easy does it, kiddo. She's not a whole lot bigger than you are."

Alyssa ratcheted back her excitement a notch and wrapped Billie in a gentle hug. "This will be my very very first ever going trick-or-treating." She squeezed Billie a little tighter. "Thank you," she said. "I love you!"

Billie looked over Alyssa's head and straight into Noah's eyes. If he didn't know better, he'd think she might burst into tears—happy tears, as Alyssa liked to say. Billie's eyes glittered, reminding him of those sweet, warm moments beside the campfire. Alyssa wanted a mom, and he wanted that for her, too. If things were different, if *he* was different—

Billie's cell phone rang, shattering the moment. Giving Alyssa's hair an affectionate tousle, she read the number in the caller ID window.

"Uh-oh," she said. "It's my mom." She pointed at the deck door. "Be right back."

Alyssa helped herself to a handful of popcorn as Billie stepped outside.

"Where did that come from?" he asked, popping a kernel into his mouth.

"I wanted a snack after Billie brought me home last night. She didn't think you'd like me eating sweets so close to bedtime, so she made popcorn."

"Good woman," he said, watching as she leaned against the railing. As she nodded. Shook her head. Shrugged. And tipped her head back to laugh. Did she throw herself wholly into *everything* this way? Yeah, something told him she did. Which made it harder still to accept that she could never be more than a friendly acquaintance.

She did a little jig. Marched in place. What in the world had her mother said to inspire that!

Noah didn't need to hear the discussion to know that Billie and her mom shared a warm, loving relationship. He'd always gotten along well with his parents, too. Oh, what he'd give to have an ordinary conversation with his mom, his dad, his sister Grace, like Billie was enjoying now! If it had been any other woman out there, enjoying an animated exchange with a family member, he'd wonder if she appreciated just how lucky she was. But it wasn't any other woman out there. It was Billie Landon, who didn't know how to do anything halfway. Exactly the type of woman who could make him break his Stay Single rule. If he had a mind to break it. Which he couldn't.

*Liar,* he told himself as she reentered the kitchen.

"For the first time in my life," she said, "I believe those doomsday people might be on to something."

Noah chuckled. "What?"

"I invited my folks here for Thanksgiving, and I knew it was going to be crowded and maybe a little crazy, but she just canceled the holiday, and that has *never* happened before."

"Nobody's sick, I hope."

"No, no, nothing like that. My brother Todd—Troy's twin—and his wife are going on a cruise, and they invited Mom and Dad to go with them." Billie grabbed a small handful of popcorn. "And they're going. More proof that the end of the world must be near, because my mother hates boats!" Laughing, Billie added,

"I can hardly wait to see Troy's face when I tell him!" She popped a few kernels into her mouth, chewed and swallowed. "Guess it'll just be the five of us, then."

"Five...?"

She tapped the kitchen table with every name she mentioned: "Troy, Bud, Alyssa, you and me."

Meaning this year they'd have a full-fledged, eat-till-you-drop meal? Sure would beat the turkey TV dinners they'd eaten the past three years. "That's three more than we're used to, isn't it, cupcake?"

"Yes. It is." Alyssa turned toward Billie. "Have you made Thanksgiving dinner before?"

Billie already looked pretty angelic, in his opinion. The woman must be easy to please, because it took only his daughter's voice to sweeten the look.

"Are you kidding?" she countered. "Why, I can whip up a turkey-day meal that will make you swoon."

Alyssa's brow furrowed. "What does *swoon* mean?"

"Faint."

"Have you ever fainted, Daddy?"

"Not that I recall. But if people are gonna be dropping like flies, I can't think of a better reason."

"Dropping like flies," Alyssa echoed, rolling her eyes. "He says old-fashioned things like that *all* the time."

When Billie aimed a sideways glance at Noah, his pulse quickened.

"I can believe that," she said.

Alyssa picked two unpopped kernels from the bottom of the bowl and showed them to Noah. "What do you call these again?"

"Flopcorn," he said.

Alyssa looked at Billie. "See? What did I tell you?"

She was gazing at him, not his little girl, when she said, "Then I guess it's a good thing I like old-fashioned things."

## CHAPTER NINETEEN

"Whoa. Uncle Hank. You look like something the cat dragged in."

O'Malley glared at his nephew. "You try spending three years in a place like this, see how *you* look." He slapped his hand on the stainless tabletop. "Park it. I won't be talked down to."

Nigel sat and folded big hands on the table. Did he realize how ridiculous he looked, O'Malley wondered, with his hair plugs, fake tan and too-white teeth? It galled him that this sycophant shopped at Chicago's exclusive George Greene, while *he* was forced to endure stiff, scratchy prison garb. He blamed his sister for a lot of what was wrong with Nigel. O'Malley sniggered. She'd named him *Nigel*....

"Do you have news for me, or did you just come here to show off your Zanone sweater?"

Nigel sniffed. "This is last year's—"

"News, Nigel. Plain and simple. What is your father doing these days?"

"*Dad* hasn't been doing anything," his nephew began, "but my *brother* has been going through my drawers again."

Thankfully, he'd remembered the plan, and picked up on the cues. "Hoping to find some Henri Lloyd socks, no doubt."

Nigel flinched as if hit. Blanched. Poor dumb fool had no idea how to proceed. Hopefully, he wouldn't look at the camera hanging from the ceiling, because if he did, the game was over.

"Nigel. You know me. Always kidding." O'Malley laughed, too long and too hard, but it bought him some time to think of a way to reassure his nephew. Time to send the coded message that he got it: "dad" meant the FBI, and "brother" the Marshals Service.

"I know perfectly well how much it upsets you when your brother pokes through your things. It upsets me, too. But don't you worry about it. Your brother will find something else to focus on soon, and when he does, he'll stop going through your stuff."

Nigel exhaled the breath he'd been holding and removed his pricy leather jacket. He'd probably paid more for it than O'Malley had paid for his first car.

"Would you believe that wacky brother of mine has a girlfriend?"

Nigel laughed, a harsh nasal sound that reminded O'Malley of the Wicked Witch.

"Can you believe it?" he continued. "A tall redhead. Nice looking. Smart. And sneaky."

Maybe his stupid nephew wasn't so stupid, after all. "How do you know she's smart and sneaky?"

"Because she loves keeping my brother on his toes. Never calls him at the same time twice, shows up when he least expects it." He leaned forward to add, "And I caught her going through his things."

"A little 'what goes around, comes around,' eh?"

Nigel's smile was proof that he got the joke, told for the benefit of the goon monitoring the camera feed.

O'Malley pretended that he'd paused to work the kinks out of his neck, while he rapidly thought this through. There was only one reason for the Marshals Service to check up on him: Nate Judson. The rat was out there somewhere, living the good life, while O'Malley slept with one eye open every night. If Nigel could get hold of Judson's whereabouts...

Hank smirked. Clenched his hands. Oh, it would feel good, balancing *that* account.

"I know your brother annoys you," he began, "but you have to do the right thing."

Nigel frowned. "Which is…?"

"Follow his big redheaded girlfriend. Find out as much about her as you can. Because if she's sneaking around in your brother's things, who knows what other secrets she's hiding?" O'Malley signaled the guard. "It won't be easy, but it's best for everyone."

Nigel nodded and looked directly into his eyes.

"You're a smart young man," O'Malley said, "and I'm proud to be related to you."

An hour later, he was seated in the library, doing his best to concentrate while the inmates around him cursed and scratched and blew smoke in each other's faces. He missed his private cell. What he needed to do next would be far easier with his personal laptop and cell phone.

The guy sitting at the next computer was taking a lot of razzing for the internet site he'd pulled up. Curious, O'Malley leaned slightly left to see what had prompted the coarse barbs aimed at Williamson—the least offensive of which was "sissy"—and the girl in the photo.

"Shut up, fools," Williamson roared. "Show a little respect. That's my sister's kid."

The men at Stateville were as different as the crimes that had put them here. It didn't surprise O'Malley to see that the pierced and tattooed giant had a soft spot for musicals. Had a soft spot for his niece, too, as evidenced by his outburst.

O'Malley recognized the old broad in the photo as the costar of a Broadway play he'd taken his wife to see, decades ago. But Williamson's niece? She reminded him of every brat he'd ever seen, smiling and posing as if she actually believed the lies her mama told about her looks and talent. He'd seen enough, and started leaning toward his own computer again. No sense calling attention to himself. A man like him had to keep a low profile.

But something stopped him. A caption under the photo that said Bonnie, with her Little Friend Alyssa. The child looked vaguely familiar. Something about the eyes, and the dainty lips. Wait…wasn't Judson's kid's name something like Alyssa?

He stood, bent close to Williamson's screen for a better look.

"Back off, pervert," the big man snarled.

"What's the matter, Will? Is the senator sweet on your little niece?"

A chorus of obscenities shot back and forth as O'Malley held up his hands. "I was looking at the woman. That's Deidre O'Toole. She was a famous Broadway star, once upon a time. Took my wife to see one of her plays when—"

"What play?"

*"Chicago." Irony,* he thought. *Y'gotta love it.*

Williamson exposed a gleaming row of gold teeth, with a diamond front and center. "Saw the movie," he said, nodding approvingly. "My favorite part was when—"

The chaos behind them escalated, making conversation impossible. Williamson got to his feet and faced the crowd, hands balled into fists as he glared at each man in turn.

"Oh, now see there?" said one. "We done woke the monster." But despite his bravado, the man looked a little like O'Malley felt: intimidated, and determined to hide it.

The tension was as thick as the gray-blue cloud of smoke above them. "You ain't s'pposed to be smokin' in here," Williamson told them. "Go ahead. Make a fuss and give them monkeys an excuse to come in here and confiscate your cigarettes." It was quieter when he sat back down.

Quieter, but certainly not peaceful. O'Malley had unintentionally become a pawn in the never-ending game of survival, for Williamson's intervention had put Hank in his debt. Having a friend who was willing to go to bat for you was a good thing—on the outside. Not so in Stateville. The inmates lived by the "choose your battles well" code, and taking this skirmish to the next level wasn't worth the price.

Yet.

O'Malley had dodged *this* bullet, but the war was far from over. Just last week, he'd seen a man killed for standing too close to another in the chow line. Anger, resentment, fear…mix them with a desire to appear invincible, and the will to survive, and the result was a dangerous recipe. A recipe that, consumed daily by the entire prison population, produced the expected outcome: volatility. A situation that, if not vented regularly, could produce a brutal explosion.

If he kept his head down and his back to the wall for the next day or two, some poor fool would do or say something that would put himself in the line of fire. And when that happened, O'Malley could get a message to Nigel, instructing him to contact his friends… the ones who'd hacked some of the world's most elaborate computer systems. The big redhead might have nothing to do with the little girl in Williamson's picture, but if her connections led him to Judson and his daughter, O'Malley could kill two birds with one shot.

## CHAPTER TWENTY

"Somebody needs to tell Mother Nature that it's only November 3," Max said, shaking snow from her hair. "It's way too early for this Chicago-like weather!"

"Better not let Alyssa hear you. She's lovin' the stuff."

Max hung her jacket on the hall tree, withdrew a fat legal envelope from an inner pocket. "Where is she?"

"Out back, trying to make a snowman." Noah laughed. "A good lesson in coping with frustration. It's melting as it hits the ground."

"She's outside? Alone?" Max felt his forehead. "Well, you don't *look* delirious from fever...."

"That's a twelve-foot fence out there—one of a hundred reasons I'm glad you didn't stick us in a subdivision ruled by a homeowners' association—and the gate squeals louder than a horror movie heroine." He patted the baby monitor's receiver clipped to his belt. "If an acorn falls, I'll hear it."

Max tilted her head and tucked clasped hands under her chin. "Aw, my little boy is growing up."

"You're a riot," he said, and using his chin as a pointer, added, "What's in the envelope?"

"Letters." She handed it to him. "Thought I'd save time and deliver them myself."

This wasn't the first time Max had chosen to become a link in the chain of events that brought mail from his family to his door. Much as he appreciated the good intentions, Noah wasn't comfortable with her decision. If the wrong person noticed the pattern, it could raise suspicion.

"There's coffee in the kitchen. Care for a cup?"

"Love some," she said, hugging herself. "It's freezing out there."

"Might be time to trade your cool 'I'm a tough cop' jacket for something more practical."

Laughing, Max shook her head. "I'd rather suffer than look like a geeky civilian."

They sat facing each other at the table, Max munching store-bought chocolate-chip cookies, Noah reading letters from his family. As he finished each, she picked them up and read them, too.

"I know I've said it before, but they seem like really great people."

"They are. This," he said, tapping the stack of mail, "would be a whole lot easier if they weren't."

He hadn't seen any of them since that last day of the trial, when O'Malley's deadly threat had echoed through the courtroom. Were they being honest, writing that all was well on the home front, or putting on a good show to keep him from worrying?

"What would happen if one of them got sick—or worse?"

"If you're asking whether or not you could go back for a visit…" Max sipped her coffee, looking grim and gloomy. "Let's just say I'd put my full powers of persuasion into talking you out of doing anything that dangerous." She set the mug down with a clunk. "And dumb."

He nodded. "I figured that's what you'd say." If he got word that something had happened to his folks, to his sister, would he stick to the WITSEC guidelines? Noah honestly didn't know.

"If something happens to O'Malley, now that he's in the general population, what then?"

"They bury him." She gave an indifferent shrug. "One less convict being fed and housed by my tax dollars."

"Yeah, yeah…but *then* what? Do I get to go back to Chicago? Pick up where Alyssa and I left off?"

Groaning, Max slapped a hand over her eyes. When she came out of hiding, she leaned forward, flattened both hands on the table. "Help me understand why all of you guys *say* that! I mean, why would you *want* to go back? You think people will welcome you with open arms? Put their hair up in Pollyanna pigtails and adopt a sunny forgive-and-forget outlook?" She aimed her trigger finger at him. "Trust me, there's no forgiveness out there. None. And if you go looking for it, well, let's just say if you think life stinks now…"

He thought she'd decided to let him finish the sentence in the privacy of his mind. He'd been wrong.

"I know what you're thinking. You're thinking your story will have a different ending, that the love and acceptance of your family and friends is all you need."

Noah nodded, amazed yet again that Max had gotten into his head and pretty much put his thoughts into words.

"Well, think about *this,* smart guy: if you go back, Alyssa is going to find out the truth about you. Everything. Up to and including the fact that if you hadn't made a deal with that devil O'Malley, her mom wouldn't be dead. You think she'll be okay with *that?*"

Heart hammering, Noah frowned. "Man. You don't believe in beating around the bush, do you?"

The agent sat back, crossed her arms and drilled him with a long, hard stare.

"Look. I like you—and you should know that I don't say that to everyone in my care. Most of the guys in your shoes are as sleazy as the people who want them dead. You're a good guy. And a great dad. I respect that. Which is exactly why you have to understand…."

She leaned forward again, and this time gripped his wrists, hard.

"It's like we're a weird family. I'm the mom, you and Alyssa are my kids. Sometimes I have to say things you don't want to hear. Make you do things—or *keep* you from doing things—that you don't agree with. Because I care about what happens to you guys."

Max let go and slumped in her chair, watching him, waiting for him to show her some sign that he got it.

"I don't mean to sound ungrateful," Noah began. "You've been good to Alyssa and me, real good. Gone way above and beyond the call of duty, all the time. No way I can repay you for all you've done for us. So thanks, Mom."

Laughing, Max said, "You have no idea how ironic that is!"

He failed to see any irony in what he'd said, but Noah knew if he gave her a moment, she would explain.

"The guys at the office think I'm sweet on you. They say I treat you like a beau, treat Alyssa like she's mine. It's one of those damned if you do, damned if you don't situations. If I deny it, they'll think they're right. If I don't deny it, they'll think they're right." She threw her hands into the air and laughed. "So thanks, *son*. Thanks a *lot!*"

They shared a moment of laughter, but Noah's heart wasn't in it. He saw her dilemma, and felt helpless to correct it. Yeah, this was her job, and she was professional enough to take the good with the bad. He felt guilty for adding to the latter.

"Sorry," he said, meaning it.

But it didn't stop him from thinking that with some serious effort and patience, he *could* make a go of it in Chicago…provided O'Malley was out of the picture.

"Don't fool yourself, Preston. There's no forgiveness and there are no guarantees, either. Even if that miserable thug is shanked by one of his own kind, you can't be sure he hasn't given one of his flunkies orders to find you, *end* you, to avenge his death."

Yet again, she'd read his mind. He would never admit it to her, but Noah was relieved that she could.

He tried not to dwell on the sad, depressing elements of life in WITSEC. Far healthier, he thought, to focus on things he could be thankful for. Like the bike shop, which kept a roof over their heads and provided enough money to meet every physical need. They had a true friend in Max, and thanks to her diligence, they'd remained safe. If the price to pay for that was never again seeing Chicago, or those near and dear who called it home...

He'd learned to live without the accolades that were a result of his former profession. The big house. The status car. But if he hadn't learned to live with the restrictive nature of the program by now, would he *ever*?

"Sometimes," Max said, "it is what it is."

"Now there's an original line. Maybe I'll have it printed on a T-shirt."

"Sorry, somebody beat you to it." She dunked a cookie in her coffee. "Bumper stickers, too. And if I'm not mistaken, wall posters, magnets, pencils—"

"Uncle," he said, waving a paper napkin. "I get it."

She wasn't smiling when she said, "I sure hope so." She slid a second, smaller envelope from her jacket pocket. "Because if you don't, you *will* get it. Literally."

## CHAPTER TWENTY-ONE

"Look, I wouldn't ask if I wasn't desperate. Be a pal and help me out here."

Noah couldn't decide if Troy was serious or joking. "She's your *mom,* not Godzilla. Besides, I thought your parents canceled Thanksgiving."

"They did, but they wanted to spend a few days with us before their cruise."

Troy looked at Billie, his hands extended. "Tell him, kid. Tell him what will happen if Mom gets here and my house still looks..." a sweep of his arm indicated the empty rooms "...like this."

Noah glanced at her, standing in the doorway between her brother's foyer and living room. Did she seem small and delicate because the arch was so large? Or because of the sympathetic look on her expressive face?

"He's right," she said. "Mom will start a one-woman campaign to fill every space with furniture."

"And doilies and knickknacks and embroidered throw pillows. See?" Troy's voice cracked slightly. "I really need your help, man!"

Noah had already agreed to loan him his truck. Alyssa might get a kick out of traipsing through a department store in search of bath towels, pots and pans, window coverings and bed linens, but it would bore Noah to tears.

"Alyssa can stay with me," Billie offered, "if that's why you're hesitating. She can go grocery shopping with me to fill Mr. Hubbard's cupboards."

Troy stepped up and opened his wallet. "Here," he said, handing her a credit card, "use that. And remember, I hate lima beans."

Was Noah thinking about saying yes because helping a pal made his life seem more normal, or because saying no would disappoint Billie?

"You'll watch her like a hawk, right?" He knew she would, so why had he said it?

"I'll pretend she's mine."

He'd seen how she tended Bud after the operation. There wasn't a nurse anywhere who would have doted on the man that way, and she'd done it gladly. Bud's cat got the royal treatment, too. If Billie could treat a snaggle-toothed black cat with that much TLC... But this wasn't an elderly neighbor or a scraggly pet they were talking about. It was *Alyssa*.

"Promise you won't let her out of your sight, even for an instant."

"I promise." On anyone else's face, he might have called that smile patronizing. But this was Billie, who didn't seem to have a condescending bone in her body.

"All right. Count me in. I'll go shopping with you." Troy clapped him on the shoulder. "Thanks, man!"

Billie reached into her pocket and pulled out two pieces of paper. She handed one to Noah, then gave the other to Troy.

Troy started reading his aloud. "'TV, computer, printer, microwave, washing machine, dryer...'" He tucked it into his shirt pocket. "When did you have time to make us lists?"

"Doesn't matter. Just follow them."

While Troy groaned, Billie pressed his credit card into Noah's palm. "It'll save time if you split up." She pointed at his list. "If you get the little stuff while he's choosing appliances and arranging deliveries, all the major stuff will be in place when our folks get here...the day after tomorrow."

Noah glanced at his paper, then looked at Troy. "Persuasive for a little thing, isn't she," he said, pocketing it.

"You think she's bad, just wait until you meet her mother."

Billie waved his joke aside. "If you call the school," she said to Noah, "I'll pick Alyssa up and we'll head straight to the grocery store. We'll get things put away, and then I'll take her to my house so she can get started on her homework."

"So much for waiting till the weekend," Troy muttered.

That's pretty much what Noah had been thinking. But it wouldn't break the bank if he closed the bike shop early. He had to hand it to Billie, though, because in a matter of minutes, she'd organized the shopping trip that would turn her brother's empty house into a home. And if he knew her, she'd pitch in and organize everything they bought, too.

After he called the school to arrange Alyssa's pickup, Billie left them to work out the final details. During the drive to the discount store, Noah tried to imagine how his daughter would react when she saw Billie arrive in his place. And how she'd look walking up and down the grocery store aisles beside her new best friend. The idea made him smile, because he could almost see them, discussing every item that ended up in the cart.

Noah and Troy parked side by side and

headed into the store, where Troy veered toward the sheets and comforters section, while Noah grabbed towels, bath mats and a shower curtain. Next, he added cookware, silverware, dishes and glasses to the cart, and Troy sought out the window blinds. They paid for their purchases, carried the merchandise to the parking lot, then went back inside for a mattress and box spring.

"Billie will be disappointed," he said, smirking as the clerk rang up the order. "She thinks our folks are staying at her place, now that I have one of my own."

And once the clerk assured a morning delivery, they went on to the appliance aisle.

Noah focused on price and energy savings, while Troy commented on color and style. A couple shopping nearby scrutinized them and gave them a thumbs-up.

Troy snickered.

"Oh, don't even—"

"Don't worry. I have too many scruples to put the moves on a guy my sister's sweet on."

Noah decided it was quicker and easier to go along with the joke than to press Troy for details. Besides, a salesman was headed their way.

"What can I do for you today?" the man asked.

Troy pointed out the appliances he'd need, and once it was determined they were in stock, the man, whose name was Victor, started the transaction. He explained the warranties and made sure Troy knew about the next day delivery and installation charges.

"Best customer I've had all week," he said while Troy signed the credit card receipt. "Almost makes me wish I wasn't hourly. Six appliances in one sale?" He whistled and tucked the paperwork into a pamphlet-sized pocket folder.

On the way to the parking lot, Troy said, "Well, I just about spent my limit, but we're finished." He checked his watch. "And in record time, too. I challenge any woman to furnish an entire house in less than two hours." Now he patted his stomach. "Who knew going broke could work up such an appetite? I'm starving."

Noah laughed. "Tell you what. I'll call Billie, give her a heads-up that I'm bringing a couple of pizzas home. And since you broke the bank in there, it's my treat. We'll consider it a housewarming gift."

"Make mine pepperoni and mushroom. And take it easy on the drive home, will ya? I'd hate to see you end up on the side of the road…"

Born and bred in Chicago, Noah knew how to drive on snow-covered roads. Maryland's sleet and freezing rain made him glad he lived and worked in the same place.

"...because I'm in no mood to watch you chase frying pan lids and shower curtains down Route 100."

"You're all heart, man. All heart."

Troy grinned. "If Billie's okay staying with Alyssa after we eat, maybe I can talk you into dropping the stuff that's in your truck over to my place."

"Sounds like a plan."

Troy started to get into his car, then said over the roof, "You're a pal, man. Really saved my bacon today."

Guy talk, Noah thought, for "thank you" and "friend."

"No problem," he said, sliding behind the wheel. Like it or not, it seemed he had a pal. How long since that had happened? In college, he'd gone to the usual after-game parties, but stayed on the sidelines. At the office, he'd attended only mandatory social functions. And much to Jillian's dismay, he'd flat-out refused to take part in block parties. Having *friends* had never been important to him. Getting ahead. Making a name for himself. Earning money. That's what mattered.

Money. Did he have enough cash for pizza? If not, he'd pretend he was Troy, and slap down some plastic. In the lot at Domino's, he dialed Billie's cell number, talking as he entered the shop.

"How do you like your pizza?" he asked.

"Anything but anchovies."

"Good. I'm bringing supper, so don't cook." He paused, covered the mouthpiece. "Two large pizzas," he told the kid behind the counter. "One plain cheese. One with half everything, half pepperoni and mushroom."

"Except anchovies," she said into his ear.

"Except anchovies."

The kid wrote it up and stuck the order ticket on the pass-through counter. "Slow tonight," he said. "Ten or fifteen minutes."

Noah handed him his credit card as Billie said, "Funny you had this idea. Alyssa was just saying it's been ages since you guys had pizza. She'll be happy."

"So she's behaving?"

"Like an angel. We had a ball. Shopping, baking, playing old maid…"

She laughed, and so did he.

"So what did you guys bake?"

"Brownies. And chocolate chip cookies."

"That's my Alyssa. She knows what I like. I'm guessing Troy should be there in five, ten minutes."

"I heard on the news that it's sleeting, so take it easy…"

"I'll find a salt truck and follow it."

"…because we wouldn't want anything to happen to you."

We? He liked the sound of that. It had been a pretty good day so far. In the span of a few hours, he'd made a pal and found out that Billie—

Noah caught a glimpse of himself in the chrome exterior of the cash register. Crooked grin, slouching shoulders, half-closed eyes… The kid stacked two pizza boxes on the counter. "Sir? Is everything all right?"

Embarrassed, and trying his best not to laugh at himself, Noah checked the labels: cheese; the works.

"Yeah." He paid and said thanks, then left the shop without a backward glance. "See you in a few," he said to Billie, and hung up.

Five minutes later, he was still chuckling to himself when traffic came to a halt. He checked his watch. Too early for the usual rush-hour gridlock.

By his calculations, he was four, maybe five cars back from the accident, but because of the curve and slight incline, he couldn't see if it was serious or not. Since they weren't moving anyway, Noah turned off the pickup, grabbed the keys and jogged forward to get a better look. If it seemed as if it might take a while to get tow trucks in place, he'd give Billie a heads-up; those pizzas were getting colder by the minute, and she'd need to rustle up something else for Alyssa and Troy's supper.

As he rounded the corner, Noah realized it wasn't one accident, but several.

An elderly woman, her beaded purse hanging from her wrist, wandered, as if she'd been rudely shaken awake from a dream.

A little girl no older than Alyssa sat on the pavement, wide-eyed and silent, a trickle of blood oozing from her left eyebrow.

No sign of ambulances or police cars, he noticed, so he withdrew his phone and dialed 9-1-1.

Crouching, he placed a hand on the child's shoulder. "Where's your mommy or daddy?" he asked. And she pointed three cars up, at the maroon minivan that lay smoking on its side.

"9-1-1," said a man's deep voice. "What is your emergency?"

"I'm on Route 100," Noah said, tucking the little girl's hair behind her ear. "There's been a multivehicle accident. Four, maybe five of them. People are hurt. I can't tell yet how bad."

"Where on Route 100, sir?"

Cars on the other side of the highway were

slowing, and all he could think was *Knock it off, you idiots, before you end up in the same kind of mess!* Noah tried to remember the last exit sign he'd seen. "Long Gate Parkway, I think. We're on the westbound side."

"Emergency personnel is on the way. Stay on the line with me, sir. Can you tell me what you see?"

"Stay right here," Noah told the little girl, "while I check on your family, okay?"

Lower lip quivering, she nodded as he stood up.

The blacktop was slick, and he took care with every step. As he walked, windshield glass crunched under his boots. "There's smoke coming from this minivan," he told the dispatcher, "and everyone inside seems to be unconscious. Two adults, one child. And there's blood. Lots of blood."

He looked beyond the van, tried to figure out what had caused it to end up on its side. "Two more cars, I think," he said, as the woman in the first one moaned. "Help is on the way," he told her, then described her condition to the operator: older model car; steering column pressed tight against her ribs; front seat shoved into the back. "She's shaking. Guess she's in shock."

"Don't try to move her, sir. Medics are en route."

Yeah, yeah, but how did he help these people in the meantime!

Noah took off his jacket and gently draped it over the woman. His dad had always carried a handkerchief in his right rear pocket, and since leaving Chicago, Noah had, too. He blotted her bloody lip with it, then kept moving.

"People are getting out of their cars. Wandering around. Not the ones involved in this mess. Just other drivers."

"Yes, sir. I can hear them. We're getting other calls about this incident now. You're doing great. What else are you seeing?"

"Two more cars," Noah said. "A pickup truck. And a jackknifed 18-wheeler. Nothing in front of it." He took a deep breath.

"Smoke's coming from the semi, too," he added. "Don't see the driver…he's too high up in the—"

And then he saw Troy's car.

Noah relayed the information to the dispatcher: the car sideways…and upside down in the lane. Dashboard shattered. Driver's door caved in. Troy dangled from the seat belt, like a marionette without a puppeteer. The airbag had deployed—fat lot of good that had done him.

"Can you check for a pulse for me, sir?"

Dark smoke stung Noah's eyes and he squinted, looking for the source of it. He placed two fingers on Troy's throat and held his breath. A faint flutter. "Yeah, he's alive. Thank God. Thank God. Thank God." And then the choking smoke started a coughing jag.

"Sir? Stay with me, sir. Tell me what you see...."

"Smoke. A lot of it." And then Noah saw tiny flickers of yellow and orange leaping up between the gnarled metal of the floorboard.

"I see the fire now. It's rolling under the front seat...down the sides.... If I don't get him out of there—"

"No. Sir. Do *not* touch him, do you understand? Wait for the EMTs. They're in transi—"

"Wait? No way. I know this man!"

The wind kicked up, blowing a blast of hot air that hit him square in the face. Stinging sparks pecked his skin. He'd heard the warnings and understood the dispatcher's no-nonsense order: let the pros handle the rescue; amateurs do more harm than good.

Well, the pros weren't here. *He* was.

Sirens. Finally! But a long way off. By the time the ambulances, cop cars and fire trucks made their way through the snarl of vehicles, Troy could be dead. How would Noah live with himself if he stood here like some simpering idiot and let that happen? He had to get Troy out of there, because every instinct told him the car would explode. Soon.

"I'm going to put my phone into my pocket," he said, "but I'll leave it on."

Ignoring the dispatcher's protests, he grabbed the door handle, drawing his arm back when it burned his palm. He looked for the source of the heat, and seeing none, decided it wasn't as important as getting Billie's brother out of there.

Noah didn't even want to think about how losing Troy would impact Billie, and their mother, who so lovingly fussed over her kids. He thought of his own little girl, who'd already lost her mother. What would become of her if, while helping Troy, something happened to him?

Noah shook off the ugly, terrifying thought and focused instead on what could go wrong if he disobeyed the operator's order. He could unintentionally snap Troy's neck while pulling him free. Dislocate a shoulder. Break an arm or a leg. Windy as it was, the fire might double or triple in intensity, and kill them both.

Then he saw the flames licking at Troy's pant legs. It was now or never.

Noah filled both hands with Troy's shirt and pulled. Pulled with all his might as the image of Alyssa flared in his mind. *She doesn't have a mom,* he reminded himself. *Are you willing to take the chance she'll lose you, too?*

For an instant, he froze. Considered letting go. He'd made a will. Named Max legal guardian if—

Troy uttered a ragged whimper as his head lolled from left to right. Noah had no way of knowing what sort of damage the impact had caused. Broken ribs, sternum, pelvis...*spine*... Based on the condition of Troy's car, from the spiderweb-shattered windshield to the concave dashboard, it was likely his friend had suffered a head injury, too.

In one second, Noah heard the car's metal groaning like a wounded bear. In the next, a deafening explosion blinded him. Threw him backward. The hard landing forced the breath from his lungs. He couldn't see. Couldn't breathe. And the pain...the pain was so extreme that he couldn't think straight.

Noah had never been much of a praying man. But he prayed now...that when Billie came to terms with losing her brother, she'd help Max take care of Alyssa.

*Sorry, cupcake,* he thought as tears stung a cut on his cheek. *I'm so, so sorry....*

## CHAPTER TWENTY-TWO

SOMETHING WAS WRONG. Troy and Noah should have arrived more than an hour ago, and neither had called to explain where they were.

She hadn't told Alyssa her dad was bringing pizza, so she wasn't disappointed when Billie served up the fish sticks and mac and cheese she'd found in Noah's kitchen.

"Aren't you eating, Billie?"

She forced a brightness into her voice that she didn't feel. "I snacked a little, fixing your supper," she fibbed. "Maybe I'll grab something later."

"After Daddy and Troy get back?"

"That's right."

"They must be buying everything in the whole entire store." The little girl dipped a fish stick into the puddle of ketchup on her plate. "Bet he'll be in a bad mood when he gets home. Daddy *hates* shopping."

"I'm not crazy about it, either." Why didn't one of them *call*?

Noah's house phone rang, startling her.

"Billie, this is Max. I'm a, uh, a friend of Noah's."

"Yes. I remember."

"Where's Alyssa?"

"Right here. Eating supper." Billie frowned, wondering what business it was of hers.

"Take the phone into the other room. I don't want her to see your face when I tell you why I called."

The woman's take-charge voice riled Billie and rattled her at the same time. Yet, like an obedient child, she followed instructions.

"There's been an accident," Max said, "and it's bad."

A tremor passed through Billie, from the soles of her feet to her scalp. She sat on the arm of the sofa.

"How bad?"

"Your brother and Noah were medevaced to Cowley."

The R Adams Cowley Shock Trauma Center at the University of Maryland's medical facility?

"But…but they drove separately to the mall…."

"I don't have all the details yet. Multicar pileup on Route 100. Tractor trailer jackknifed and started a chain reaction. No word yet why, but they're blaming the weather. In your shoes, I'd be wondering why they called me."

Maybe later, Billie thought, when the news sank in. At the moment, it was all she could do to accept the facts as she knew them.

"They called me," Max continued, "because I'm the closest thing to family Noah has. He keeps my contact info in his wallet. The cop I talked to said he kept muttering something about Troy, so I put two and two together and came up with *you*."

The phone trembled in Billie's hand. "Will they be okay?"

"I've made a few calls, but it'll be a while before the first responders file reports. Soon as I hear back from my contact at the shock trauma center, you'll be the first person I call."

Max paused, and Billie heard the steady click-click-click of a turn signal.

"You're phoning from the road? Are you on your way down there?"

"No, I'm on my way to you. I'm going to stay with Alyssa while *you* go down there." There was another pause before she said, "Noah keeps instructions in his wallet, so the docs don't need next of kin signatures. But your brother—"

"You mean…you mean they think Troy and

Noah might…" Billie couldn't say it. Wouldn't say it!

"It's too early to know anything yet, except that they're both critical. Now listen, Billie. You need to pull yourself together. You've spent enough time around Alyssa to know she's supersensitive to people's moods. Walk back into that kitchen sounding like you do now, and nothing you say will be a comfort. No point scaring her until we know what's what."

"Good advice. She's already been through so much."

"Exactly. I'm parking out back right now. I know where Noah hides the key, so head straight for the bathroom and splash some cold water on your face."

Max hung up, and Billie's brain went into overdrive. She'd need to find her GPS if she hoped to locate the hospital without getting lost. And break into her emergency stash of cash for the parking garage. Grab a handful of change for the vending machines, because she intended to stay until she had definitive news for her parents. For Alyssa, too.

Billie reentered the kitchen, resolved to behave as if the little girl's world—and her own—wasn't spinning out of control.

"Was that Daddy on the phone?"

"No," she said on her way to the bathroom,

making sure Alyssa couldn't see her face, "it was Max, calling to see if it was okay to stop by."

Billie heard Alyssa's exuberant "Cool!" through the bathroom door.

No need to splash water on her face, because she hadn't cried.

Yet.

But Max was right—she did need to gather her wits, not only for Alyssa, but for Troy and Noah, too. The last thing they needed was to see fear in her eyes. Besides, unless she wanted to end up in there with them, she'd need to focus on maneuvering the icy roads safely.

She sat on the edge of the tub and looked at the pale blue walls, lavender towels, pink contour rug and colorful butterfly-infused shower curtain. The apartment offered all the comforts in a compact nine-hundred-square-foot space. Noah had let Alyssa decorate their only bathroom. He was a good man. A good *dad*. He had to be all right…for Alyssa's sake.

Tears stung Billie's eyes and a sob ached in her throat. He had to be all right for her sake, too. Why had it taken *this* to make her admit how much he meant to her?

On her feet now, she returned to the kitchen to find Max with Alyssa.

"Where are you going?" Alyssa asked when Billie slipped into her coat.

"I…well…a friend of mine is in the hospital, so I'm going to pay him a quick visit."

Max nodded, as if to say, "Good answer."

"I cleared my schedule," she stated calmly, "so I can stay with Alyssa until…"

Billie understood why Max had stopped talking so suddenly. She couldn't very well say "until Noah gets home" because not even the doctors knew when—or if—that might happen. And because Billie didn't trust herself to speak, she grabbed her purse and waved a silent goodbye.

The drive from Ellicott City to the shock trauma center wasn't nearly as treacherous as she'd expected, yet when Billie arrived, her hands were shaking and she had the hiccups. The guard at the E.R. entrance walked her to the information desk, and before he left her there, said, "Nobody comes in here for fun. Just remember that and you'll calm right down."

Not likely, Billie thought, but she thanked him and punched the elevator button.

"If those hiccups don't go away in a few minutes, try my technique. Swallow ten itty-bitty sips of water, one at a time, while holding your breath. Trust me," he added as the doors whooshed shut, "works every time."

When she arrived in the surgical unit, a nurse explained that Troy was in surgery, and that, based on what little she knew so far, the team would perform a craniectomy to relieve pressure on his brain.

"Don't quote me on this, because I'm not supposed to speculate," the woman said, "but I'm guessing they'll do a laparotomy, too, to relieve pressure on his abdomen."

"And what about Mr. Preston. I was told he was brought in with my brother."

"How are you related to Mr. Preston?"

"He's...he's...." Billie's hands trembled as she twisted her wedding band.

Nodding, the nurse picked up the phone, asked a few questions about Noah, and after hanging up, said, "I'm due for a break. I'll walk you down there." At the elevators, she added, "Ever been to Multitrauma before?"

"I've never even heard of it."

"Well, just to warn you...your fiancé might look a little rough, so brace yourself."

Evidently, the woman had assumed that because Billie asked about Noah Preston, instead of her husband, Noah was her fiancé. And because rules were rules, she didn't correct her. For the first time since the divorce, Billie was glad she'd never found the courage to remove her wedding ring. When Troy and Noah were home and on the mend, she intended to throw it into the Patapsco River. The nurse pointed. "He's just around the corner."

Billie held her breath, footsteps slowing as she summoned the strength to deal with whatever came next.

"Want me to stay with you?"

She shook her head. "No, but thanks. Go ahead and finish your break."

The nurse hadn't exaggerated. If not for those perfectly shaped eyebrows and enviable lashes, Billie might not have recognized him.

"I'll just stay long enough to explain what's going on." The nurse grabbed Noah's chart, slid a finger down the first page and shook her head. "Hmm…looks like he was hit by a lot of flying debris when the car exploded."

Exploded! Billie cringed, but did her best not to show fear.

"There was a lot of blood in his abdominal cavity. Lost more than three liters during transport. Lucky for him, he's type O, and it isn't a holiday weekend."

In other words, they'd transfused him.

"He's doing as well as can be expected. If he survives the golden hour, his chances are good. Real good."

"The golden hour?"

"Blocks of time lost at the scene, during transport, in surgery, time in recovery, building up his reserves again, avoiding infection."

How many times had the nurse been pressed to deliver that explanation? Billie wondered. Too many, if her quiet monotone was any indicator.

Billie couldn't take her eyes off Noah. The breathing machine. The heart monitor. The tubes and lines and clear bags hanging from stainless poles. "How did they do all this in the short time between the accident and now?"

"9-1-1 call came in at four. Six hours isn't a short time in a place like this. Besides, like I said…it isn't a holiday weekend. Plenty of staff available." She headed for the door. "A word of advice?"

Billie met her eyes and nodded.

"Think positive thoughts when you're talking to him. I happen to be one of those who believe people in his condition can hear and understand what's going on."

"Is that true for Troy, too?"

"Way too early to tell," she said. "After your brother is out of recovery, we'll know a lot more. Meanwhile, if you believe in prayer, this might be a good time for it."

AS THE DAYS passed, it got harder to sidestep Alyssa's pressing questions about her dad. One night, long after Billie had tucked Alyssa in, she nodded off on the couch. Fractured dreams kept waking her, born, she supposed, of what her imagination made of the information delivered by the first responders. After half an hour of channel surfing, she dozed off again. And again the nightmare images pummeled her brain: an ear-splitting crash. Glass raining onto the pavement like blue diamonds. Fire and black, billowing smoke. And a blast that shook the ground until—

"Billie," Alyssa whispered. "Billie, wake up."

She opened one eye and looked at the wall clock. Two thirty-five. "Hey, sweetie. What are you doing up at this hour?"

"I couldn't sleep."

Billie opened her arms, and Alyssa went willingly into them.

"I want my daddy. When can I go to the hospital and see him?"

*When he doesn't look like a cross between the Mummy and the Incredible Hulk,* she thought. But that kind of sarcasm would offer no comfort to this frightened, lonely little girl. Trouble was, Billie had no idea how to tell her that her daddy was still unconscious, still breathing with the aid of a machine, still being nourished by an IV drip.

But she had to try.

"Remember that movie we watched a little while ago, *While You Were Sleeping?*"

Alyssa nodded.

"And you remember how Peter got hurt, and ended up in a coma in the hospital?"

Alyssa's eyes filled with tears as she nodded again.

"It's okay, sweetie. The coma is helping your daddy rest, so his body can heal from the accident." Billie gave her a sideways hug. "Things turned out pretty well for Lucy and Peter, didn't they?"

Rubbing her eyes, Alyssa nodded yet again. "So Daddy looks like Peter? Like he's sleeping?"

Billie rested her chin amid soft blond curls. The staff did their best, keeping patients clean, preventing bedsores, but, unlike patients in the movies, there wasn't a blessed thing they could do about whiskers and matted hair, or skin so pale it almost blended with the bed linens. If he were clean-shaven, hair combed, it might be safe to let her see him. But those often-open, staring eyes sometimes gave *her* the willies. How much more difficult would it be for his innocent, seven-year-old daughter to see him that way?

"I'm not a baby," she said, brow furrowed. "I know he got in a crash. I heard you and your mom talking…." Alyssa turned, gazed straight into Billie's eyes. "I heard you say you don't know how to prepare me for how he looks. Why don't you just *tell* me?"

Billie didn't know whether to laugh or cry, so she gathered Alyssa close and said, "Are you sure you're only seven years old? Because you sure don't sound seven, and you *absolutely* don't act it!"

She felt the child inhale a shaky breath and release it.

"Does that mean you'll take me to see him?"

"How about this. I'll talk to his doctors, and Max, and see what they think."

"And if they say yes?"

"I'll take you to see him."

"Promise?"

Billie's right hand formed the Scout's salute. "Promise."

Another deep sigh…much too deep and sad for one so young.

"I'm hungry," Billie said.

"Me, too."

"Ice cream? Or brownies?"

Alyssa made an attempt at a smile.

"I know," Billie said, "how about ice cream *on* brownies!"

## CHAPTER TWENTY-THREE

"HARDLY SEEMS FAIR, does it?" Troy said.

Billie gripped the wheelchair handles tighter, but said nothing. Noah looked so fragile, lying there. Not at all the strapping, broad-shouldered man who could easily hoist a bike with just one hand, or rearrange a stack of heavy cartons without breaking a sweat.

"He saved my life. I was in and out of it," her brother said, "but I sorta knew what was going on. I wanted to tell him to get away from me, but I couldn't get the words out."

She squeezed his shoulders. "It wasn't your fault."

"I'm not a moron, Billie. I understand the whole 'accidents happen' thing. That doesn't make it easier, knowing Alyssa might become an orphan. And for what? To save my sorry—"

She walked around to the front of the chair and knelt beside him. "Troy. Please don't talk that way. Especially when Mom is around."

Their parents had canceled their cruise to

make sure their son was okay, and Billie was glad for their company.

"Can't you look on the bright side? You have a new home, beautifully decorated, thanks to me. No charge for running up and down the highway, picking up all the stuff that blew out of your car, by the way."

"Weird. I said something like that to Noah, right before we hit the road that day. And you're all heart, *by the way*."

"Oh, don't be such an old sourpuss," she said, mussing his hair.

He swatted her hand away. "Where are Todd and Dani? I thought they were coming into town today."

"Tomorrow." She'd told him that, half a dozen times. But the doctors said that repeating himself, problems with short-term memory, even his surly attitude was normal after a head injury like his.

"Well, tell them to turn the lights off when they leave a room. I'm broke." He grunted. "*And* broken."

She'd told him that Jeff had agreed to pay his salary until he was well enough to go back to work, but Billie told him again.

"Work? What a joke. I put in six lousy days before…"

Troy's gaze focused on Noah, and he took

a deep breath, wincing when the chest brace put pressure on his broken ribs. "Get me out of here."

Rising slowly, she just looked at him for a long, silent moment.

"Is everything all right?" their mom asked as she entered Noah's room.

"Troy is tired," Billie said, wheeling the chair into the hall. "He wants to go back to his room."

"Let me take him. Your father went to the Courtyard Cafeteria. He's supposed to call my cell phone once he sees what's on the menu today." She leaned forward and kissed Troy's cheek. "Maybe Dad can bring you something, so you won't have to eat that awful hospital food."

"Not hungry," he said. "Can we go to my room now?"

Billie and her mother exchanged a worried glance.

"Sounds like my boy needs a nap."

Troy shook his head, and their mom shrugged helplessly.

"Are you coming, honey?"

"No, I think I'll sit with Noah for a while."

When they were gone, Billie slid the bedside chair closer. "You'd better get well, and do it fast," she said, patting his bandaged forearm, "because you need to talk some sense into that fool brother of mine."

It was disconcerting, watching Noah. If she positioned herself just right, it seemed as if he was looking at her. But the blank, lifeless stare told her that, although his eyes were open, Noah wasn't seeing anything. She was beginning to doubt the theory that comatose patients could hear and understand what was going on around them.

"So I'm thinking it's time to bring Alyssa here, so she can see for herself that you're alive and breathing." Not much else, she thought, but it was something to be thankful for, at least.

She walked to the window and, cupping her elbows, described the scene outside. "You should see the traffic. Where *are* all those people going? Not here, I hope."

Billie leaned on the sill. "I wonder what it cost the developer to plant all those trees and shrubs," she said, tapping the glass. "And there must be a thousand mum plants out there." Laughing, she said, "But you're a man. You probably wouldn't know a chrysanthemum from a dandelion, would you?"

She told him about the park benches and water fountains, and the decorative trash barrels positioned here and there. "You know what's missing? One of those glider swings.

Not the wood-slat kind…a green metal one, like my grandmother used to have on her back porch. Can you hear it now? *Squeak-squeak, squeak-squeak…*"

Billie sighed and watched the people down on the ground level. From five floors up, it was hard to tell if they were students of the university, professors or visitors headed for the trauma center.

"Sor-r-ry."

She whirled around. Surely she'd been hearing things. Because how could he say "Sorry," or anything else for that matter, with a breathing tube down his throat?

Billie stepped up to his bed, rested both palms on his bandaged arm. "Between you and Troy nearly dying, I swear, you're driving me nuts."

For the first time since the trauma team had put him in this room, his eyes moved. Blinked. And locked on hers.

Billie would have raced into the hall to find his nurse, but he slowly shook his head, once. At least, she thought he had.

"Well, I hope you're happy," she said. "You've succeeded at driving me nuts. I would have bet my next design contract that you said sorry, *and* you moved your head just now." A nervous laugh escaped her lips. "And you're going to know it for sure when you hear that I almost prefer that vacant stare of yours to this. Almost…" Billie wasn't smiling when she whispered, "…because it feels like you're reading my heart and my mind at the same time."

His eyelids drooped, then slowly closed, and a tiny tear tracked down his cheek.

Billie plucked a tissue from the dispenser on his tray table. His eyes had watered a lot that first day, and the nurse explained that happened occasionally to patients with a sensitivity to the tape that held their eyes closed during surgery.

Gently, Billie blotted the tear. "I shouldn't be surprised. A guy who risks his life to save someone else has to be pretty darned sensitive." She held her hand against his cheek a little longer than necessary. "On the way here tomorrow, I'm going to buy one of those electric razors and clean you up." Leaning close to his ear, she added, "Although I kinda like the rugged, unshaven movie-star look. And if you tell anyone I said that, you'll be sorry."

Noah's eyelids fluttered slightly, and she couldn't be sure if it was because he wanted to open them—and couldn't—or a dream had begun forming in his poor, bruised head.

"I better go. I promised Alyssa I'd teach her how to make tuna salad, Billie style."

On her way to Troy's room, she ran into her dad, who was carrying a cardboard drink tray and a white paper bag.

He handed her the bag, and as they walked down the hall, he threw an arm over her shoulders. "You're lookin' a little weary and worn, kitten. You doin' okay?"

"Yeah, I'm good." She looked up into his mustachioed face. "You and Mom sleeping okay over at Troy's?"

"You know me," he said as they entered Troy's room. "I can sleep standing up, like a horse."

"Eats like a horse, too," his wife teased, relieving him of the drinks tray. "Ate every morsel of food in Troy's kitchen."

Billie looked at her brother, who was staring out the window, not paying attention to his family.

She helped herself to a soda. "That's what it's there for, but restocking is a good idea. Todd and Dani will be here tomorrow morning, right?"

"Around noon," her dad said, "unless they hit traffic."

"And then you'll move over to my place?"

"That's the plan, if it's still all right with you."

"Of course. There's a key under my mat."

She heard Troy shifting and sighing in his chair, and she knew that meant he was itching to get rid of their parents. Poor guy wasn't accustomed to so much parental interaction.

Their mom walked over to kiss his cheek. "Well, we'll get out of your hair. Try and take a nap, will you? You look horrible."

"I just had major surgery—two of 'em," Troy said, "four days ago. Of course I look horrible."

"Oh, now, you know I didn't mean anything." She kissed him again. "We're leaving. Take a nap, all right?"

"Have fun," Billie teased. "Take lots of pictures of Troy's new house."

When they were gone, she looked at her brother, who was slouching, battered and bruised. He seemed beyond sad, and her heart ached for him. There were so many reasons Noah just had to get better, and one of them was sitting in a wheelchair near the window.

She opened the paper bag, withdrew a wrapped sandwich. "Bacon, lettuce and tomato on toast. Triple decker, sliced in triangles, secured with blue-and-red-fringed toothpicks!"

"Looks good," he said. "Thanks, but I'm not hungry."

"If you don't eat, how do you expect to get your strength back?"

"Yeah. Right. Like BLTs are health food."

Well, at least he was smiling. Sort of. She sat beside him and helped herself to a sandwich wedge. She'd almost finished it when he said, "All right. I give up." He held out one hand, and Billie unceremoniously plopped a quarter into it.

"Noah looked at me today," she said.

"He never stops looking. Poor guy's eyes are—"

"Troy, I'm serious." Billie leaned forward. "He turned his head—not much, but he turned it and *looked* at me. And after a minute or so, he closed his eyes." She fidgeted with the cellophane decoration on a toothpick. "I was talking about how, between the two of you nearly dying… Anyway, a tear escaped his eye."

Her brother stopped chewing. "A…a what?"

"A tear."

"It's probably because he hardly ever blinks. Or maybe it's clogged tear ducts or something."

"It could just as easily be a sign that he's coming out of the coma." In her excitement at the possibility, she grabbed his arm, gave it a little shake.

"Ow! Yeesh," he said, wincing.

"Oh. Sorry." She patted his arm, gently this time. "But…that's great news, isn't it?"

"Yeah. Yeah, it would be great."

A nurse stepped into the room. "BLTs," she said, one hand on her hip. "Really?"

Billie stood behind Troy's wheelchair as the nurse waved an orderly into the room. "Jerry here is going to help you onto the gurney, and then he'll take you down to X-ray."

She looked at Billie. "By the way, there's a tall redheaded woman in your fiancé's room, and she's asking for you."

## CHAPTER TWENTY-FOUR

"You're looking a little peaked," Max said. "Did you overdo it in physical therapy today or something?"

"Nah. I've had this low-grade fever, almost from the start."

"But they just changed your meds again. Yesterday, right?"

"Yeah. And if this doesn't work, it means more exploratory surgery to look for the source of the infection."

"Listen to you...you're starting to sound like one of them."

Noah cringed. "Oh. Man. See there? I have *got* to get out of this place!"

They enjoyed a moment of easy laughter, and then he said, "Worst part about it is it means more time with *them*. Which means more time away from Alyssa."

"I know." Max nodded slowly. "But she's handling it like a trouper."

"Yeah, but I know my girl. She's trying hard to hide it for my sake, but she's scared." And he could hardly blame her, because he knew how close he'd come to dying. He still wasn't out of the woods, and that scared him, too.

"She'll be okay. She's a good kid and she has a great dad…."

He knew Max. That tone of voice meant she had more to say. Some might call him crazy for inviting trouble, but he said, "Let me have it."

"When are you going to do something about Billie?"

"Sometimes I wonder if this happened because the powers that be think she'd be better off without me."

"That's insane."

"I know. Most of the time, anyway. But when I think of all the mistakes I made, all the things I did to bring me to this point…"

"You know that old joke—patient says, 'Doc, it hurts when I do this.' And the doctor says, 'Then don't do that.'"

"Who doesn't know that one?"

"Well, there's a lesson in there, genius, if you listen for it. If rehashing the past depresses you, knock it off! It isn't as though you don't have plenty of other things to concentrate on. Good things, like…you're making slow but steady progress. A miracle in itself, all things considered."

He'd heard that half a dozen times since

the accident. Years from now, when all this was a distant memory, he might ask to see the pictures. If he was here years from now. And wouldn't that be the ultimate irony, he thought, to have spent years in hiding from what O'Malley might do to him, to be taken out by a *germ*.

"You have Alyssa, the bike shop, and before you know it, you'll be as hale and hearty as you were before…." Max frowned. "Y'know, in the interest of accuracy, I'm not sure whether to call it an accident or an explosion."

"How about penance?"

She rolled her eyes. "Look. I know you're in pain, and I know you want to get out of this awful place, but self-pitying talk like that isn't helping matters."

Self-pity. He didn't like admitting it, but Max was right. And he told her so. "Maybe what I need to do is get it all out there in one fell swoop. I've never done that before."

"There you go again, waxing all dramatic."

"Huh?"

"You have a law degree and don't know Shakespeare?"

"A law degree, but no license to practice law, ever again, thanks to trying to take the easy way out of bankruptcy and foreclosure by climbing into the sewer with vermin."

It all poured out, fact by ugly fact, starting with the deal his former boss had put on the table after presenting him with the damning telephone recording, where then-Senator O'Malley had soothed his fears of getting caught by detailing the payoffs and "people who mysteriously went missing."

Without Noah's testimony, the prosecutor had explained, O'Malley's team of lawyers would claim it was someone else's voice on the tape. He was their only hope for conviction, and after securing their promise to reduce his sentence to time served, community service and revocation of his law license, Noah had agreed to testify…or serve years in federal prison.

But O'Malley had friends in high places, and heard about the deal. "Keep your mouth shut and do your time," the senator had said, "or bad things could happen to good people." Like an idiot, Noah had reported the visit to his boss, who didn't believe a word of it. A week later, when Jillian died in a car wreck, his self-righteous boss refused to believe the fatal accident—weather-worn brake line on her nearly new, garage-kept vehicle—had been sabotage. It wasn't until an armed thug in a ski mask tried to abduct Alyssa at her preschool that they'd taken Noah seriously.

"Wow. Maybe it's a good thing they don't give us all the gory details when assigning us to people like you," Max exclaimed when he'd finished.

He knew her well enough to hear the smile in her voice, but that didn't make it easier to hear her lump him in with all the other criminals she'd babysat during her career.

"I would have been better off serving time."

"Even in your weakened, fevered state," Max said mockingly, "you don't really believe that. If you *had* survived prison—and what were the chances of that, bearing in mind how many guys were in there because you put them there—you would have been under O'Malley's thumb, doing his dirty work, forever."

When she was right, she was right.

Max got up and threw her jacket over one arm. "Gotta go," she said. "My turn to watch the brat." And winking, she added, "If you're a good boy, I'll let you see the video of her doing her thing onstage last night. I took the disk from my camera to Costco so you could see pictures of her in the play, and I'm picking them up on my way back to your place."

He didn't know how to feel about that. On the one hand, it would be great, seeing the performance he hadn't been able to attend in person. On the other, who knew how many other pictures there were of her, floating around out there, falling into the wrong hands?

"Another instance of my weakness," he grumbled. "I just hope saying yes to that play doesn't come back and bite us in the butt."

Max groaned. "Okay, Mr. Sunshine, I'm outta here." She leaned over and kissed his forehead. "Wow. You *are* warm, aren't you?"

He felt worse now than when he'd first come to, but maybe Max had a point. Positive thinking couldn't kill him. "This too shall pass."

It had better, he thought as she left the room. But just in case, he should probably update his will. A good time to remind himself how this whole downward spiral had begun. He reached into the nightstand and grabbed his wallet. Even that small exertion made him wince, and he flopped back against the pillow until the worst of the pain passed. Then he removed the newspaper clipping he'd been carrying for nearly four years, folded into a two-inch square and tucked into a photo sleeve between a picture of Alyssa and his driver's license. If Max knew he'd been carrying it all this time, he'd never hear the end of it. But even if she knew, he'd insist on keeping it, because it was the bare-facts reminder of what he'd done...and what he'd been before entering the witness protection program. He'd read it so many times that the article felt more like cloth than paper. Taking care not to tear it, he unfolded it and read:

Assistant D.A. Accused of Planting Evidence

By Riley Smith

CHICAGO (APB)—*Judge orders mistrial and sentences Assistant D.A.*

Criminal Court Judge Abe Burns yesterday ordered a mistrial in the case of Bartholomew Miller, alleged serial rapist accused of attacking the 16-year-old daughter of Hon. Sen. Henry (Hank) O'Malley. At the same time, Burns sentenced Asst. D.A. Nate Judson for allegedly tampering with evidence.

"I draw no pleasure in reaching this decision," Burns said, slapping Judson with an 18-month jail sentence—the stiffest allowed under Illinois law. "Officers in the criminal justice system have a duty not only to administer justice, but to follow the letter of the law and demonstrate to society that every defendant will receive a fair trial."

Judson was freed hours later pending an appeal, court officials said.

*Second trial for Miller*

The judge's dramatic move came at the start of the trial of Miller, 30, also charged with drug trafficking and the rape of women employed by his escort service. Burns declared a mistrial in the case after Judson allegedly failed to provide defense attorneys with transcripts of statements by witnesses, all of whom recanted their testimony and stated that sex with Miller was consensual, court records show. A separate trial earlier this year, charging Miller with kidnapping, assault and battery, and rape, ended in a hung jury.

*Questionable evidence*

Miller's second trial had just begun when, according to court documents, Judson produced a hand towel that he claimed Miller used to clean himself after allegedly attacking the senator's daughter. Judson further claimed, court records show, that while preparing for trial, he found the hand towel during a second sweep of Miller's apartment. Consequently, defense attorneys demanded a mistrial, arguing they had been blindsided by the revelation, and accusing Judson of planting the new evidence.

Out of earshot of the jury, the judge agreed with the defense. In a six-page de-

cision, Burns described Judson's claims—
that he had suddenly discovered the hand
towel—as "implausible and improbable."
The judge noted that neither the police
officers who initially searched the apartment, nor the evidence clerk who logged
items from the apartment, made any ref-
erence to the hand towel, which Judson
claimed had been overlooked during the
first search of Miller's apartment. Burns
also noted that two of Judson's fellow
prosecutors, both of whom helped prepare
for the case, were unaware of the hand
towel until it was suddenly produced and
introduced into evidence on the second
day of the trial.

*Constructive contempt*

The judge then ordered a mistrial and
cited Judson for constructive contempt,
described under Illinois law as "an act…
tending to obstruct or interfere with the
orderly administration of justice."

It was not immediately clear whether
prosecutors would have enough cause
to bring Miller to trial a third time. The
judge's order barred prosecutors and defense attorneys from discussing the case
with the media.

Duly humbled, Noah put the article back where it belonged, dropped the wallet into the drawer and slipped into a deep and fitful sleep.

BILLIE HAD GROWN accustomed to watching him sleep, and took comfort from listening to his slow and steady breaths. It felt good, knowing the pain meds were working, providing a few minutes of much-needed, healing rest.

On days like this, when Noah's body writhed in pain, she felt helpless. Maybe music would soothe him....

Billie called up a song on her phone, one by his favorite singer, Bonnie Raitt, and hit Play. Instantly, the room filled with the husky, sultry tones of the blues singer's voice, singing with a depth of emotion that reached out to someone, somewhere who couldn't love her as she loved him. Billie closed her eyes, remembering how that same song had had the power to reduce her to a sniveling mess when she'd thought of how Chuck had given up on her.

The lines were still hauntingly meaningful, but now, thanks to the passage of time, maturity and the quiet affection of the big man beside her, she could simply enjoy the beauty of Bonnie's voice, and the eloquence of the poetic words.

Noah's agitation increased. Should Billie

wake him, put a stop to whatever thoughts were causing his distress? Call for a nurse to administer another dose of painkiller?

"...living a lie," he whispered.

Billie leaned closer. "What's that?"

"...lies, just...lies and more lies..." He levered himself onto one elbow and, facing her, opened his eyes.

But it was immediately apparent that he wasn't seeing her. Had he slipped back into the coma? "Oh God, no," she said, grasping his hand. "Don't leave me again, Noah."

"Love you," he rasped, "so much."

Billie froze. Was he just rambling, the way he had soon after the operation? And was he talking to her...or someone else who'd slipped into his semiconscious, fevered mind?

She'd never been jealous of another woman. Not even the one who'd added the final straw that broke up her marriage. But she envied Jillian, because Noah had loved her, truly loved her, and Billie didn't know if it was possible for him to love anyone that way again. The only certainty: she would settle for whatever sliver of his heart he was willing to give *her*.

Random words spilled from his lips. *O'Malley. Testify. Federal charges. Prison.* He fell back onto his pillows, his breathing ragged.

Then arbitrary phrases, like *not an accident* and *almost kidnapped*. Something that sounded like *lipstick*. And one grammatically correct, perfectly enunciated sentence that made her blood run cold:

"I would have been better off serving time."

# CHAPTER TWENTY-FIVE

NOAH HAD NEVER felt more grateful for an old recliner than right now.

He was finally well enough that Max, Billie and Troy no longer felt the need to hang around, making sure he had everything he needed, right within reach. The doctor hadn't cleared him from climbing stairs more than once a day, but that, too, would come in time.

For two nights in a row, he'd been able to tuck Alyssa in just like he had before the explosion. And now, as she slept contentedly right down the hall, he kicked back in the chair and flipped through the TV channels. Bypassing black-and-white reruns, replays of Ravens games, a Civil War documentary on the History Channel, he stopped in time to catch the awkward Thanksgiving scene in *Scent of a Woman*. It brought back memories of his own Thanksgiving, weeks ago in the hospital, when facing a bland meal served by staff who'd rather be anywhere else. It had seemed it would be grim, indeed.

But thanks to Billie, the day had been anything but grim. He still hadn't figured out how she'd slipped coolers of hot and cold foods, a small folding table and chairs, linens and fancy dinnerware past the guard.

And though Troy had been released weeks before, he'd returned daily to enforce long walks through the maze of hallways, and seemed to feel no guilt, trouncing Noah at chess, checkers and cribbage. That morning, they'd taken advantage of the sunny day to walk outside for a change. He remembered Troy getting a phone call, and his sudden desire to head back to Noah's room.

*Tricky,* Noah thought now, remembering the small crowd that had gathered there to surprise him: Billie, Alyssa, Max, Troy, his twin and sister-in-law, Billie's parents, and even Jason, the once-troubled kid Noah had hired to help run the bike shop.

He had first met Jason when he'd hired Hunter, Deidre's grandson-in-law, to replace the stairway leading from the back alley to the apartment. The kid had seemed surly and rebellious, but by the time Stone Contracting had returned to rebuild the stairs, his attitude had softened considerably. No one would have guessed that Jason had been mere days from juvie when Hunter had taken him under his wing.

A little "good example" went a long way, Noah thought. And no one offered better evidence of that than Noah himself...though in his case, having time to reflect on his past had wrought permanent changes.

It hadn't been all that long ago when Max had told him to quit feeling sorry for himself, to count his blessings. Admittedly, they were many, and he was smiling at the realization when a commercial piqued his interest....

"Up next," the announcer said, "Nobel-winning journalist Clancy Flynn interviews the nation's most notorious inmates."

First up, Charles Manson, whose wild eyes and fearsome mind-set had not been tamed by prison life. Next, Terry Nichols, famous for his role in the Oklahoma City bombing. Then former FBI agent Robert Hanssen, convicted of passing classified information to the Russians. And the once-esteemed Senator Hank O'Malley, former federal judge and one-time contender for president of the United States.

In his late sixties now, O'Malley had not aged well. Gone was the cultured gentleman whose financial prowess had kept his name on the Forbes 500 list right up until his conviction. In place of the distinguished politician who'd been the go-to guy on all the news channel talk shows was a cold-eyed thug who seemed more than comfortable with inmate jargon.

He talked about the trial. How he'd been framed. "If this could happen to me," he snarled, tugging at the stiff orange sleeve of his prison-issue jumpsuit, "it could happen to any of *you*." After detailing the lies told by a crooked D.A. that had put him in his predicament, O'Malley leaned close to the camera and glared into the lens.

"Didn't get away with it, did ya, Judson? You might not be in a penitentiary, but you're in prison, all the same. Witness Protection is a joke. You *know* I have the means and the wherewithal to find you. It's only a matter of—"

The tape stopped and Flynn's face filled the screen. "We apologize, ladies and gentlemen, for that abrupt interruption. Now a word from our sponsors, and when we return, my interview with Matthew Hale, founder of the Neo-Nazi World Church of the Creator."

Noah's pulse thundered in his ears. He'd been giving a lot of thought to telling Billie everything, because he wouldn't feel right about asking her to marry him without coming clean about his past.

*Well, you can't do it now, can you?*

Because as long as O'Malley lived and breathed, he was a threat to anyone close to Noah.

Might be time to move on, he thought. Wouldn't be easy, now that Alyssa was wholly adjusted to her new life. But she was a tough kid. It would require time and patience, but she'd accept and adapt, just as she had following the move from Chicago.

He thought about Billie, and all the ways she'd shown him how she felt. Oh, he'd miss her. Miss her like crazy! But after hearing that interview, he was certain that leaving, starting over, was his only alternative.

If only he could be so sure about his own adjustment to life in the new place, wherever it was…without Billie.

BILLIE HAD SPENT the day sorting through her Christmas decorations. Items in the boxes in the middle of the living room would decorate her home, inside and out. Those stacked near the door were for the bike shop, and the ones beside that, for Noah and Alyssa's apartment. The largest carton contained the seven-foot artificial tree Chuck had bought the year before their split. Billie didn't know why she'd held on to something that served as yet another painful reminder of their failed marriage, but it would be perfect for the father and daughter for whom Santa's deliveries defined the holiday.

Side by side at her computer this afternoon, she and Alyssa had surfed the 'net for cookie recipes, and printed out their favorites. She'd set aside the Saturday before Christmas—just two weeks from now—for baking. This weekend they'd scour the mall for gifts, wrapping paper, ribbon and bows, and then get busy hanging lights and garland, and arranging ceramic snowmen and reindeer on the mantel and tables.

Her favorite news program flickered on the TV as Billie wrote up the grocery list that included cookie-making ingredients. The host was discussing famous criminals, starting with Charles Manson's 1969 killing spree, and switching to the Oklahoma City bombing. She understood how they'd become icons for evil. What she didn't get was why stories like this turned up, year after year. She was about to change the channel when the reporter began naming less violent criminals, such as the D.A. who'd disappeared after his testimony put presidential front-runner Senator Hank O'Malley into prison.

O'Malley. The name Noah had muttered in his fevered delirium that day in the hospital. She put down her pen and paper and zeroed in on the screen. So many things made sense now... Noah's almost fierce refusal to let Alyssa out of his sight. The lack of background information about him. His avoidance of all conversation having to do with his past. And how his wife had died.

O'Malley sat facing his interviewer and looked right into the camera when he said that he had been framed by a man named Judson, the alleged "crooked assistant district attorney." Billie wrote the name in the margin of her grocery list, thinking to look the story up later. The senator's malevolent voice stopped her.

"Didn't get away with it, did ya?" he growled. Witness Protection, he claimed, was an exercise in futility, because he had the money and the connections to find Judson. Now something else Noah had said made sense. She'd wondered why he would mutter "lipstick" over and over. Now she realized he'd been saying WITSEC.

Billie began to tremble, and barely heard what the journalist said before going to commercial.

A little research helped her better understand WITSEC, the reasons for its existence, and the steps—and risks—U.S. Marshals were willing to take for people living under its protective shield. She couldn't imagine a fate worse than the fear and desperation that drove witnesses into hiding, leaving loved ones, jobs, homes behind.... Max, Billie decided, must be the agent assigned to Noah.

She typed "Nate Judson, Chicago" into her search engine, and found listing after listing describing the charges filed against the assistant D.A. and the senator. At first it seemed odd that the few photos she'd found of Judson were too blurry or distant, making identification—or comparison to Noah—impossible. But it didn't matter. Noah Preston and Nate Judson were one and the same. After seeing the raw, unbridled hatred in O'Malley's eyes as he'd uttered his fearsome threat, she understood why Noah had lied about his past. His reasons for getting involved with a man like O'Malley... Billie needed time to process those facts. Because which persona had she grown so fond of? The man who'd lied and cheated and partnered with known criminals to defend his treasured material possessions? Or the one who'd gone deep into hiding to protect his precious little girl?

No. She didn't need time. She loved him. It was just that simple...and that complicated.

But did she love him enough to spend the rest of *her* life looking over her shoulder, pretending she didn't know the truth?

## CHAPTER TWENTY-SIX

NIGEL NODDED, AND from that smug look on his face, O'Malley knew he'd come to deliver good news.

"Out with it, nephew."

"I'd think sitting here with someone who won't stab you in the back is worth a little patience."

Oh, he needed to get *out* of this place and back in control of his life!

He'd learned to forecast the political climate, and had sensed well in advance that the government had a case against him. To prevent them from seizing his assets, he'd moved everything into separate accounts, and put Nigel in control of them all. Before the trial, he'd been confident of the decision, because he believed in his nephew's trustworthiness. But he'd believed in Judson's loyalty, too, and look where that had gotten him.

With every visit, Nigel gained more confidence, and O'Malley lost more control. A dangerous thing—for the nephew of a desperate man who trusted no one.

"Just spit it out, Nigel. You know I have no patience for guessing games."

Nodding, his nephew said, "My IT guys dug up some stuff on Judson. We haven't confirmed it yet, but things look promising. Real promising."

O'Malley ran a hand through his hair. "Are you determined to give me a stroke? Why are you beating around the bush?"

Six months ago, the boy would have shrunk back in fear. Today, he shrugged, nodded and continued, "We locked on to a U.S. Marshal by the name of Maxine Coleson. Five years ago, she transferred from Chicago to D.C., and now she's working out of the Baltimore office."

"As a WITSEC agent?"

Nigel smirked. "Yup. I've already got a tail on her. Once we track her, get some pictures, we can make our move." He adjusted the knot of his tie. "Which is what, exactly?"

"You're kidding, right?"

"I know what I'd do, but you're the boss. I just want to make sure I don't step over the line."

O'Malley leaned forward, narrowed his eyes and lowered his voice. "It's really quite simple. *End. Him.*"

Nigel didn't even blink before he said, "Done." He stood and signaled the guard.

"If I had a son..." O'Malley said. And nodding, he added, "I'm proud of you, boy."

A moment later, the door opened to the processing center, and Nigel walked unwittingly into an ugly skirmish between two inmates. The guard tried to diffuse the situation, whirling his baton, bellowing for backup as he tried to get between Nigel and the bedlam. By the time the door-open buzzer sounded, one inmate, the guard and Nigel lay motionless on the bloody floor, victims of a carpenter's square-turned-knife.

As the attacker dropped his handmade weapon, rage boiled in O'Malley. Sick of ducking and cowering at the whims of other prisoners, he pounded on the door. To his surprise—and delight—it opened, and he charged into the waiting area like a grizzly.

In the next moment, he picked up the blade, slashing wildly at Nigel's killer...until an advancing guard stopped him with a well-aimed club to the temple.

When he came to in the infirmary, his wrists, ankles and chest were strapped to a stainless-steel table. The warden, leaning nonchalantly against the door, flicked a cigarette into a deep stainless sink.

"Looks like we're gonna be spending a lot more time together than you expected," he said. "As you're no doubt aware, our noble legislative body, always with an eye to improving our great state, abolished the death penalty. Which means your six and a half years at Stateville just became a life sentence."

"Don't make me laugh. It was self-defense."

"Not according to the guard who clocked you," he said, pointing at the goose egg on O'Malley's temple.

He was looking at years of hearings and appeals, even before the trial. Without Nigel to act as his defense attorney—or release funds for another lawyer's retainer—the state would stick him with some snot-nosed public defender fresh out of law school. O'Malley felt like the meat in a Life Gone Wrong sandwich, and it was all Judson's fault. *Every*thing bad that had happened to him since the trial had been Judson's fault!

He had one card left in his hand: Nigel's wife. He would ask her to solicit his former partners' aid in securing his early release. He'd pay any price for the freedom to even the score once and for all, even if it meant dying an old man, right here at Stateville.

## CHAPTER TWENTY-SEVEN

A LIGHT SNOW was falling, and Alyssa stood, nose pressed to the window, watching.

"Do you think we'll have a white Christmas, Daddy?"

"Anything is possible," he said, stepping up beside her.

"Do you think it'll snow enough to make a snowman?"

It wasn't likely, but why burst the kid's bubble? "You never know. You could wake up in the morning and find a foot of the stuff on the ground."

She wrapped her arms around him, and he winced. The stitches from that second surgery to find the source of the infection were healing nicely, but the site was still tender to the touch. Thankfully, she didn't see him flinch; it would have upset her, because she'd been especially protective of him since his release from the hospital.

"I can't wait for it to get dark. I haven't seen our decorations with all the lights off."

"I'll bet the place will look gorgeous."

She and Billie had strung lighted garlands around the banister leading down to the shop, and strung twinkle lights from the valances. They'd rearranged the living room to make space for the tree, and hung a hundred colorful ornaments from the branches. Jillian used to say she'd rather have no tree at all than put one of those fake things in her house. Noah wondered what she'd say about this one, draped with graceful folds of white gauze and guarded by a satin-gowned angel that held a tiny candle in each porcelain hand. A deep red cloth covered the dining room table; in its center, a three-tiered stand held an assortment of homemade cookies, brownies and small pies. Three battery-operated flameless candles, positioned amid artfully arranged evergreen branches, stood in shallow wooden bowls on the end tables, and there were doilies—*doilies!*—on top of the TV and stereo.

For the first time in a long time, he looked forward to Christmas.

And Billie Landon was solely responsible for that.

"And wait until you see what we did downstairs," Alyssa said.

"In the bike shop?"

"Oh, yes! Billie says your customers will *love* it."

"Maybe after supper you can show me around."

"Can we call Billie? I bet she'd love to see if you like it."

"Sure. Then I can thank her in person for helping you make the whole place look so pretty."

Alyssa clapped her hands, grabbed the phone and hit the autodial button. He'd programmed Ike's Bikes in the number one position for those rare days when she stayed home sick and he couldn't shut down the shop. Max got the number two spot because, well, because she was Max. And now this. He wondered if Billie knew what an honor it was to come in third.

"Did you program that, all by yourself?"

"Billie showed me how."

Alyssa spent the next minute or so chattering happily with Billie about the snow, then invited her to join them for what she termed "Light Up the Night!" Next thing Noah knew, he was making popcorn and hot chocolate, and setting the table with dessert plates…pale blue with snowflake decals.

"Where did these come from?"

"Billie made them," Alyssa said, "when she

was only ten years old." She picked one up and showed him the underside. "See? She signed her name and wrote the date."

Sure enough, thick black curlicue letters spelled out BILLIE. He tried to picture her at age ten, hunched over the unfired, unglazed ceramic, tongue between her teeth and brow furrowed as she concentrated on dotting her *I*'s with tiny black hearts. A strange warmth fluttered in his chest, and he quickly pushed it away. He couldn't afford to let his feelings deepen. Even if he hadn't decided that he and Alyssa should leave town after the first of the year, it wouldn't have been fair to any of them—or safe.

"She said she's going to walk, because it's faster than driving."

Thick red mittens muffled the sound of her knock, he found, when he'd limped to the door to let her in. When he saw her, a hand on either side of her face to block the glare of the porch light, the flutter returned. He needed to get back to his hammers and screwdrivers and pneumatic lug wrench, because all this sitting around, reading and watching romantic comedies on TV was making him think a lot about love and romance.

"Well that didn't take long," he said, opening the door.

Billie shook snow from her Orioles cap. "Took me less time to walk here than it took you to open the door!" she teased.

"Oh. Yeah. Left my cane in the kitchen," he explained.

"I wasn't talking about how long it took to *get* to the door. I meant…" Laughing, she hung her coat on the hook nearby. "Do I smell popcorn?"

"Alyssa thought it would be nice to have a little something to commemorate Light Up the Night."

It wasn't quite dark enough yet to get the full effect of the decorations, so the threesome had their snack before, rather than after, their celebration. When the hot chocolate and popcorn were gone, they turned on the Christmas lights, switched off everything else and stood in the middle of the living room to admire the sight.

Noah didn't know which glittered more, the mini bulbs and candles or Billie's big, beautiful eyes.

Alyssa decided it was the perfect occasion to watch *Miracle on 34th Street*. Noah prepared more cocoa, Billie made more popcorn and Alyssa set up the DVD player and put cookies on plates. They sat side by side on the sofa, with Alyssa between the adults, holding the big bowl on her lap.

An hour into the movie, Noah's right arm stiffened up. He stretched it across the back of the sofa, and when he did, Alyssa leaned into him…and Billie leaned into her. His hand was going numb, so he worked out the kinks—open, closed, open—until Billie stilled his flexing by slipping her right hand into his.

He worried that his heart might leap from his chest. Could she hear it, hammering against his ribs? If not, surely she could feel the pulse pounding through his fingertips. Alyssa was asleep. He could tell by her soft, steady breaths.

Billie gave his fingers a gentle squeeze. "My very favorite part of the movie is coming up," she whispered.

By Noah's calculations, there were two, maybe three minutes remaining. "You didn't like the rest of the movie?"

"Yes, but…" She pointed, and right on cue, John Payne wrapped Maureen O'Hara in a fierce hug and kissed her, long and hard, right there in the lovely, empty house that would one day be theirs.

Noah looked at Billie. Watched the action on the screen flicker light and dark across her face.

She looked at him, too. If there had been

any doubt about how she felt about him before now, that affectionate glow emanating from her eyes removed it. If he'd given it a moment's thought...if he'd considered the consequences of his actions...

Gently, he brought her closer, closer, until he could feel her soft, quick breaths puffing against his chin. Noah tipped his head and this time, *this* time, nothing stood in the way.

So he kissed her.

And she returned it.

Oh, he was in trouble, because since that near miss beside the campfire, he'd wondered what it might feel like. Now that he knew, now that he'd tasted these cocoa-sweet and popcorn-salty lips, he'd never forget it. Already his heart was breaking, and he hadn't even talked to Max about leaving yet.

"Daddy?"

He pulled back, only slightly, and it surprised him a little to see that Billie had lingered, eyes closed, a dreamy expression on her pretty face. He would have kissed her again if Alyssa hadn't wriggled, stretched, then looked up at him with sleepy eyes.

"I'll tuck her in," Billie said, her voice thick with emotion.

He couldn't let her do that. If he did, they'd be alone once Alyssa was out for the night, and he didn't think he'd have the willpower to avoid a repeat performance.

"Nah," he said. "I'll do it."

Billie looked a little confused, a little hurt, so he added, "I missed a lot of nights, tucking her in, while I was lying in that hospital bed."

"Oh, of course." She smiled, making him glad he'd tacked on that little qualifier.

"I should have known better. You go ahead and get her settled, and I'll clean up here…"

*You're a genius,* he thought. Because he'd created a stalemate…with himself.

"…and then I'll head home."

Noah nodded and held out his hand to Alyssa. "C'mon, cupcake. Daddy can't carry you just yet."

His daughter padded toward her room without taking his hand. "I'll brush my teeth and get into my pajamas," she said, "while you kiss Billie goodbye."

Billie inhaled a tiny gasp, then quickly began stacking popcorn bowls and cookie plates, and disappeared into the kitchen.

The bathroom door began to swing closed, and just before the latch would have clicked, Alyssa stuck her little face in the opening. "Well," she said, "are you going to kiss her again or not?"

"It's already way past your bedtime, kiddo.

Get those teeth brushed while I turn down your blankets."

He snapped the blinds shut and tossed back the quilt. When he glanced toward the door, there stood Billie, hair tucked under her baseball cap, snugging her jacket around her.

"My folks are coming down for our annual Christmas Eve dinner. Todd and Dani, too. And of course, Troy will be there." She tugged the cap lower on her forehead. "If you and Alyssa don't already have other plans, dinner is at six."

Noah watched her walk toward the back door. Watched as she let herself out. At the window, he separated the blinds and watched as she ran down the stairs. Then she turned the corner and stepped out of sight, leaving nothing but tiny boot prints in the snow.

And he missed her already.

## CHAPTER TWENTY-EIGHT

"THE TABLE LOOKS beautiful, honey. I love that centerpiece!"

"She made one just like it for our table," Alyssa said. "Only ours has sugar cookies and brownies and little pies on it. All sitting on paper doilies."

Ellen sighed. "Oh, Billie and her paper doilies. Do you know that when she was your age, she made a thousand things out of paper doilies?"

Billie lit the candles on the mantel, and the ones on the buffet, too. The past six years or so, it seemed her mom designed Christmas dinner around a theme, and God help the poor soul at the center of it. Last year, it was the Troy Had Lots of Girlfriends theme, which didn't sit well with Victoria. The year before that, Frank the Golf Addict took the heat. Todd and Dani bore the brunt of things the year they'd earned The Couple Who Won't Have Children title. If it was her turn this year, Billie supposed it could be a whole lot worse than 101 Uses for Paper Doilies.

"Did you hear from Troy?" she asked.

"He and Todd and Dani should be here any minute now. And your tree is lovely, too," Ellen said from the doorway. "Wherever did you get the idea to wrap clear mini lights in white toile?"

Clearly, a rhetorical question, because her mom had already joined Noah and her husband in the living room.

Billie was cracking ice into a plastic tub when Alyssa stepped up beside her.

"When I was little, we had a refrigerator that dropped weird-shaped little ice cubes right into people's glasses." She picked up a loose ice chip and popped it into her mouth. "Mommy liked it."

That day in the hospital, when Noah had bared his soul, he'd said "love you" and "so much." At the time, Billie hadn't been sure if he meant her or Jillian or the nurse who swapped his green Jell-O for tapioca pudding. Lately—especially after that kiss the other night—she'd begun to think maybe he *had* been talking to her, and that he'd meant every word. But Noah had loved Jillian first, and Billie wasn't at all sure he'd ever love anyone as much.

"Did you know chewing ice is against the dentist's rules?" Alyssa asked.

Billie walked around the table, dropping ice into stemmed water glasses. "You know, I think I did hear about that one."

"What kind of things did you make from the doilies, Billie?"

"Let's see…there were butterflies and ballerinas, birds, clothes for my Barbies…."

"You played with Barbies? Like me?"

Nodding, Billie said, "I sure did. And nothing was too good for *my* dolls. They had a van, and a Corvette, and a town house with an elevator."

Ellen came back into the kitchen, laughing. "And little suitcases filled with clothes and shoes and accessories…not counting the doily outfits she made for them."

"I think I would have liked being your friend when you were a little girl. It sounds like you were nice and fun then, too."

Nice and fun. If only Chuck could hear that!

The doorbell rang, and Alyssa said, "I bet that's Troy. Can I answer it?"

On the way to the foyer, Billie remembered Noah's fevered confession. "That's okay, sweetie. You've worked hard enough for one day." It wasn't like O'Malley would come calling on Christmas Eve, she thought, opening the door, but she wasn't taking any chances where Noah's little girl was concerned.

"Bud," she said, "you have a key."

"I know, but then I wouldn't get to play with this weird little doorbell of yours." He gave it a crank, then stepped inside.

"Merry Christmas," she teased, hugging him. "Dad and Noah are in the living room. Make yourself at home."

Troy, Todd and Dani arrived right behind him. And after them, Max.

Troy joined her in the kitchen. "Anything I can do to help?"

"Thanks, but everything is ready."

"Noah's looking well, don't you think? I mean, except for that limp, he's almost good as new."

It was good to see her brother looking healthy *and* happy, and she knew Noah's recovery had a lot to do with it.

"And determined as he is, I doubt he'll need that cane much longer, either."

He took a step closer and whispered conspiratorially, "You two—or should I say three—have been spending a lot of time together lately. You planning to make an announcement today?"

"Announcement?" She transferred mashed

potatoes from the saucepan to a serving bowl. "What kind of announcement?"

"You know…" He looked left, right, and eyes closed, he puckered up.

Billie dabbed a fingerful of potatoes onto his lips. And handing him the biscuit basket, she said, "Carry that to the table for me, you big nut, and tell everyone dinner's ready."

Fifteen minutes later, Billie sat back and looked around the dining room. She'd often wondered why her mom made such a big deal about family get-togethers, but now she understood. Days of cleaning, shopping, cooking and baking were forgotten as steaming sides made the rounds amid laughter and amiable chatter.

She'd never understood the need for a seating chart, either, so it surprised her, once everyone settled where Ellen put them, how *right* it felt, looking across at Noah. He'd just taken a big bite of ham, and caught her staring. Eyebrows raised, he stopped chewing as a slow smile slanted his mouth.

"Now that everyone has a full plate," Ellen said, "it's time to initiate my favorite part of a Landon Christmas Eve dinner. And since some of you don't have a clue what I'm talking about…Frank? Will you do the honors?"

Billie's dad put down his fork and cleared

his throat. "My Christmas wish," he began, "is to have the time and good weather for at least one round of golf every week." He looked at Dani, who sat on his other side. In her typically shy and quiet way, Billie's sister-in-law wished for good health for everyone, all through the year. Todd looked forward to another profitable year for his accounting firm, and all Troy wanted was to make Jeff glad he'd taken a chance on him.

Max wanted a promotion, and when the family asked what she did for a living, she said, "Next!"

As it happened, that was Bud, who wished Inky would stop darting out of the house every chance he got. "And I wish people would stop parking on the sidewalk in front of my house. Folks have to walk in the street to get around them, and one of these days..." He punched his right fist into his left palm, startling Alyssa, who almost jumped in her chair.

"Why don't you tell us how you *really* feel, Bud," Billie teased. "But I guess it's my turn, isn't it?"

Todd chuckled. "You don't think just because you organized this shindig you get a pass, do you?"

No, she didn't. Soon after it was decided she'd host this dinner, Billie had started thinking about what she'd say. Not the truth—that she wished peace of mind and safety for Noah and Alyssa—because that would expose them to the exact opposite. She couldn't wish that what he'd said that day in the hospital really *was* intended for her, because then she'd have to decide whether to tell him what she knew.

"I wish…" If she looked at Noah, even for a second, she might lose her nerve. "I wish everyone's wishes come true this year…the ones you've shared and the ones you're holding close to your heart."

"Oh, honey," Ellen said, "that's so sweet!"

While her brothers groaned, Billie chanced a peek at Noah, whose expression told her that he got the message hidden in her wish.

"Alyssa, dear," Ellen said, "you're next!"

Giggling, she hid behind her hand and said, "I wish I could open all my presents right after dessert instead of waiting until tomorrow morning!"

When the "Awws" and "Isn't she cutes" ended, she said, "I'm just kidding. That isn't my real wish." She looked at Billie. "My real wish is…that Billie could be my mom."

Following a drawn-out, uncomfortable pause, Ellen said, "And *my* wish is…" she leaned forward to look around her husband

"...that someone around here will decide to make me a grandmother!"

Relieved laughter lightened the mood...for everyone but Alyssa, who sat quietly staring into her lap.

Billie thought she understood how the poor kid felt. She'd bared her soul, and probably expected everyone to agree. If not everyone, at least *Billie*. Noah had recognized her disappointment, too, as evidenced by his pained expression. It touched her deeply that his father's heart ached for his little girl.

He cleared his throat, pressed his forearms to the tabletop and said, "Alyssa, I think Billie will be a great mom...when she's ready. And speaking of ready, are you ready to go?" He softened the blow by adding, "The sooner you get to sleep, the sooner Santa will come with your presents."

Alyssa's shoulders sagged and she sank lower in the chair. "Can I have dessert first? I promise to eat fast...."

"Speaking of fast," Bud injected, "you might *think* you got away with pulling a fast one, Noah, using your innocent little girl to get out of sharing your wish, but you're wrong."

Todd, Troy and Frank voiced their agreement, and put the pressure on to coax Noah's cooperation.

He nodded, then shook his head, and smiling, said, "My Christmas wish is that no matter where we go or what we do, we'll never forget each other."

Billie didn't hear any of the comments that followed, because as Noah's gaze fused to hers, she read the unspoken message in his heartfelt little speech: he was thinking about leaving Ellicott City. Something dreadful must have happened to make him consider uprooting Alyssa again. Billie didn't need to hear details or reasons. Only one thing could raise that kind of desperation.

O'Malley.

## CHAPTER TWENTY-NINE

THE DAY AFTER Christmas could be depressing…if she allowed it.

With her parents, brother and sister-in-law on their way back to Philly, the house seemed ghostly quiet and empty, despite the wrapping paper, ribbons, foam electronics protectors and cardboard boxes scattered throughout the first floor. Billie decided to tackle the kitchen first, hoping the rest of the mess would seem less daunting once the hard jobs were behind her.

With the dishwasher humming and pots and pans stacked in the drying rack, she headed for the dining room. She put the furniture back in place and had just finished vacuuming the area rug when the doorbell rang.

"Figured you'd be up to your elbows in cleaning solution," Troy said when she opened the door, "so I brought lunch." He held up a brown paper bag and led the way to the kitchen. "How does sushi sound?"

"Like you're a mind reader." Billie slapped paper plates and napkins onto the table. "I've been thinking about sushi, trying to remember the last time I had it."

"I made sandwiches that day."

"Oh. Yeah." He shook his head. "Will this head of mine ever get back to normal?"

"Of course it will. Just be patient with yourself."

She grabbed two bottles of water from the fridge. Tough times for Troy. Not as tough as the accident, but traumatic all the same. "But all that's behind you now."

He shrugged and unsheathed his chopsticks.

"What does that mean?"

Another shrug.

"Troy! No way. Victoria is back in the picture?"

Using a chopstick, he pointed at his forehead. "This old bean got beat up pretty bad, but I'm not completely brain dead. I remember telling you that she deserves better that I can give her, and nothing has changed."

Billie sat across from him and helped herself to a California roll.

"Go easy on that wasabi," he warned. "These guys make it themselves."

"Quit beating around the bush. Out with it. What has Victoria done?"

"Well, it all started day before Christmas Eve. She called to tell me her grandmother died. I felt like a heel. We'd spent tons of time with the woman, and because of how things ended, Victoria said she didn't feel like she could call and tell me."

"Give me a break. It isn't as if you're an ogre or anything."

"In all fairness, I did behave like a lout, there at the end." He winced. "I yelled. Slammed doors. Even broke a lamp. On purpose."

"Hey. I didn't know her nearly as well as you did, and she made *me* want to throw lamps on a couple of occasions." Billie snickered. "At her butt." Billie paused. "*But*…I sense there's more…."

"I asked for information, you know, so I could at least send flowers to the funeral home and a card to her mom. She hemmed. And hawed. So I typed her grandmother's name into the computer. Didn't find a death notice anywhere. To make a long story short, turns out there was a good reason for that."

Billie huffed. "No way," she said again. "Her grandmother didn't die?"

"She's happy and healthy, still living on her own in a retirement village."

"Why would anyone make up a story like that?"

"Who knows why crazy people do anything. But she did me a favor in the long run."

She failed to see how, and waited to see how her brother would explain *that*.

"Victoria loves to be the center of attention...unless she looks like a fool. I called her back, thinking once she knew I'd caught her in the lie, it would balance out the way I ended things. *That* didn't end the way I thought it would, either."

"I don't get it."

"She read me the riot act. Told me I had a lot of nerve, rubbing her nose in—and I quote—'the one little mistake' she made."

"There had to be more than that. I know you." Billie dabbed wasabi onto a California roll. "You wouldn't have ended it if she'd met you halfway."

"There you go again, giving people the benefit of the doubt."

It's what he'd said after Chuck left and refused to acknowledge the pregnancy. She took it to mean Troy had made more than just one mistake in the relationship, too.

"So is it finally over, then?"

Waving a chopstick like a conductor's baton, he sang the exit song from *The Sound of Music*.

"Leave it to you," Billie said, laughing, "to turn a sour note sweet." She handed him the last shrimp roll. "What did she say when you told her you nearly died?"

"Didn't tell her. Didn't see the point. She already thinks I'm a jerk. Why add fuel to the fire by proving it?"

"I don't get it," Billie said again.

"If I told her, she'd think I was trying to bury my bad behavior under that sad story. Last thing I want is her pity."

Billie only nodded.

"Have you seen Noah since Christmas Eve?"

"No. But I'm sure he's been busy, being Santa and all."

"Uh-oh. Something tells me your two tickets to paradise got canceled."

"Paradise. Right."

"Hey, you know me. What goes in here," he said, pointing to his left ear, "stays in here."

She grinned at his self-depreciating joke. "It isn't that I don't trust you. It's just…I had a feeling this would happen if I let myself get too involved."

"Had a feeling what would happen?"

She thought of the almost kiss, and the one that had been anything *but* almost. Remembered what Noah had said when the fever weakened his typically steely self-control. Pictured the way he'd looked at her while sharing his Christmas wish…

Troy sat back, crossed both arms over his chest. "If I tell you something, you have to

swear you'll keep it to yourself. You can't tell
anyone. Not Mom or Dad. Not Bud. Especially
not Noah…"

In high school, when she'd caught their
brother, Todd, sneaking into the house after
curfew—drunk—he'd promised never to do it
again…if she didn't snitch on him. She hadn't
told her dad about the speeding ticket and re-
sulting court hearing that her mom hid for
years. She'd honored Troy's request to keep
quiet the details of the deal he'd made to sidestep Victoria's lawsuit threats. If only he knew
how well she could keep a secret!

"Couple of times while I was visiting him,
Noah let things slip. Little things at first.
Like…how would he let you know he wanted
more than a business relationship. And then
he worried you might reject him if he ever
screwed up the courage to ask you out. Couple days before the accident, he said you deserve better than a guy like him. Said some
crazy stuff about baggage. And this morning,
he came as close to telling me he loves you as
a guy can get."

Billie didn't know what to say, or how to
feel, especially after learning the reasons for
Noah's sometimes peculiar behavior.

"I didn't realize you guys spent so much

time together. But why are you just now telling me all this?"

"Didn't think of it until just now, to tell you the truth. But what difference does it make? He sent every signal a guy can send. You're smart. And intuitive. I can't believe you didn't figure it out on your own." He smirked. "Evidently, you don't know everything."

"If that's the impression I leave you with, I'm embarrassed. And sorry, too."

"I'm telling you all this because I think if you gave him a sign that you're interested, he'd eliminate the middleman. Namely, *moi*."

She ought to tell him how, on two separate and very different occasions, she'd all but thrown herself at Noah. That would give her brother a good laugh.

"Remember Dave, that guy you dated in high school?"

"How could I forget the guy you ran up the flagpole—literally—because he dumped me two days before prom? You nearly got suspended."

"And it would have been worth it. Guy's gotta look out for his kid sister, y'know?"

"I appreciate it. And I love you, too."

"So anyway, my point is I wouldn't tell you to…I don't know, flirt or whatever…if I thought Noah was a bum." Troy shrugged, then broke into song again. "Nobody better hurt you, or make you cry-y-y...."

"That's three songs in a row. But at least you have good taste in music."

They shared a moment of quiet laughter. Then Troy shoved the sushi containers aside and leaned both elbows on the table.

"Correct me if I'm wrong, but I get the feeling you fell for the guy, weeks ago. So what do you have to lose, letting Noah know?"

Billie wanted to cry. She put too much wasabi on a sushi to hide it. "All right," she said around a bite, "I admit it. I have...I have feelings for Noah. But I can't give him a sign."

"Why not?"

Because, she thought, one night—probably soon—he would simply disappear without a word, the way he'd left everything and everyone in Chicago. Here one minute and gone the next, like the fog that clung to the rocky banks of the Patapsco.

Troy nodded. "I get it. It's a leap of faith. A big one. After what Chuck did to you, I can see why you're leery. But the only thing Noah has in common with that self-centered jerk you married is..." Troy paused, then said, "I was going to say gender is the only thing they have in common. But Chuck is not a man."

Billie blotted her eyes.

"Told you that wasabi was powerful. Maybe someday you'll listen to me."

"Maybe."

"Go for it, kid. What do you have to lose?"

Nothing. Everything. Billie sighed and dipped another California roll into another deliberately huge dollop of wasabi, let the tears come…and blamed them on the sauce.

"I KNOW IT'S last minute, so if you're busy, I understand."

Billie couldn't believe her ears. Noah Preston, inviting her to Alyssa's birthday party tomorrow, and thinking she might have other plans. It was almost laughable.

She could play it cool. Pretend there was something on her calendar that she'd have to rearrange. Decline, to reinforce the "That'll teach you to make *me* an afterthought!" attitude. But she'd never been any good at those silly, passive-aggressive games. Life was complicated enough without trying to control others. Relationships shouldn't be that much work, either.

"I wouldn't miss it," she said. "What can I bring?"

"Just your pretty self."

He made a noise—something between a groan and a cough. Proof that a little unintended truth had slipped out, and he didn't know how to react to it?

"It's funny you called, because I was going to call *you,* to ask when I could bring her present."

"You didn't need to get her anything. That kid has more toys than she knows what to do with."

Billie heard the grin in his voice, and it touched that sweet, warm spot in her heart. "Of course I did. I love you guys."

She slapped a hand over her mouth and hoped she hadn't made the same "oops, what have I said" noise he'd just made.

"You okay with burgers and dogs on the grill?"

"Sure. I'll make my world-famous potato salad. Who else is coming, so I know how much to make?"

"Half a dozen kids from Alyssa's class and a parent or three. Bud, Troy, Max... I know it seems too cold outside to grill, but there's a method to my madness. I'm not good with small talk, and the deck isn't big enough for that many people."

So, she thought, a *real* party, then, and not just something thrown together on the fly.

"Did you already order the cake?"

She heard his hiss of frustration. "Darn. I knew I was forgetting something."

"Relax. You worry about the paper plates and plastic utensils—"

"Sheesh…"

He'd forgotten those, too? Well, he had time to pick some up.

"—and I'll bake the cake."

"You'd do that?"

*Anything for you, Noah, Nate…whatever your name is.*

"It'll be fun, dragging out my decorating tools."

"Thanks. See you at—"

She looked at the receiver to check the reception, which was dumb, because he'd called her house phone.

"Um, see you at three. And thanks, Billie. You're a sweetheart. Thank you."

*Sweetheart, indeed,* Billie thought as he hung up. She grabbed her keys and headed for her parking pad out back, thinking *idiot is more like it.* She and Noah didn't even have a relationship, yet here she was, feeling hurt and rejected. Which was ridiculous and unfair, since he hadn't made any promises.

Maybe she had become one of those women that stylists and their customers talked about at the hair salon, the kind who ignore the signs of trouble and plow ahead when things go awry, determined to make the impossible work. She'd be the one all her friends and relatives tried to match up with their coworkers, bachelor neighbors and recently widowed former schoolmates.

The errands, at least, would divert her attention from what promised to be a strange and sad future. By hitting the grocery store while most people were eating supper, she could get in and out with the ingredients for the cake and potato salad, some balloons and streamers, and still get home by six. While the cake was in the oven, she'd start the potato salad, and while the spuds were boiling, she'd make baked beans. Barring unexpected interruptions, she'd have everything ready before she turned in for the night.

What a joke, Billie thought, grabbing a cart. She'd probably lie awake all night, wondering if they'd have any time alone together while she decorated and got the buffet table set up for Alyssa's guests.

As predicted, Billie logged three, maybe four hours sleep. But she didn't feel the least bit tired. Too excited, she guessed, about performing duties that could be described as wifely and motherly. She showered and took her time with her hair and makeup. Took her time choosing an outfit, too. If this turned out to be the last time Noah saw her, she wanted the memory to be lasting…and positive.

She packed the car with everything she'd bought and baked and cooked, and drove to Noah's. He'd offer to help carry things, but he wasn't physically ready for climbing and toting. Smiling to herself, Billie wondered how long she had to put her birthday decorating plan into motion.

Her Uggs boots—soft, warm and quiet—allowed her to dart up the steps without making much noise. As she reached the landing, she made a mental note to sweep and salt the steps, just as soon as she'd put the groceries away, to keep Alyssa's guests from slipping. Then Billie would put Alyssa to work, tying helium balloons to the chair backs and weaving crepe paper streamers through the railing pickets. And Noah? He could help hang the Happy Birthday banner and—

A peculiar sound stopped her in her tracks. Billie didn't move, scarcely breathed, trying to identify its cause and source. Craning her neck, she peeked between the spindles. She saw Noah's shoes first…then dark blue socks and the rust-colored stitches that hemmed his jeans. Billie didn't need to see more to know he was crying.

Every womanly instinct said, "Get up there and comfort him!" But common sense—and lessons learned from being raised with two older brothers—stopped her. Noah was a proud man who'd gone to extremes to protect his privacy. If she went up there now, he'd only resent her for witnessing his temporary weakness.

Billie took care, heading back down the staircase. She opened the car door, then intentionally slammed it with every bit of power she could muster. Might as well grab some of the groceries, she thought, as long as she was down here. So she made lots of noise opening and closing the trunk, too.

It wasn't easy, stomping back upstairs in her soft-soled Uggs, but she managed to produce an audible thump with every slow step. She wanted to give him as much time as possible to pull himself together.

"Hi," she said, forcing cheeriness into her voice that she didn't feel. She wanted to know what had happened to cause his tears. "What are you doing out here in the cold?" she asked. "You'll catch your death!"

He didn't answer, but held the door open instead. Billie hurried inside, wondering if after-accident pain had driven him outside in the snow....

"Just one more trip," she told him on the way back down.

She decided to talk. A lot. About the party and the guests. About the weather. About anything that would distract him from the pain. When she returned with the last of the food and decorations, Noah closed the door behind her, and after hanging their jackets on the hall tree, began poking into the packages lining his counter.

"What's all this?" he asked. "I thought you were just bringing a cake and some potato salad."

"Can I help it if the cooking-baking bug bit me?" She hid her amusement by sticking her head in the fridge, pretending to look for places to store everything until party time.

"Guess I forgot to tell you what time the party starts."

"Three o'clock, right?"

"Right…"

"I'm early, I know. I just thought you might need a hand setting things up. Answering the door. Keeping the kids corralled while you're outside grilling."

She shut the fridge door and started unpacking the decorations as Alyssa ran up and wrapped her arms around Billie's waist.

"I'm so glad you're here!" the little girl said.

"Me, too."

It was hard to believe she'd started out disliking this kid, that in the beginning, she hadn't *wanted* to like her. Now? Now she looked forward to the enthusiastic greetings and surprisingly exuberant hugs, and it felt so good, knowing that every time she blurted "I love you!" she meant it. Billie didn't know how to define her feelings for Alyssa, but she cared. Deeply.

When Noah left—if Noah left—she wouldn't worry about him. He was a full-grown man who'd proved himself very capable of taking care of himself. Alyssa, on the other hand, needed more than his protection. She needed stability. A woman's guidance. A mother's love. And Billie wanted to provide it. If that was love, so be it. Adjusting to life without Noah would be hard. Adjusting to life without Alyssa...

Billie shook off the horrible thought.

"Want to help me decorate?"

"Yes!"

She showed Alyssa what to do, then looked for Noah. She found him at the window of his room, left hand tucked into his side pocket, right fingers wrapped around the curve of his cane. Billie walked up beside him, linked her arm through his.

"Hey."

He looked down at her. "Hey, yourself."

"You feeling okay?"

"Better, now that you're here."

In the past, Billie had prided herself on being decisive. When she made a promise, she kept it. When she chose to do something, she did it, and she never knowingly started things she couldn't finish. Trying to save her marriage to Chuck had been proof of that. Since meeting Noah, though, only one word described her: *fickle*.

Not ten minutes ago, she'd had every intention of talking nonstop to keep his mind off his troubles. But now she thought talking was exactly what *he* needed to do.

"I don't want to pry, Noah—and I know everyone says this—but I'm a good listener. And when I give my word to keep things to myself, I do."

Noah nodded. "I believe you." He looked out the window again. "Don't worry. I'll snap out of it before everybody gets here."

Snap out of what? she wondered. His fingers opened and closed, opened and closed around the grip of his cane. She rested her free hand atop his knuckles.

"Are you in any pain?"

"Not the kind you think." He focused on

their hands, and without looking up, said, "Any of that stuff on the counter need refrigeration?"

Billie knew a dismissal when she heard one. But she didn't intend to give up just yet.

"Only the potato salad. And the whipped cream."

"Why do we need whipped cream?"

"Can't have strawberry shortcake without it."

"Strawberry shortcake? For a little girl's birthday party?"

"Of course not. The cake with the roses and fancy trim is for the party. I made the short-cake for you."

His brows drew together slightly. And then he stared out the window again. "I prefer mine plain."

"I think there's some kind of law against that."

He looked at her again.

She almost said, "I guess as a former D.A., you'd know the law." Instead, Billie said, "Well, guess I'd better get the perishables into the fridge." She didn't know what to make of the way he was looking at her.

"Don't worry. I've almost snapped out of it," he whispered, gently grasping her upper arm.

"Almost?"

"Guy can't enjoy his kid's party," he said,

turning her slightly, "with a thank-you hanging over his head."

"I wouldn't let self-pity ruin my kid's party."

He took a half step closer. "And I apologize for not thanking you. For coming over here early, baking the cake, bringing side dishes and party decorations."

"Sure you did. Last night. On the phone. Twice. Three times, even." She raised her eyebrows. "Remember?"

His arm slid around her waist and he pulled her close, so close that she could feel his heart beating hard against her chest.

Noah buried his face in her hair. "If only," he whispered, and then leaned back to study her face for a long, agonizing moment.

If only what? she wondered as he licked his lips. Would he kiss her? And if he did, would it mean "I care," "Goodbye" …or both.

His lips touched hers, gently at first, then more insistently.

And Billie knew that if his situation demanded another escape, she wouldn't let him go without her.

## CHAPTER THIRTY

"Jeff throws a huge New Year's Eve party every year," Troy said, handing her an invitation. "From what I hear, it's top of the line, all the way."

"He's inviting *me?*" She laughed. "I have absolutely no desire to attend a black-tie gala, all by myself."

"You won't be alone. He invited Noah, too."

"Right. Noah. Who won't walk ten steps away from Alyssa—" Billie pointed at the line in the invitation that said Four Seasons "—driving half an hour to the Inner Harbor. You're a laugh a minute!"

She dropped the card on the kitchen table. "I guess you have to go, though, huh, since Jeff is your boss."

"Hey. Have you *met* me?" Her brother laughed. "When have you ever known me to turn down free food? And since it includes a night at a fancy-pants hotel, I wouldn't say no, even if Jeff wasn't my boss." He wiggled his eyebrows. "Besides, I'm not going alone."

"What?" Billie sat at the table. "Park it, brother, and start talkin'."

He told her about the woman he'd met at the office.

"She's older than me," he said, "but doesn't look it. Her husband died eight years ago, left her to raise two kids, who are in high school now. She's smart and sweet and funny. I tell ya, Billie, I've never met a woman who could make me laugh the way she can. Knows exactly who she is and what she wants."

"And you hope that's you?"

"Yeah." An odd, shy little smile lit his face. "Yeah, I guess so."

He looked so happy that Billie didn't have the heart to voice her concerns.

"I can hear the wheels spinning from all the way over here. What are you thinking?"

"Only that if she ever hurts you, I don't care if she's a ninety-year-old female Sumo wrestler."

"Female Sumo…is there such a thing?"

"I have no idea."

They shared a moment of laughter, and then Troy said, "So how was Alyssa's birthday party?"

"Nice. Real nice. The kids had fun, I think, and Noah is a pretty good host…for a shy, secretive, overprotective, too-stubborn-to-admit-he's-in-pain dude."

Troy's eyebrows rose. "The leg's still giving him problems, is it? I feel rotten about that. If he hadn't pulled me out of the car—"

"You wouldn't be here. I'm sure he has no regrets. You'd have done the same for him."

"I certainly hope so." He ran a hand through his hair. "So how was the party? Did Alyssa make a good haul?"

"I'll say! I have no idea how it's all going to fit in her little room. I think she was a bit disappointed that you couldn't come to the party."

"She said that?"

"Didn't have to. When I left there last night, she was still working on a special art project to thank you for the DVDs. Just wait until you see it."

*Thank you.* Would Billie ever hear that phrase again without thinking of those intense, sizzling moments in Noah's room? She exhaled a sigh. Not likely.

"She's a sweet kid. Just the kind I'd want… if fatherhood was in my future."

Ah, Billie thought. So he had considered the likelihood that his new lady friend didn't want more children.

"You've always wanted kids, so why wouldn't fatherhood be in your future?"

"I'm not getting any younger."

"Please. I could name a dozen movie stars who fathered kids long into their seventies."

"If this thing with Sheila goes where I think it might…" Troy shook his head. "She doesn't want any more kids."

And there it was, the answer to her question. Funny, but it made Billie sad, because Troy would make a great dad.

"At least she was honest with you. If having kids is still high on your priorities list, it's early enough in the relationship to move on, find someone who shares your goals, before either of you gets hurt."

"Is that what you're doing with Noah? Keeping a safe distance because you're planning to move on?"

"There's nothing to move on from, Troy."

"Could've fooled me."

The comment—and the undercurrent of disappointment in his voice—surprised her.

"You *did* fool me," he continued. "I would have sworn you were falling for the guy. That you were crazy about the kid, too." He shrugged. "But then, I remember what you used to say about kids…that they're messy and loud. Rude. Grabby." He shook his head. "It's your life. That's all I'm going to say."

And then he left to update Jeff on the franchise owners he'd met with earlier in the week. He'd no sooner gone than the phone rang, and dread swirled in her heart when she saw Noah's number on the screen.

"Hello, Billie. It's me, Alyssa."

The last person she wanted to hear from right now. She needed time to process the truths Troy had unearthed.

"Hi," Billie said. "How's the birthday girl?"

"I can't find places for my new toys. My room looks *awful*. When Daddy saw it, he said, 'Think like Billie. She's the most organized person I know.'" Alyssa sighed.

Surely, Noah didn't really expect her to go over there, help his daughter put her room in order. The better question was what if Alyssa was lying about this, the way she'd lied about the allergy pill? Why, Billie would look like a fool, barging into his home to rearrange his little girl's room!

"Will you take the phone to your dad for me?"

Billie heard the receiver hit the kitchen counter with a clunk. A small voice, a baritone...then heavy footsteps.

"Hey, Billie. What's up?"

"Couple of things, actually. Wondering what

you're going to do with your invitation to Jeff's New Year's Eve gala, for starters."

"RSVP a polite no, of course." He hesitated, then said, "Why? Are you going?"

"No." She felt like a fool admitting it, even to herself, but she didn't want to go if he wouldn't be there, too.

"You could come over here. Alyssa has been pestering me to call you all day, to see if you'd help her figure out how to arrange things in her room. I don't expect you to, of course," he quickly added. "But I'm sure she'd get a kick out of watching the ball drop with us."

Billie spotted some tickets on her desk, where they'd been since last week when a client had given them to her. "I have tickets to watch the fireworks from the top of the science center. I was going to give them to Jeff and his family, since they'll be downtown anyway, but if you think she'd enjoy it…"

"She'd love it."

If he thought she was going into that crowd with Alyssa by herself, he had another think coming!

"I have four tickets." Hopefully, he'd get the hint.

"What time do we need to be at the Inner Harbor?"

"I'll pick you up at nine-thirty," she said.

"That way, you don't have to worry about getting behind the wheel with Percocet in your system."

"I can skip a dose."

"But you won't. I have parking passes, so that'll save you having to walk from one of the garages."

A long pause followed her offer, and Billie wondered what excuse he was cooking up to back out. She stood straighter. If he thought she was going to let him hear regret in her voice, well, he had another think coming on that score, too!

"Why wait until nine-thirty to come over? If you get here at six or seven, we can order a pizza."

"That's a great idea."

Her instant reply didn't surprise her nearly as much as the disappointment she felt, looking at the clock and realizing it was only four o'clock.

HE HADN'T EXPECTED a visit from Max.

"Don't you have any life of your own?" he asked when she let herself in. "It's New Year's Eve, for the love of Meb."

"For your information," she sniffed, "I have a date."

Only when she opened her coat did he realize she hadn't worn her hip-length leather jacket.

"Wow," he said, taking in her sparkly red dress. "Tight as that thing is, where will you stow your badge?"

She patted the small purse hanging from a thin strap draped over her shoulder. "Be quiet and sit down," she said, faking a sneer. "I stopped by to give you some good news."

Max reminded him that several weeks earlier, O'Malley's nephew had walked into the wrong room at the wrong time during a visit to Stateville, and never walked out again.

"Seems the senator didn't appreciate having his only conduit to the real world shut down that way," she continued. "He picked a fight with the inmate he thought was responsible for Nigel's death, and ended up in the infirmary...where he died of a stroke a couple of weeks ago."

Noah wished he'd taken her advice to sit down, because the news rocked him.

"No way." He'd been looking over his shoulder for so long, he wondered if he could stop. "O'Malley is dead. Really?"

"Really."

She was smiling, but only a little, and Noah

didn't know what to make of that. He dropped heavily onto the seat of his recliner and looked up at her.

"Does that mean I get my life back? Or did that… Did he pay someone to keep the heat on, in case he died in prison?"

Max sat across from him. "I've spent the past two weeks on this, Noah. Not just me, three other marshals, too. With Nigel gone, there's no one left to deliver orders…or payments. So near as we can tell, it's over."

When he first went into the program, Noah used to dream something like this would happen. But as the months turned into years, he'd decided it was healthier—and less painful—to accept his fate. But now?

"You're sure. O'Malley is really dead."

"I can probably sneak the death certificate over here if you need proof."

"I—I don't know what to say." He shook his head. "I just can't wrap my mind around it."

Max got up, and halfway between the couch and the recliner, she nodded. "Happy New Year, Noah Preston," she said, sitting on the arm of his chair. And sliding an arm across his shoulders, added, "Unless you'd rather go back to being Nate Judson."

She told him it was safe to reconnect with

his family. Safe to take Alyssa back to Chicago. Safe to admit his feelings for Billie…

And make Alyssa's Christmas wish come true.

But first things first. He picked up the phone and dialed his parents' number.

BETWEEN RECONNECTING WITH his family and physical therapy, Noah found the weeks sped by. When he called to reserve a small, private dining room at Tersiguel's, he expected to hear that, this close to Valentine's Day, the restaurant was fully booked.

"You're in luck," said the reservations clerk. "We just had a cancelation."

Noah didn't ask if there was a waiting list, or why the top name on it didn't qualify for the special table. He saw it as a sign, and jumped on it. Then he called Max, who was only too happy to stay with Alyssa. After making two additional calls, he went and found Alyssa in her room, humming as she rearranged furniture in her Barbie town house.

He sat on the corner of her bed. "Hey, cupcake. Come sit with me for a minute," he said, patting the mattress. "I have a question to ask you."

"What?"

"Remember at Billie's on Christmas, when you wished she could be your mom?"

His daughter frowned and went back to moving tiny tables and chairs. "Yeah, I guess that was a dumb thing to say, wasn't it?"

Noah hadn't known what to expect. Surely not that. "What do you mean?"

She sat back on her heels and looked up at him. "Do you think it made Mommy sad, hearing me say I wanted a *new* mother?"

"Aw, baby." He sighed, pulling her onto his lap. "No. No way. Your mom knows how much you love her, that you'll never *stop* loving her. But she knows you need somebody in your life. Somebody who can tell you things and teach you things that I don't know anything about, because, well, because I'm a *guy.*"

"Somebody like Billie…"

"Somebody like Billie," he echoed. "It won't hurt Mommy's feelings if you love Billie. In fact, I believe if she could, she'd tell you how happy she is that a really nice lady has come into your life, to take care of you, to love you, to help you do girl stuff."

Alyssa stared at him for a moment, then said, "Whew." She tugged at a loose string hanging from a button on his shirt. "Bet Mom's glad for someone to take care of you, too."

He chuckled. "Yeah. I bet she is."

"Do you miss her, Daddy?"

Noah swallowed. Dangerous territory, he told himself, considering…

"Yeah, I do. I guess I always will, in some ways. But you know what? I don't miss her nearly as much as I used to. Thanks to Billie."

Alyssa laid her head on his chest. "Me, too."

He kissed her forehead. "So if it's okay with you, I'm going to ask her to marry me. Tonight. Over dinner at Tersiguel's."

She hopped off his lap and stood in front of him. "Really?" She rested her palms on his knees. *"Really?"*

"Really."

She glanced around her. "I hope we can live at her house. After the wedding, I mean."

He took the ring from his pocket. "Can you keep a secret?"

Eyes wide, she stared at the minuscule jewelry box. "Yeah…"

Noah opened the box. "This is Billie's engagement ring. Well, it will be, if she says yes."

"Oh wow, it's so sparkly!" And then Alyssa climbed onto his lap again. "If she says no, I'll take it!"

Laughing, he hugged her tight.

"Do you think Billie will wear a pretty white dress and a long white veil? And she'll hold a big bouquet of roses? And we'll have a giant cake all piled up with frosting flowers?"

"Let's not get ahead of ourselves. She has to say yes first."

"Oh, she will. Why wouldn't she?"

He could think of a dozen reasons without even trying. For one thing, he intended to tell her the whole ugly truth. But with any luck, Billie would overlook it all.

"So anyway, Max is going to stay with you tonight."

"Too bad Max can't cook. We could make a special cake while you're gone. One that says Happy Getting Married, You Two!" One tiny forefinger popped up. "Hey! I know! We can make one of those—what do you call those giant signs, like the ones that say Welcome Home and Happy Birthday?"

"A banner?"

"Yeah. We'll make a banner. And hang it so it's the first thing you see when you get home."

"You're that sure she'll say yes, huh?"

"Oh yes. Because she loves you, a *lot*."

He might have asked how Alyssa knew such a thing, if she hadn't darted off to dig through her art supplies. Might have pointed out that Billie had never said she loved him. That he hadn't said the words, either. Oh, he'd *dreamed* about saying it. Dreamed she'd echoed the words.

Tonight, Alyssa's wish and his dreams would both come true...if Billie said yes.

"OH MY," SHE SAID, opening the door, "you clean up pretty good."

"And you...you're a knockout."

She'd spent two hours, showering and fussing with her hair and makeup, trying on dresses, matching them with heels and jewelry.

"Oh, this old thing?" she said, lifting the corner of her skirt. "I just grabbed the first thing I saw in the closet."

"Uh-huh," he said. "Now get your coat. We have ten minutes to make our reservation."

He helped her into it, and after she locked up, he offered her his arm. "Gorgeous night for a walk, isn't it?"

"I love living here, where you don't feel completely dependent on a car."

"And walking is great exercise." He looked down at her and winked. "Not that you need it."

"It's supposed to snow tonight," she said as they made the turn onto Main Street. "Might not be such a pleasant walk home."

"We'll see. Worst case scenario, I'll call us a cab."

"To go a few blocks? That's silly."

"Well, you can't walk in the snow in *those* shoes." He pointed to her three-inch heels and they both laughed.

The maître d' escorted them up three flights of stairs to a small dining room. Ornate draperies cloaked windows that overlooked Main Street. The paintings and dinnerware echoed a Parisian theme made warmer by the fire crackling in the tiny woodstove in the corner.

"Oh, Noah," she said, "it's beautiful."

Once their waiter left to place their order, Noah reached across the candlelit table, blanketed her hands with his own.

"There are so many things I want to talk about. I really don't know where to begin."

"You know what they say…."

He nodded. "I know…start at the beginning. See, that's the trouble. There isn't just one beginning in my crazy life."

Maybe she should spare him the ordeal of reliving his painful—sometimes shameful—history.

She picked up her water goblet, took a small sip. "I talked to my folks today…."

His eyes widened slightly, confirming her suspicions that they'd talked to Noah earlier, just as she'd suspected. Her mom had no talent whatever for keeping secrets. Good thing she'd never need to disappear into the program, Billie thought.

"Oh? How are they?"

"Fine. Dani is pregnant, and Mom is over the moon at the prospect of becoming a grand-mother."

"That's great news."

"Did you know that Troy has a girlfriend?" She told him all about the woman who'd made her "I love kids" brother consider a future without any of his own.

"How's your leg?" she asked.

"Almost as good as new."

"You're amazing. Seems like only yesterday I sat beside your hospital bed, worried that I might lose you. I think you must be part cat."

One eyebrow lifted, and then he nodded. "Never thought of it that way before, but I guess it does seem like I have nine lives, doesn't it?"

Their dinners arrived, and as the waiter stood by to make sure they were well attended, the conversation turned to less personal things. The weather. The price of gasoline. Congress's latest tax hike.

The waiter cleared the table, then delivered dessert. "May I get you anything else?" he asked.

"Just a little privacy."

The men exchanged a knowing glance.

"You know him?" she asked when the young man left them…and closed the door.

"A little. He bought a bike from me."

Billie had a feeling that this was more than a Valentine's Day dinner. More than their first official date. More than his way of thanking her for everything she'd done for him and Alyssa since the accident. But she and Noah hadn't exactly shared a normal relationship. And he wasn't exactly a run-of-the-mill man. Making assumptions about the real reasons for this dinner might come with a serving of major disappointment.

"I'm sorry," he said.

"Sorry? This night has been perfect! Sorry for what?"

"That I can't get down on one knee." He dragged his chair to her side of the table and sat down beside her. "So I guess we'll have to settle for this…."

He took her hand in his, placed a tiny box onto her palm—a perfect cube, wrapped in shiny red paper, topped off with a silver bow.

"It's almost too pretty to open," she whispered.

"Billie. You're killin' me here."

She removed the bow. He looked puzzled when she tucked it into his shirt pocket.

"I have a feeling I'm going to think of that as a keepsake," she said, peeling away the wrapper. She added it to the pocket. "That, too."

She removed the top of the glossy red outer box, shook the red velvet box inside it onto her other palm.

Noah relieved her of it. "Your hands are shaking. Let me take it from here."

His hands were shaking, too, as he pulled back the creaking lid.

"Your dad said if you say no, you're grounded."

She couldn't decide which shimmered more, the round diamond in the box, or the tears that misted in his beautiful, loving eyes.

"If you don't put it on my finger, right now, you're grounded," she said.

And then she kissed him.

# *EPILOGUE*

*Noah and Billie's 10th Anniversary*

"HOW DID YOU arrange this?" she said as they entered Tersiguel's Tower Room.

"Pulled a few strings, buttered a few palms, worked a little magic...."

"Well, it's the best present you could give me," she said. "Dinner in the same place where you proposed."

"Getting the room was easy compared to talking Alyssa into babysitting. I had to promise she could use the car, three weekends in a row."

Billie laughed. "I still have trouble believing she's old enough to drive, let alone wrangle deals like that."

"She wants to be a lawyer. Guess she figures she needs the practice, wrangling."

"Speaking of practice, the twins will start soccer practice in a few weeks."

"Think they'll both make the same team?"

"They'd better. I do *not* want to drag a lawn chair from field to field, like I did last year."

"What will you do with Buddy while the girls are on the field?"

"There's a playground beside the practice field. If I position my chair just right, I can watch all of them."

"Funny, I was thinking about the original Bud the other day."

"Wondering what he'd say if he knew we named our li'l guy after him?"

Noah nodded. "Well, we couldn't name the kid after me."

"We could have, if you had let me flip a coin. Heads, Noah. Tails, Nate."

"Either way, he'd be a junior. I went to school with a boy named Junior. Kids can be mean. No way I want Buddy going through that."

"So what's in the box?" she asked, pointing.

"Yeesh." He laughed. "You don't have a romantic bone in your body, do you?"

"That isn't what you said last night." She wiggled her eyebrows, then reached into his pocket and withdrew a box…exactly like the one he'd given her that night, right here at this same table, a decade ago.

"Your mom called this morning," she said, fiddling with the bow. "Wished us a happy anniversary, and asked if it's okay for them to fly out next week."

"I'm glad they haven't developed a fear of flying. With the kids' schedules, it makes it easier to see them often."

"It would be easier still if they'd move in with us. I mean, we chose our house because of the in-law suite."

"They might. Someday."

Billie opened her purse and withdrew a narrow rectangular box that she'd wrapped to match the one he'd just delivered.

They opened their gifts: his, a stainless-steel calendar watch; hers, one-karat cushion-cut diamond earrings to match her engagement ring. Billie wasted no time putting them on.

"How do they look?" she said, turning her head left, then right.

"Gorgeous. And so do you. You like 'em?"

"I love them."

Winking, he said, "You can thank me later."

"Ditto," she said, batting her eyelashes.

He reached across the table and grasped her hands. "All joking aside, thank you. For the best ten years of my life. For being the best mom to Alyssa and the twins and little Buddy, and making a wonderful, happy home. You're my hero. I hope you know that."

Billie's eyes filled with tears. Yes, she knew

it. And no matter how many times she told him, Noah didn't feel comfortable when she returned the compliment. Maybe ten years from now, as they celebrated another happy decade together, he'd believe her when she said the past didn't matter...that it had never mattered. Maybe he'd believe it when she told him that he was living, breathing proof that people really *can* change.

She'd been a bitter, broken young woman when they met, but he had changed all that.

"When you turned your whole life upside down and inside out all those years ago, you saved Alyssa, but I need you to understand that you saved me, too."

As expected, he started to protest. Billie shook her head and held up a forefinger.

"Shh," she said. "Your sherbet is melting."

Noah picked up his spoon.

"And by the way," she said, as he sipped it, "if you ever get it into your handsome head to go undercover again, well, don't. Because I'll make it my mission in life to hunt you down and drag you home."

"Nothing like that has ever entered my—"

"Because I love you," she interrupted. "Understand?"

He nodded. "I've understood that from the day you hobbled into the bike shop. You're stuck with me, Mary Margaret Elizabeth Landon Preston."

She laughed at the way he sing-songed her name.

"Ditto," she said.

"Ditto?" Noah rolled his eyes. "You're a hopeless romantic," he teased.

"Shh," she repeated. "You know how much you hate melted sherbet."

* * * * *

# LARGER-PRINT BOOKS!

## GET 2 FREE LARGER-PRINT NOVELS
## PLUS 2 FREE MYSTERY GIFTS

*Love Inspired®*

### Larger-print novels are now available...

# *ReaderService*.com

## Manage your account online!

- Review your order history
- Manage your payments
- Update your address

---

**We've designed
the Harlequin® Reader Service
website just for you.**

---

## Enjoy all the features!

- Reader excerpts from any series
- Respond to mailings and
  special monthly offers
- Discover new series available to you
- Browse the Bonus Bucks catalog
- Share your feedback

*Visit us at:*

## ReaderService.com

RS13